Praise for the novels of Christie Ridgway

"Christie Ridgway writes with the perfect combination of humor and heart. This funny, sexy story is as fresh and breezy as its Southern California setting."   —Susan Wiggs

"Delightful."   —Rachel Gibson

"Tender, funny, and wonderfully emotional."
                                                —Barbara Freethy

"Pure romance, delightfully warm, and funny."
                                                —Jennifer Crusie

"Smart, peppy."   —*Publishers Weekly*

"Funny, supersexy, and fast-paced . . . Ridgway is noted for her humorous, spicy, and upbeat stories."
                                                —*Library Journal*

"Christie Ridgway is a first-class author."
                                                —*Midwest Book Review*

"Christie Ridgway's books are crammed with smart girls, manly men, great sex, and fast, funny dialogue. Her latest novel . . . is a delightful example, a romance as purely sparkling as California champagne."   —*BookPage*

"Ridgway delights yet again with this charming, witty tale of holiday romance. Not only are the characters sympathetic, intelligent, and engaging, but the sexual tension between the main characters is played out with tremendous skill."   —*Romantic Times*

Titles by Christie Ridgway

HOW TO KNIT A WILD BIKINI
UNRAVEL ME
DIRTY SEXY KNITTING

CRUSH ON YOU

Crush on You

CHRISTIE RIDGWAY

BERKLEY SENSATION, NEW YORK

R

THE BERKLEY PUBLISHING GROUP
Published by the Penguin Group
Penguin Group (USA) Inc.
375 Hudson Street, New York, New York 10014, USA
Penguin Group (Canada), 90 Eglinton Avenue East, Suite 700, Toronto, Ontario M4P 2Y3, Canada
(a division of Pearson Penguin Canada Inc.)
Penguin Books Ltd., 80 Strand, London WC2R 0RL, England
Penguin Group Ireland, 25 St. Stephen's Green, Dublin 2, Ireland (a division of Penguin Books Ltd.)
Penguin Group (Australia), 250 Camberwell Road, Camberwell, Victoria 3124, Australia
(a division of Pearson Australia Group Pty. Ltd.)
Penguin Books India Pvt. Ltd., 11 Community Centre, Panchsheel Park, New Delhi—110 017, India
Penguin Group (NZ), 67 Apollo Drive, Rosedale, North Shore 0632, New Zealand
(a division of Pearson New Zealand Ltd.)
Penguin Books (South Africa) (Pty.) Ltd., 24 Sturdee Avenue, Rosebank, Johannesburg 2196,
South Africa

Penguin Books Ltd., Registered Offices: 80 Strand, London WC2R 0RL, England

This is a work of fiction. Names, characters, places, and incidents either are the product of the author's imagination or are used fictitiously, and any resemblance to actual persons, living or dead, business establishments, events, or locales is entirely coincidental. The publisher does not have any control over and does not assume any responsibility for author or third-party websites or their content.

CRUSH ON YOU

A Berkley Sensation Book / published by arrangement with the author

PRINTING HISTORY
Berkley Sensation mass-market edition / June 2010

Copyright © 2010 by Christie Ridgway.
Excerpt from *Then He Kissed Me* by Christie Ridgway copyright © by Christie Ridgway.
Cover art by Tetra Images/Punchstock.
Cover design by Lesley Worrell.
Interior text design by Laura K. Corless.

ISBN: 978-0-425-23513-3

BERKLEY® SENSATION
Berkley Sensation Books are published by The Berkley Publishing Group,
a division of Penguin Group (USA) Inc.,
375 Hudson Street, New York, New York 10014.
BERKLEY® SENSATION and the "B" design are trademarks of Penguin Group (USA) Inc.

PRINTED IN THE UNITED STATES OF AMERICA

10 9 8 7 6 5 4 3 2 1

For Micki Plummer,
with thanks for your encouragement and friendship!

And, as always, for Rob.

7/10

Wine gives courage
and makes men more apt for passion.

—OVID

1

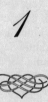

If God were a woman, Alessandra Baci thought, holding her breath as she struggled to fasten the thirty buttons behind her back, a wedding dress would fit forever.

Knuckles rapped on her closed bedroom door. "Allie?"

At the sound of her name, Alessandra gave a guilty start, losing both that puff of breath and grip on the latest pearl-sized fastening.

"Allie, let me in," her sister Stephania called from the hallway.

Glancing at her bedside clock, she called back, "Not right now." She didn't want anyone seeing her like this.

"But, um, Allie, we have a little problem."

No kidding. Alessandra sucked in another breath and tried a second attack on the buttons that marched up her spine. The dress wasn't designed to don solo, especially five years and seven pounds past its due date.

Her mind flashed back to the first morning she'd stepped into the frothy layers. She'd been twenty years old and standing in this very bedroom, in front of this very mirror, but surrounded by her two sisters and the other four bridesmaids. A hairdresser had already pinned the jeweled tiara in her updo and the filmy veil had brushed her bare shoulders.

She'd been wearing a lace demi-bra that she'd fore-gone today, just like the veil, though the little crown was perched on her unbound, dark and wavy hair. Instead of the sheer, thigh-high stockings and matching panties she'd been wearing on her wedding day, this morning she'd left on her striped cotton pajama bottoms.

Still, she could exactly recall her excitement—the hollowed-out feeling of her belly and the kamikaze butter-flies winging inside it—as she dressed in the strapless gown with its layers of tulle for the eleven o'clock ceremony.

A knock rattled her door again. "Allie," a new voice said, sounding impatient. It was her oldest sister, Giuliana, joining the hall-to-bedroom conversation. "Look, we need to reconsider this vow thing."

Alessandra frowned. "What are you talking about?"

"I'm talking about the vow we made to Papa on his deathbed. We can't—"

"A promise is a promise," Alessandra hissed, giving up on the buttons to glare at the closed door, knowing neither of her sisters had the guts to say such a thing to her face. "A promise is a promise is a promise."

"I know you feel that way, Allie," her sister responded, her voice softening, and she could imagine Giuliana's big brown eyes full of sympathy. "And I know *why* you feel that way. You didn't get to make . . . well, you know. But we might not be able to do this."

Alessandra pressed two fingers against her forehead, just above the bridge of her nose. She didn't want to cry. Not yet. Dropping her hand, she glanced around to locate the white satin wedding shoes.

"Let us in, okay?"

"No." This was Alessandra's private pity party. Her

sisters wouldn't understand and would only worry if they knew that she annually dressed the part, then drenched herself in memories, allowing herself to feel every drip of romance before every drop of regret. "We'll talk later."

"Allie—"

"Papa's been gone three months," she said. "Will another hour or two really matter?"

"Every minute matters," Giuliana muttered. "When we promised him we'd save Tanti Baci we didn't have any idea what a mess he'd made of it."

"He didn't make a mess of the winery," Alessandra spit back. "He . . ." He'd made a royal mess of the Napa Valley winery that had been in the family for generations.

She pressed her fingers to her forehead again, guilt adding to her mix of emotions. Of the three sisters, as the only one employed by Tanti Baci—Many Kisses, a play on their last name—it was she who should have guessed the dire state of the family business. But she'd been just as staggered as the other two when Mario Baci had confessed his concerns as he lay dying.

His three daughters hadn't hesitated to swear they'd save Tanti Baci. They must! It was their legacy.

"If you won't let us in, Allie, then you have to come out," Stevie said. "Liam Bennett is here, and he has one of the bastards with him."

As if that would get her moving, Allie thought, resettling the tiara on top of her head. The Bennetts were just another thorny issue she didn't feel like facing right now. They were their neighbors and their competition . . . and despite an old feud, also part owners of Tanti Baci. Liam and his younger brother Seth had lost their father not long ago, too, and though the Bennett patriarch had left their family's winery and other financial holdings in good shape, his will had publicly acknowledged two children who were the products of his heretofore secret affairs.

One of those "bastards" must be on a wine country visit. She felt a twinge of curiosity about the newcomer as she spied her satin shoes and slipped them on her feet.

"Allie . . ."

"I can't come out just yet," she replied, glancing at the clock by her bed.

It read 10:44.

Her sisters' interruption forgotten, Alessandra's pulse dipped to a slow thud, as ominous as a funeral dirge. She met her own eyes in the mirror, trying to push away the hovering dread in order to recapture those last moments of delighted anticipation on her wedding morning. She had been so happy. Her dreams came true.

Every year, on the anniversary of that day, she made herself replay those hours. The good parts included—in an effort to remember that life held moments of supreme joy. To remember, and to hope—

The LED flicked to 10:45.

Grief slammed into Alessandra, just as it had at that exact moment years ago, a bitterly cold wave that took out on its tide her happiness, her joy, and the determined belief she'd held in happy endings. Then, surrounded by her bridesmaids, she'd been told about Tommy and she'd shuddered in her sisters' arms as her heart contracted to the size of a stone.

Five years later, Alessandra shuddered again.

"Allie," Giuliana said, her voice more insistent. "Look, this is really urgent."

"What?" she asked, her throat so tight that the words were half-whispered. "What is it?"

"You've got to come out."

"No." She couldn't. Not wearing the wedding dress and not with sorrow carving at her insides like a knife. Bowing into herself, she pressed her fists against the hard, shriveled rock of her heart.

"It's about the cottage."

Alessandra's head came up. The raging grief gave a little hiccup. "What?"

"The cottage. That's the problem we've been trying to tell you."

A contractor was renovating the historic residence of the original founders of the winery, Anne and Alonzo Baci. The cottage was an essential element of Alessandra's brainchild—that of offering the winery as a wedding destination. This service would provide a new revenue stream for the family business and the success of her plan would prove to the bank, to her sisters, to everyone, that Tanti Baci should remain in their hands. To that end, she'd already jumped through hoops to get the right zoning, building, and events permits.

She took a step toward the hall. "What kind of problem?"

"The guy you hired says he has a better offer. He's packing up right now and claims he's not coming back."

"No!" A flush of rage shot over Alessandra's skin. She flew to the door, wrenching it open and then pushing past her sisters even as she noted their startled faces. "You're wearing . . ." Giuliana choked on the rest of her words as her gaze took Alessandra in from head to toes.

Following her sister's eyes, Alessandra saw her white satin high heels. With a little growl, she kicked them off, then reached down to yank Stevie's rubber thongs right off her feet. Wearing them herself, she rushed away, feeling her tiara sliding as the hem of her wedding dress fluttered in the breeze of her outrage.

Her pajama bottoms flapped around her ankles and her heaving breaths threatened to lift her breasts right out of their boned nest. She'd never managed to get the dress completely buttoned, she realized, which meant God must be off somewhere enjoying a fly-fishing tournament.

Behind her, she heard her sisters sputter as they trailed her down the stairs.

"Maybe you should change first . . ."

"There are, um, people out there who might get the wrong impression . . ."

Not a word they said stopped her. Nothing could do that.

Even her flinty heart couldn't weigh her down. As a matter of fact, she welcomed its stoniness now. If anyone looked at her twice, if anyone got between her and the success of the weddings she'd booked for Tanti Baci—the weddings that would save the winery—she was going to rip the worthless thing from her chest and use it to murder the one who got in her way.

~

In the middle of a leafy vineyard, leaning against the warm side of his half brother's Range Rover, Penn Bennett decided his first day in Napa had all the elements of a great night of television. He should know, as the "star" of *Penn Bennett's Build Me Up*, a four-year-old prime-time show that had been in Nielsen's top ten for the past two seasons. When asked to describe the program's premise, he'd once quipped that it was about improving deserving families' homes as well as their self-esteem, one low-flow toilet at a time. Yet he knew the appeal had nothing to do with water conservation and even went beyond watching muscled men wield power tools.

It was all about the story, man.

Liam, the oldest of the two legitimate Bennett siblings, ran his hand through dark blond hair that had surprised the hell out of Penn the first time he'd seen him. It was the exact shade of his own, and the physical similarity didn't end there. Before this, Penn had never known a soul who looked like him.

"Sorry about the delay of your wine country tour," the other man said. "I know I told you this was going to be a brief stop."

Penn waved the concern away. He wasn't on a tight agenda—he was on an escape mission. Here, miles from the mistake he'd made in L.A., he intended to enjoy a few weeks of pure R & R. No work. No women. No trouble.

Liam frowned, shoving his hand through his hair again. "You're being damn decent about all this."

Penn settled himself more comfortably against the vehicle. "All this," he knew, referred to the recent revelations in Calvin Bennett's will. They'd surprised Penn, true, but it was obvious the news of his father's extramarital affairs had rocked Liam's well-ordered world. A half-smile crossed Penn's face. Yeah, good TV drama in the making.

Big family shake-up: check.

His head tilted back to take in the blue sky that was a perfect match to the seventy-five-degree sunshine. A raked-gravel parking lot separated the torn-up bungalow from the entrance to wine caves carved into the hillside. Standing as sentry on either side of the caves' double doors sat two dwarf lemon trees planted in halved wine barrels. Orderly rows of paper bag–brown grapevines with their lush, spring-green growth covered the rolling acres surrounding them. Penn's showbiz-trained brain imagined an aerial view of the countryside in the opening credits.

Sweeping visual appeal: check.

Just then a woman came into sight, flying toward them from the direction of a simple, two-story farmhouse. Ah, yes, he thought. The final element to complete the necessary triumvirate of Hollywood small-screen success.

Beautiful, busty young woman: check.

His eyes narrowing on the oncoming figure in the white strapless number, Penn straightened. Based on her determined expression and the strange getup she was wearing, the TV show he was building in his head might be pitched with a logline that went something like "*Desperate Housewives* meets *Say Yes to the Dress*." When he caught himself moving toward her, he forced his body back against the warm metal of the car. Knight errant wasn't a role that suited him.

Liam, however, let out a muffled oath and seemed unable to stifle the same impulse that had struck Penn a moment before. He surged forward to intercept the small figure with her cloud of dark hair, her froth of wedding dress, and her—were those pajama bottoms? But she shoved Penn's half brother out of the way without a blink, her rubber thongs flapping against the soles of her small feet as she sped toward the battered Ford F-150 pulled alongside the cottage.

A couple of Hispanic men were loading tools in the bed while the truck's owner, a sweaty guy with a stubble of hair on his nearly bald pate and a beer belly stretching out his grubby T-shirt, looked on. Wedding Dress Girl didn't hesitate to get a handful of that dirty cotton in her small fist. "Newton Smalls, what do you think you're doing?"

Newton Smalls backed away from her evident temper, but his movement only served to further stretch his stained shirt. He blinked down at her, both hands raised in a placating gesture. "Now, Alessandra . . ."

"We had a deal, Newton."

"I *gave* you a deal, you know that. But I can't afford to turn down a better paying job. My sister's husband called. He needs me for a spec house in Oregon and the pay is good if I get there right away."

Two more young women hurried up, obvious kin to Wedding Dress Girl. Dark-haired, dark-eyed beauties, all three. One of the newcomers was tall and capable-looking. The other was shorter, with sharper edges, or maybe that was just because of the look she threw like a knife at Liam.

His half brother stiffened. "Christ, Jules, I'm just the messenger. You can't blame me for Newton bugging out because I'm the one who discovered it."

"You're trespassing," she hissed at him.

He sucked in a breath, his expression hardening.

"Giuliana, the Bennetts may be silent partners, but we still have a stake here."

The taller young woman took her life in her hands and stepped between the invisible blades swishing through the air. She held out her hand to Penn. "Stephania Baci—Stevie. That's my older sister, Giuliana, and the strangely dressed creature is Alessandra, the youngest of the three of us."

"Penn Bennett," he said, accepting her firm shake.

"The bastard," she added, then grimaced. "Sorry. Maybe you don't care for irreverence."

"I'm a big fan of irreverence," he assured her. He liked this forthright Baci, though his gaze wandered toward Wedding Dress Girl again. She'd left off manhandling the construction foreman in order to reach into the truck bed and lift out one of the items just loaded.

"You'll need this to get back to work." She was so little, the air compressor nearly toppled her over.

Penn found himself stepping forward again, only to halt as Newton plucked the heavy contraption out of her hands. "Alessandra, I don't have time for this."

"I don't have time to find someone else to do the job!" she countered, and wrapped her hands around a 2 x 4 that she drew from the top of a stack of wood resting in the truck's bed. As she pulled, a sparkly thing caught in her hair fell free. She tripped on it, going to the ground in a tumble of white skirts and striped-cotton legs.

Penn closed half the distance between them before she was up on her rubber thongs again, her temper at fever level if the flush on her face and on her over-exposed breasts was anything to go by. She had a small mouth with puffy lips that were two shades redder than her cheeks. It was one of those mouths that had a man thinking of something more than kissing. Put that together with the dark wavy hair, and he could just imagine twisting his fingers in those silky strands to urge her forward and, well . . .

If he wasn't a guy burned out on trouble and women, then he might have been seriously turned on by the small, sexy package. Except he *was* a guy burned out on trouble and women and if the odd outfit she was wearing was anything to go by, a bad temper wasn't her worst fault.

She was trying to get to the items in the truck again, but Newton was blocking her way. Steam came out of her ears and she stomped a foot, scattering gravel. "This isn't right!"

"We agreed, Allie. The price I quoted you was so cheap you told me I could take a better offer if one came my way."

"One wasn't supposed to come your way!" Gravel flew beneath her rubber thong again.

Her sister Giuliana made a cautious approach. "It's going to be okay. We'll figure out something."

Alessandra's head whipped around. "Like forgetting about our promise to Papa? Like selling the winery? Is that what you mean?"

Stephania started forward. "Allie—"

"You, too?" The girl in the wedding dress and pajamas spun to confront her other sister, anger still blazing across her delicate features. "You're willing to let go of our birthright, our heritage, our history? This place is our *heart*, Stevie."

Liam stepped forward. "Still, maybe it's time to call it quits."

At his quiet words, all the fire in Alessandra was quenched. Her gaze took in the united wall of her two sisters and Penn's half brother. Her shoulders slumped, her head dropped.

A moment passed, then she took a long breath and turned to Newton again, looking up at him through her tangle of dark lashes. Her voice was husky and halting. "You can't leave me like this," she told the man.

The atmosphere instantly changed. Where minutes before it had been charged with the rioting atoms of Wedding Dress Girl's fit of pique, now it was a different emotion coloring the air.

Bemused, Penn crossed his arms over his chest and leaned on the Range Rover again to take in the little show. Alessandra's small face tilted up and she turned those velvety brown eyes—was that a sheen of tears?—on the construction worker. "Please, Newton. You can't leave me like this," she repeated.

Newton appeared on the verge of crying himself. "Allie . . ." he whimpered. From the other side of the truck, Penn heard the two guys muttering to each other in Spanish. *Idiot!* he heard one say to the other. *He's looking her in the eyes. Everyone knows not to look her in the eyes.*

Who did they think she was, Medusa?

"Newton . . ." Wedding Dress Girl implored again, one perfect tear dangling at the end of one perfect bottom lash.

Surely the guy wouldn't fall for this. Penn glanced around, ready to share a laugh at her so-obvious ploy, but was astonished to see everyone else frozen, their stricken gazes glued to the little drama queen. How come they were so taken in? Had four seasons of assisting histrionic preteens select bedroom decor given him a special bullshit detector? Nah, it wasn't the tweenies who had honed his sense of the over-dramatic, it was the woman who'd walked away with a wheelbarrow full of his cash and, well, his wheelbarrow, among other things, that had done that.

So, fine, maybe he was a tad more cynical than most.

Newton whimpered again. "Okay, Allie. All right. All right, I'll stay."

Sunshine didn't come brighter than her sudden smile. She rushed the contractor for an exuberant hug, and then gave one to each of his workers, too. Giuliana came next, then Stevie, and even Liam managed to take her embrace without his stiff spine breaking in half.

Penn should have seen it coming, but he was stupefied when she turned and flew toward him, her next victim. But before contact could be made, she scuttled back and let out an embarrassed laugh.

"I'm sorry," she said, an adorable dimple that she was certainly supremely aware of winking beside the corner of her adorable mouth. "We haven't even met. You must be one of the Bennett bas . . . ." Her adorable dimple disappeared to make way for an adorable blush.

What a player! "I'm Penn," he said, voice matter-of-fact.

"Penn." She beamed him a ray of that practiced sunshine. "Nice to meet you."

Despite how much he despised manipulative women, it didn't change the way her bright smile and plump breasts thickened the blood chugging through his veins. He plucked at his shirt to force a breeze past his now hot skin.

For a guy still smarting over the last female who'd sailed past his common sense, his reaction to Alessandra Baci was completely unwelcome and only served to piss him off. Little Wedding Dress Girl was sexy as all get-out, but obviously she was damn spoiled, too.

"And congratulations to you," he said, not disguising the edge to his voice.

Her gaze narrowed, a quick contraction of her eyelids before her expression turned guileless again. "I don't know what you're talking about."

He leaned closer, and spoke in a near whisper. "They don't know what hit 'em."

"What?"

She had the innocent thing down pat, and he hardened himself against it. "That little break in your voice," he said. "The single tear—brilliant. We'll have to see about a booking on *Inside the Actors Studio*."

The Kate Winslet wanna-be didn't answer. With a little flounce, and another spit of gravel, she turned and headed back up the lane, her sisters once again following. As Newton and company started pulling equipment from the bed of the Ford, he and Liam were left looking after the three Baci women.

"Good God," Penn said, shaking his head. There were like a million little buttons trailing down the back of that crazy outfit—only half of them fastened—and the almost-undressed aspect ignited his imagination nearly as much as her generous breasts and pretty mouth. He could see his fingers working on the remainder of those tiny pearls, his calluses catching on silky fabric as he hurried to bare her for his eyes. For his touch.

His thickened blood moved southward and he groaned. "Lord help me."

Liam glanced over. "What's wrong with you?"

"Wedding Dress Girl—Alessandra. She's one hot little mama, isn't she?"

Liam's eyes widened. He looked almost . . . shocked.

Okay, from the get-go the other man had struck Penn as somewhat unbending, but at the basest of levels XY was XY, wasn't it? He cleared his throat and snuck a quick glance at the swinging hips receding in the distance. "I mean, surely . . ." It was just two guys, so he plowed forward. "C'mon. The body. That mouth. I'd like to—"

"Stop," Liam said. "Stop right there."

Something shot through Penn—disappointment? Nah, he wasn't really interested in the youngest Baci sister, so it made no difference to him that his half brother had a prior claim. "Sorry, I didn't know you and she have a thing."

"We don't. No one does, not with Alessandra. And you won't be messing with her, either. Not with the Nun of Napa."

"Disaster averted then?" Clare asked.

Alessandra nodded, squinting a little as the bright sunlight coming through the beauty shop's wide front window glinted off her friend's space-Afro. There was no other way to describe the do created by the layered sections of Clare's foil-wrapped hair. Though Alessandra wasn't here for her own appointment, she'd taken the neighboring stylist's chair in order to keep her friend company during the chemical process. "I promise the cottage will be ready for your wedding day."

It had better be, that was sure. Clare's "I do" would be the first uttered at Tanti Baci this summer, but Alessandra had hopes that there would be bookings for most every weekend in the months ahead. Of course, that couldn't guarantee the winery would be saved, but she avoided that uncomfortable truth by gazing out the window onto the quaint main street of her birthplace. Located toward the northern end of Napa County, Edenville, population 6,100, was a one-square-mile walking town, with a block-sized central plaza of grass, paved paths, and shaded benches. The downtown's wide sidewalks were edged by mature trees and ran along the clapboard storefronts, some fancied-up with eye-catching paint and Victorian embellishments.

Bright color and ornamental woodwork signaled the more upmarket establishments. A gourmet food shop was in avocado and lemon, the trendy bistro painted a silver-touched salmon, the owners of the homewares boutique on the corner had chosen the blue and white of a willow pattern. These tourist magnets shared space with the more modestly decorated county library, small grocery store, and no-frills deli patronized by the town locals.

Clare raised her voice over the sound of gushing water from the shampoo sinks at the rear of the salon. "So what did you think of the bastard Bennett?"

Alessandra winced. It wasn't a very sensitive way to refer to him, though they'd begun calling him that when he was nothing more than tantalizing gossip. Now that she'd met him . . . "I don't want to think about that man," she told Clare, "or ever see him again."

But life hadn't been going her way the last five years, and as if she needed more proof of that, she noted a shiny truck pulling into a parking space in front of Oliver's Ristorante across the street. "Though you can check him out yourself. Looks like he's heading for Overpriced Ollie's."

Clare wiggled in her seat. "That's what I love about small towns and big picture windows. Sooner or later everybody passes by."

Crossing her arms over her chest, Alessandra wasn't so pleased. She watched his long legs emerge from the truck's cab. There was a kid with a table on the sidewalk outside Ollie's, soliciting funds for some good cause, but it didn't make her like the bastard any better when he drew out a couple of bills from his pocket.

We'll have to see about a booking on Inside the Actors Studio.

What the heck did he mean by that? And he'd said it with such a cynical smile on his handsome face, too.

While she watched him hand over the money, he smiled again. But then his head turned toward the street as a car came to a sudden stop behind his vehicle. The skinny passenger in the beat-up sedan shot his torso out the side window and stripped off his shirt.

"Build me up!" The guy yelled it so loud she could hear it through thick plate glass and whirring beauty appliances. "Penn Bennett, build me up!"

Smile growing to a grin, Penn reached into his truck and withdrew a T-shirt that he balled up and threw to the half-naked man. A fist-pump later, the car took off with a screech of tires.

"Okay, I know my experience with the male animal has been somewhat limited, but . . ." She glanced over at Clare, who was staring out the window, her jaw dangling.

Her friend transferred her gaze toward Alessandra, showing wide eyes. "The bastard is *Penn Bennett*? You didn't tell me that! Penn Bennett of *Build Me Up!*"

Alessandra blinked. "Which would happen to be . . . ?"

"Just the hottest home renovation show on television. His team repairs and remodels homes of needy people. I almost cry every time he leads the grateful family into their now-beautiful house. He makes them feel so special."

"Really?" While Alessandra could believe the guy was on TV—he was Hollywood handsome—she couldn't imagine him as an altruistic do-gooder.

That little break in your voice, the single tear— brilliant.

Remembering the words, she frowned and figured mean and spiteful was the guy's true character. "The thing is, Clare, this *Build Me Up* show—it's a job for him, right? He gets paid to make nicey-nice and appear all sympathetic."

Clare opened her mouth, but Alessandra kept on talking. "Don't get taken in by what you think you know about Penn Bennett. If you ask me, he's—"

"Waiting with bated breath to hear your assessment of his character."

Ah, damn, Alessandra thought, the skin at the back of her neck prickling in belated warning. *Just another reason to dislike the guy.* Real men didn't enter beauty salons and catch disgruntled women discussing them over peroxide and bobby pins. Slowly, to give the embarrassed heat she was feeling a chance to fade from her cheeks, she shifted in her chair to face him.

His hazel eyes took a lazy pass over her lacy camisole, short watermelon-red cotton skirt, and bare legs. "Liam said that 'Nun of Napa' thing was just a nickname, and now I'm sure he's right."

Clare snickered.

Alessandra decided not to dignify the remark with an explanation. It wasn't her fault that the residents of Eden-ville and its environs had put that tag on her. But there were worse things someone could call someone else. Like arrogant. Like too good-looking for his own good. Over-confident, that was certain. She could imagine a bare-chested Penn Bennett flexing in front of a mirror, hear him singing to his amazing reflection. *I'm too sexy for my shirt.*

Clare apparently didn't share her vision as she gave the man a friendly smile and held out her hand. "I'm Clare Knowles."

"Nice to meet you, Clare Knowles."

He had an ease about him that got on Alessandra's last nerve. Just looking at him rubbed her the wrong way, and the surprise of that wasn't lost on her. Her job at the winery was public relations, which meant she was good at getting along with people—and also good at getting people to do what she wanted. With that in mind, she sent Penn her own smile. Sweet. Very sweet. "I'm sure you need to go away now."

He laughed. "No," he said, running a hand through his layered hair. "I'm here for a cut."

Men in Edenville went to Manuel's Barber Shop, closer to the highway. It had the requisite barber pole outside and ESPN played on a TV in the corner. In Manuel's back room it was said he pulled molars with rusty pliers and handed out herbal cures for the clap. "This is a beauty salon," she said, gesturing to encompass the lavender walls and framed headshots of female models.

"What?" he asked, all cheeky grin and sparkling eyes. "I'm not beautiful?"

The fact was, he *was* beautiful, in a wholly masculine way that involved long lean muscles and the grit of golden stubble on his chin. But Alessandra hated his studied, I-don't-give-a-damn looks, and she hated that he wasn't taking the hint and moving on. Worse, she hated his perfect knowledge of just what was going through her head, clear from the smirk on his lips and the laugh in his eyes.

"Why don't you try squeezing out a tear or two, little nun," Penn said softly, that sly smile still on his face. He moved into her personal space, leaning close enough that she could smell his lime-and-sin aftershave, even over the combined scents of sweet shampoo and acrid hair color that permeated the salon's air. "That usually gets you what you want, doesn't it?"

Clare choked out a sound that Alessandra ignored in order to thread his black heart on the skewer of her gaze.

"When you look at me like that I'm even more certain you're less than holy," Penn said. "Though Liam declined to share exactly why—"

"Girls!"

Alessandra jumped, then peeked around Penn's wide shoulders to see Clare's mother, Sally—who was also Alessandra's almost-mother-in-law—hurry toward them.

Tall, with elegant cheekbones and a shiny wedge of silver-threaded hair, Sally strode across the floor in a pair of cropped linen pants and matching turquoise leather loafers. "I've been trying to catch up with both of you all morning. Do you have your cell phones turned off?"

Clare slid down in her chair, looking as if she'd like to slide under it, out of sight. "Uh, that's a requirement of the stylist, Mom."

Her mother tilted her head, her gaze narrowing on the foiled layers of Clare's hair. "I thought we decided not to try highlights so close to the wedding."

"*You* decided I shouldn't highlight so close to the wedding. *I*, on the other hand, wanted to."

Her mother opened her mouth.

"And Jordan thinks it's a great idea," Clare added.

In a blink Sally went from battle-ready to soft surrender. Mention Clare's groom-to-be, and Clare's mother went marshmallow. The older woman was gaga over Jordan's stellar career and social standing. Sally Knowles had always wanted only the best for her children.

When she'd embraced Alessandra as a suitable wife for her beloved son Tommy, she'd been flattered and grateful.

Sally turned toward her now, her body stiffening as it became obvious she registered the presence of a male in their midst. "Oh," she murmured. Her gaze darted from Penn to Alessandra. "Do you have a . . . a man friend, Allie?"

"No." She realized the bastard Bennett was still standing too close, so she jumped out of the chair and put a decent distance between them. "*No.*"

"I didn't think so," Sally said. "You wouldn't . . ."

"I don't," Alessandra hastened to assure her, and the relief on the other woman's face made her eyes sting. With a knuckle, she blotted away an errant tear. "I won't."

"Allie was just telling me that everything's advancing nicely at the winery," Clare put in.

Blinking away a second tear, Alessandra took up the

new subject. "That's right. We had a little scare with Newton, but he's back on board."

"I heard about that scare," Sally said, frowning. "That's why I was looking for you this morning. Are you sure the construction is back on schedule?"

She nodded. "I'm sure. Nothing's going to ruin Clare's day."

"That Newton, though," Sally said, shaking her head. "I'm not sure we can count on him to get it right. I don't want Clare and Jordan stepping inside the cottage unless we're 100 percent certain the roof won't come tumbling down."

"I think we should be more worried about Jordan being there at all," Clare murmured.

Sally shot her daughter a look. "What? What's going on? Are you and Jordan in a fight?"

"Forget I said anything," Clare mumbled again. "It's not important."

"Not important!" Sally started.

"I'm just whining about his frequent business trips," Clare hastened to say. "He's making noises about missing his own bachelor party."

Sally visibly relaxed. "If that's all . . ."

"Gil is going to a lot of trouble to organize it," Clare said. "With the best man in Florida, I volunteered him for the job and I'll feel bad if the guest of honor's a no-show."

"What's Gil actually planning?" Sally scoffed. "Opening a bag of pretzels and putting a tacky DVD on the player at his greasy auto shop?"

Clare bristled, just like she did every time her mother disparaged Gil and his car repair business. He'd been Clare's best friend since kindergarten. "Mom . . ."

Now seemed a good time to step in and redirect the discussion. "Sally," Alessandra said. "Newton is doing a fine job, but if it would make you feel better, drop by and check out the progress for yourself."

The distraction worked. Sally frowned again. "But I don't know anything about construction."

"Maybe I could offer my expertise," a smooth voice said.

Alessandra glanced over her shoulder. Penn was still there! She'd thought ignoring him would make the man go away. If not, the wedding chatter should have done the trick. "We don't need you," she told him.

He sidled up to her, too close once again. "You might just be wrong about that."

Sally was staring at him, as if really seeing him for the first time. "You're . . . you're Penn Bennett."

"Yes, ma'am." He proffered a hand, which she shook.

"Penn Bennett," Sally said again, obviously dazzled. "You're famous."

Alessandra rolled her eyes. "He's not famous."

"Yes I am."

"Yes he is."

Penn and Clare spoke at the same time.

Alessandra rolled her eyes again. *Note to self, never watch* Build Up My Ego, *or whatever it is Penn Bennett calls his show.*

"Absolutely I'll feel much better if Penn goes over Newton's work," Sally announced. "What do you say, Allie?"

She had said she never wanted to think about Penn Bennett or ever see him again, but how could she refuse a request from Tommy's mom? Alessandra's tone was grudging, but she managed to force out the invitation. "Sure, Penn. Come by. You're welcome anytime."

Anytime after hell freezes over, that is.

~

From her second-floor bedroom window, Alessandra could see a light bobbing in the vicinity of Anne and Alonzo's cottage. With a resigned sigh, she headed downstairs then outside, collecting a flashlight and shoving her cell phone in the pocket of her shorts along the way. She strode off into the early evening darkness, wondering just how many times she'd shooed lovers out of the trysting place they'd made of the bungalow.

If her middle sister was here, she'd probably let them at it, but Stevie lived a few miles away in a duplex near town. Giuliana, who was subletting a condo in Edenville, would applaud her youngest sister's resolve, citing legalities or liabilities or something like that.

Alessandra just didn't want anyone messing with her wedding venue.

It wasn't that she resented other people their chance for a sexual encounter. Or not much anyway.

Instead of tromping along the gravel, she kept to the grassy edges of the lane. The surroundings were quiet, with the vineyard manager's lodgings a half-mile north and the doors to the wine caves/tasting room locked as they always were by four p.m. Alessandra didn't worry about being alone, though. She had her cell phone if there was trouble, and a pair of randy teenagers was an unlikely threat.

There wasn't a car in the guest parking lot, but she didn't expect to see one anyway. They strung a chain across the winery's turn-off from the main road at night. The usual M.O. of uninvited visitors was to leave their ride there and then travel down the drive on foot.

Ah-ha, she thought as she reached the bottom of the bungalow's steps. She was right about after-hours company. A flashlight glimmer glowed from inside the old residence. The new double front doors had yet to be installed, though Newton and company had finished gutting the interior, careful not to damage the massive river-rock fireplace that Alonzo was said to have built himself. The bungalow's interior was now the size of a small chapel and would seat seventy.

The new construction plan called for a few smaller rooms to be partitioned at the back and the walls were already framed in with two-by-fours. Some of the Sheetrock was even in place, the seams of the panels not yet taped. At the rear left was a small alcove where the groom could wait, on the right, a much larger boudoir that was designed for the bride's final primping.

The light came from the entrance to that room.

Alessandra stood at the cottage's main threshold and pitched her voice in that direction. "Hello?"

There was sudden surprise in the air.

She sighed. "Don't panic. Believe me, you're not the first I've discovered here." Not even the twenty-first. The location held a cult status for area lovers. "I've found wilted flowers on the floor. A velvet-lined ring box once. And don't get me started on the condom wrapper count."

The thought of that made her eyes narrow and sharpened her words. "C'mon, now. You're busted."

Another silent moment passed, then footsteps clapped along the hardwood floors that were yet to be restored. The beam of a flashlight traveled in her direction.

His voice reached her first.

"Will you read me my rights, or are we going straight to the strip search?"

"Oh, fudge," she muttered. She would have used stronger language, but it didn't seem fitting in this place where people were going to pledge everlasting love. "What are you doing here?" she demanded as Penn Bennett stepped into the main room.

It wasn't as if he wore a tuxedo, but even in jeans and a light sweater pushed up to his elbows, he managed to make her feel awkward and underdressed. She yanked on the hem of her sweatshirt and her bare toes curled in the confines of her running shoes. His shadow moved against the wall like a dark giant as he approached, and the image made her shiver.

"If I recall correctly—and I have excellent recall," he said, "you invited me to make an inspection."

She frowned at him. That had been three days ago and since the beauty shop she hadn't caught one glimpse of his wide shoulders or taunting smile. In the dark, she couldn't tell if he'd gotten that haircut he'd said had brought him into the salon that day, but even from several feet away she knew his scent was the same, tangy lime combined with a heated note of male skin that would smell even more delicious paired with crisp white sheets.

Shaking her head to dispel the idea, she shoved her hands in her pockets, dragging them down so that her shorts covered more of her legs. She couldn't swear that he was looking at them, but she could feel *something* traveling across her body, something like a hot breeze or a callused touch. "In case you hadn't noticed, the winery's closed for the day."

" 'You're welcome anytime,' " he quoted, repeating her words. "And I was out for an early evening walk when I remembered the offer."

The Bennett property adjoined that of Tanti Baci, and years ago, when they were still being civil to each other, her sister Giuliana and Liam had worn a shortcut that still survived. It didn't mean she had to like that Penn was using it. "Yes, but—"

"Don't be mad." His white teeth flashed and his voice lowered to a husky whisper. "I do my best work in the dark, little girl."

"Oh, please. Can the innuendo, will you?" Not for a million dollars—which she could really use right now, by the way—would she let him see how that sexual burr in his voice made the skin along her spine prickle.

"If you'll can the crying," he countered, his voice all-business again. "I caught you at it that first day, and then again at the salon. So you know, I find crocodile tears a huge turnoff."

"I'm not trying to turn you on! I don't want to turn you on!"

"But surely you're old enough to have learned . . ." He stepped closer and out came that seductive burr again. "You don't always get your heart's desire." The pad of one finger stopped short of her cheek, but he stroked the air a millimeter off. Though the faux-touch stopped at her jawline, she felt it travel like a poison-tipped arrow down the center of her body.

Poison-tipped, because it was infecting her with a sudden awareness of her female parts—her breasts, the softness between her legs, the smooth skin of her face that would be reddened by the kisses of a man with lean muscles and a hard mouth surrounded by golden stubble.

The sickness was lust!

She stepped back, stumbling over the threshold. Penn's hand shot out, but pulse whomping, she managed to avoid his fingers and retain her balance. Still, her feet put more inches of distance between them.

"Do I scare you?" he asked, sounding amused. "Why are you so jumpy?"

"You're nothing to me." Pushing away the impulse to run back home, she stepped back inside. He wasn't going to get the best of her. "But since you're here, why don't you give me your opinion of the cottage?"

"Beyond my surprise that you bothered trying to save the place?"

She'd heard that before, from the other Bennetts. From her sisters. From the bank. "Do you know the history of the Tanti Baci winery?"

"The *Cliff's Notes* version. Alonzo Baci and another guy—"

"The other guy was the first Liam Bennett who is your great-great-grandfather."

"—partnered up in a silver mine and when the ore ran out they invested their profits in land."

"This land," Alessandra confirmed. "Alonzo had learned about growing grapes and making wine in his homeland of

Italy, and Liam Bennett went along for the ride. Though later Liam bought some adjoining property that the Bennetts developed into their own vineyards, this place has been jointly owned since the beginning."

Glancing over her shoulder, she thought how the land had been then—not tamed with ordered rows of vines, but growing wild with long grasses and dotted with oaks and evergreens. It had taken sweat and will to clear the acres and Papa had claimed you could taste the area's natural fecundity as well as its settlers' grit and dreams in Napa Valley wine.

Penn's voice interrupted her musings. "From what I hear, Alonzo thought Liam's woman was a joint project, too. He stole her away, causing a grudge that's never been settled."

Alessandra shook her head. "Those are sour grapes passed down your family line." Decades of tangled business dealings had kept the Bennett–Baci feud at varying stages of simmer, though it was true that the original rift had started with two men loving one woman. "Liam wanted Anne, but it was Alonzo the Italian immigrant who won the beautiful San Francisco society girl. She and Alonzo were the real thing, and this is the home where they lived out their happy marriage. It lasted over fifty years."

"Which makes it the perfect location to hold the Tanti Baci winery weddings."

She glanced up at him, surprised he made the connection. "It makes sense to you too, then?"

He shrugged. "I'm in the entertainment business. You always need a hook, and this one's yours."

His understanding made her feel a bit more charitable toward him. "And it's a nice parallel to one of our signature products, too."

"The sparkling wine," he said. "Liam mentioned that to me as well."

Which probably meant Penn knew the dire financial

straits Tanti Baci was facing. "That's right. We've been offering it to the public for forty-nine years—the golden anniversary of the first commercial sale is next summer. We keep
a ledger detailing every bridal couple that has poured it on
their wedding day and not one of them has ever divorced."

"Bullshit."

Well, yeah, probably, but that's not the way it played in
the brochures in the tasting room and across the pixels that
were the Tanti Baci website. "Apparently you don't believe
in happily ever after."

"I'm pretty much a cynic, which comes with the ter-
ritory of being the son dear-old-dad never acknowledged
until he was dead and gone."

She winced. "Your father—"

"Had an affair with a bar waitress, knocked her up, and
then went back to his life here. Calvin Bennett could have
left it at that, but he complicated things by coming clean in
his will. So here I am, in part because Liam and Seth feel
guilty and want to share their heritage."

When the secrets of Cal Bennett's past had surfaced after his death seven months ago, his widow Jeanette had
immediately moved to her native upstate New York. Her
sons, Liam and Seth, hadn't had the luxury of ducking
the scandal that burned up the phone lines in the valley.
They'd stayed, continuing to run their family business and
apparently reaching out a hand to their illegitimate brother.
Cal had sired a daughter out of wedlock, too, but no one
seemed to know where she was.

While the news had been difficult for Liam and Seth to
swallow, Alessandra didn't imagine it was easy for Penn
to come into their lives and see the upbringing and life-
style he'd missed out on. Her family had never had much
besides the Tanti Baci land, but the Bennetts could boast
of fat bank balances and other business interests besides
wine. They were wealthy and their home and toys were
testament to that.

Liam and Seth feel guilty, Penn had said. And how exactly did *he* feel? Despite herself, she softened toward him, applauding his desire to forge a relationship with the more privileged sons. Without thinking, she reached out, though without quite touching him. "It was nice of you to come here . . ." she started.

" 'Nice'?" He barked out a laugh. "I came because it was convenient. I needed a break from L.A." He stepped closer, until they were nearly chest-to-chest. She meant to move back again, even sucked in a breath in preparation, but then his scent refilled her lungs. Combining with the spring smells of fertile earth and budding vines, it made her head spin and that infection of lust-sickness caused her body to bloom and her blood to heat once more.

His voice lowered to a whisper and she could feel his hot breath against her cheek as his mouth neared hers. "But I'd have come sooner if I'd known the town included a sexy nun who needed me."

She stood there, mesmerized by the heat radiating from his body, by the masculine form so close to hers. Both she and he were panting, she realized, and the harsh sounds made her aware of how very silent the vineyard had become. It was as if everything else in it was holding its breath in anticipation of what came next.

A kiss.

She'd never wanted a kiss so badly in her life. She needed . . .

Her mind snapped into focus. His last words replayed in her head. *I'd have come sooner if I'd known the town included a sexy nun who needed me.*

She jerked away. "Need you! No way do I need you! I don't need anything." Particularly from a man who had the looks of a movie star and the machismo of a motorcycle hellion. "I'm going back to my house."

She thought he might laugh at her vehemence, or at least

make some final mocking remark, but instead he stared at her, his eyes unreadable. Then he sighed.

"Before you leave, you should see this." He reached into his back pocket and withdrew a white sheet of paper. "I found it nailed to a wall in the back room."

Alessandra snatched it from him, frowning. As she unfolded it, he trained the beam of his flashlight onto the page. Glancing down at the sheet, the first thing she noticed was that it was letterhead from Newton's construction business. The second thing to strike her was that the nitwit couldn't spell.

Left for Orgun.

"Oh, *fudge!*" She really let the semicurse fly this time as comprehension dawned.

She'd been wrong. She needed something after all.

Worse, she needed some*one*.

3

Penn stared at his half brother Liam, sitting on the other end of the leather couch in the Bennett game room. He couldn't believe that the same man who days ago had warned him off was now trying to hook him up—in a manner of speaking, anyway—with the nun.

Yeah, that one. Alessandra Baci, the Nun of Napa. Penn still didn't know why the hell she was called that, and he'd decided to make it a point not to find out. Hadn't he learned his lesson about getting over-involved with strangers?

So instead of responding to Liam's request that Penn complete the work on the wedding cottage, he jabbed the buttons of the video game controller, focusing on the Halo 3 game projected on the big screen that took up nearly one wall. Obliterating one of the Brutes didn't calm his uneasiness. "Should we be playing something more civilized, do you suppose?" he wondered, looking around him.

The Bennett game room featured a teak-and-felt billiards table and in the opposite corner marble chess pieces sat ready for action. From his place on the long leather sofa, he could see dominoes resting in an inlaid box, a cribbage board that might have belonged to George Washington, and a backgammon set worthy of a European prince.

Liam's younger brother, Seth, spoke up from his sprawl in a nearby overstuffed chair. "You're the one who wanted to battle the Covenant."

Which was strange, because he was much too cynical to act on the belief that he could eradicate evil from the world. He glanced at the younger man—Penn was sandwiched in age between Liam and Seth—and once again was startled by the resemblance he saw to himself. For a kid who'd grown up sleeping on the sofa in an apartment living room, making himself a dinner of Cheerios every night while his mom, blue-collar Debbie Penn, worked the bar at Mr. G's, it was going to take more time to adjust. It was still hard to believe that when he'd been keeping company with late-night TV and the neighbor's cat, four hundred miles away these near doppelgangers had been living in a Tuscan-styled villa with a game room, eight-car garage, and enough bedrooms for a football team, including its cheerleaders. Living with their father, Calvin Bennett, who apparently strode around town unconcerned by the secrets he'd left behind. Secrets who had grown up fatherless.

And they called Penn a bastard.

He thought again of that skinny boy who'd been himself, the kid scared shitless by things that went bump in the night, the kid just as scared his mom wouldn't earn enough tips to cover the next month's rent. Maybe it wasn't such a surprise that there came the day when he'd been suckered in by a sob story.

Never again, though. He'd wised up and remembered all the lessons he'd learned in his rocky childhood. Every pair of wide eyes wasn't innocent. Not every trembling mouth told the truth.

Liam closed down the game, the screen going dark.

"Look, about the cottage. I know you're here to relax, but—"

"It's not that," Penn said. The truth was, he wasn't used to hanging around watching other people go about their daily business. Seth worked as the Bennett corporate lawyer and suited up every morning for offices in Napa, so Penn was left to tag along with Liam as he walked the vineyards, talked on the phone, walked the vineyards some more, and talked some more on the phone. It wasn't exactly stimulating.

"If you agree to finish up the work, you'll be doing yourself a favor," Seth put in. "We have a financial interest in Tanti Baci. If the place is kept afloat with this wedding thing, then we all benefit."

So far Penn had avoided talking about the economic aspects of being Cal Bennett's son, but he couldn't help himself from probing a little now. "So the Tanti Baci winery's not already nose-down?"

Liam shrugged. "Papa Baci drove the place into the iceberg some time back. Nobody noticed, because my— our—father embraced the 'silent' in 'silent partner' and let Mario have his way with it. Then Dad had his heart attack and Mario's cancer showed up and combing the books was even further from anyone's mind. By the time Mario confessed to his daughters on his deathbed, the water was rushing in the windows."

See, here's what Penn didn't get. Liam was an eyes-wide-open kind of man. No nonsense, and sometimes Penn thought no sense of humor, as well. "So why aren't you putting the place on the market ASAP? I know the Bennetts and the Bacis have a long history there, but you don't strike me as the sentimental type, Liam." He looked over at the younger man. "You either, Seth."

The two brothers exchanged a glance. "Well, see . . ." Seth started, obviously lacking a good explanation. "Um . . . Alessandra . . ."

Penn groaned. Were his half brothers the suckers now? "If it's a sound business decision, it's a sound business decision. But if it's men falling all over themselves because a pretty girl winks out a tear or two . . ."

"It's not like that," Seth protested. "Allie's had a really rough time—"

"I don't want to hear it." Penn stifled the impulse to put his hands over his ears. Not that he thought he could be conned by a woman and her woeful tale of hard luck ever again. Still, losing the contents of a juicy bank account and various other items of value could make a man wary. Bitter, even.

"You don't understand," Liam said with a sigh. "I think I should tell you about Alessandra."

"Don't." Suddenly, the woman in question was standing in the game room doorway. "Don't," she repeated. "I don't want you telling him anything about me."

Both Liam and Seth got to their feet, and to his own surprise, Penn found himself rising from the couch, too. Manners. Who knew he had them?

The corners of her mouth tweaked in a little smile of acknowledgment. "Sit down, sit down." She moved to perch on the arm of Seth's chair. "Charlene let me in," she added, referring to the Bennett housekeeper. Then she addressed her next remark to Liam. "You told me to stop by at two—that you'd have spoken to him by then."

Liam shifted on his cushion and glanced at Penn. "Yes, well . . ."

Alessandra turned her head to pin him with her big brown eyes. "I take it you're not interested in Newton's old job?"

"I—"

"Don't bother apologizing. I supposed it was a long shot. No surprise that my little construction dilemma isn't of interest to some big-shot TV star."

He hadn't planned on apologizing! And his refusal had

nothing to do with him being "some big-shot TV star." Good God. Folding his arms over his chest, he frowned at her, taking in the little dress she wore—a sleeveless shift that matched her lime-colored kitten heels. Her fingernails gleamed with a fresh, ladylike manicure, and she'd tamed her tumble of dark, wavy hair with a pink headband the exact shade of the lipstick on her I'm-not-that-innocent mouth. He wanted to—

No. This was why he wouldn't comply. In a wedding dress, in a sweatshirt, in something a second-grade schoolteacher might wear, she had him thinking about sex acts. His blood was already taking the bullet train southward and he knew, just knew, that his reaction was something she practiced, counted upon, had used a dozen times with dozens of men. Only an expert at manipulation could snare Penn Bennett like this when he'd been so recently burned.

Nun of Napa, my ass.

She clapped her pretty hands together and stood up again. Penn stared at her knees, just skimmed by the hemline of her dress, and realized that even they were turning him on. "See you later," she told the men.

He and his half brothers were standing again. Seth cleared his throat. "What will you do now?"

"Something will turn up," she said, her voice just the craftiest bit husky. And maybe Penn was wrong, but could that be yet another sheen of tears in her eyes? "I'm going to make some calls. Look around town."

She'd already tried that, Liam had said so, which is why Penn had been approached as last resort. He knew any reputable business would already be booked at this time of year, leaving Alessandra's only option that of picking up day laborers from the street corner. Yet if she managed to round up workers with the kinds of skills she needed, who would supervise them? He couldn't imagine this spoiled, sexy little bundle with a splinter, let alone with wood stain under her nails and plaster dust in her hair.

And didn't that just piss him off? She wanted what she wanted, but she planned on cajoling—or worse, crying—to achieve her ends. Certainly Alessandra Baci had never worked up a good sweat outside of the bedroom.

His gaze ran over her again, from her gleaming waves of hair to her delicate high heels. The tip of her nose was pink, he decided, definite proof of incipient tears.

What she needed, he thought, was to know what over-taxed muscles and an aching back felt like at the end of the day. That would really give her something to cry about. "I'll do it," he heard himself say.

"What?" She stared at him.

Liam and Seth were surprised, too. But it was a good idea. The experience he had in mind would teach Alessandra Baci a lesson—and prove to himself that he'd learned the one Lana Lang had taught him four months ago in L.A.

"There's a condition," he added, hoping he was disguising his evil grin.

Her pink mouth pursed, and he noticed her lipstick matched her fingernail polish, too. If he got his way she wouldn't be thinking about makeup and manicures for the next few weeks.

"What condition is that?" she asked, and the look she gave him wasn't the least bit teary. Her brown eyes were as suspicious as Penn should have been of Lana and her hard-luck story.

But it was Alessandra Baci he was thinking of now and he let his evil grin go free. "That I'm Job Boss and that you, baby, are Laborer Number One."

~

Alessandra's life had dished up unpleasant tasks before—including not getting married on her wedding day and picking out the headstone for her father's grave—so agreeing to work with Penn Bennett for the next few weeks should seem like recess in comparison.

But this didn't feel like jump rope.

She popped open the passenger door of Penn's truck the minute it rocked to a stop in front of Edenville's old-school hardware store, eager to exit the close confines of the cab. As a kid, she'd looked forward to recess—and she'd been good at jump rope, too—but she definitely wasn't good at this. In Penn's presence she was edgy and almost breathless, and if she didn't get a hold of herself he was going to notice he made her . . . what was the right word? Nervous?

Yeah. Nervous.

She couldn't wait for his snarky comments regarding that . . . Not.

They stepped into the street at the same time and in a replay of the incident she'd witnessed from the beauty salon days before, a car screeched to a halt behind them. This time it was the driver who shouted a muffled "Build me up!" as he struggled out of his ripped and dingy wife-beater. Wearing his trademark grin, Penn obligingly reached into the backseat of the truck's cab, found a T-shirt, and then tossed it at his fan.

Alessandra watched the guy drive off, now covered by a new, royal blue and white shirt emblazoned with what she assumed was the logo of Penn's show. Before she had a chance to remark on it, a snazzy convertible paused in the middle of the street. A blonde waved to get Penn's attention. "Penn Bennett!" With her car still running, she kneeled on her seat and stripped off a tight nylon shirt. Underneath she wore a sportsbra that made a stunning presentation of her centerfold-sized cleavage. "Build me up!"

"Sorry, I'm all out of T-shirts," Penn said, his smile not the least bit apologetic. The big liar wasn't even pretending to look the woman in the eyes.

Alessandra leaned back inside the vehicle. Her searching hand immediately found a healthy stack of T-shirts. In two seconds she'd peeled one off and thrown it in the direction of her "boss." It caught him smack in the face.

Still, he remained smiling as the woman, now decently covered, accelerated off. "Thanks for helping me out," he said to Alessandra, though his focus was on the receding vehicle as he waved a reluctant good-bye to the buxom blonde.

Alessandra smoothed out her scowl. "Sartorial upgrades, too?" she questioned sweetly. "When they said you were an expert at improvements, I had no idea just how far that went."

He turned his head. "Truth? I'm nothing more than a glorified handyman." His gaze trickled down, taking her in from pale work shirt to lightweight hiking boots. His smile went seductive. "But I will say I'm good at what I do. You have something in need of repair, sweet thing?"

The way he said it, the way he looked at her, sucked the air from her lungs and caused her skin to prickle like a sunburn. "Just the cottage," she choked out, turning away from him. "That's all we bargained for."

The bell rang as she opened the hardware store's door. Inside, the smell was a pungent combination of bubblegum balls, WD-40, and rosebush food. She didn't bother to ensure Penn followed before the door swung shut. It was easy to ascertain he was on her heels. The curiosity stamping the faces of the owners, Ed and Jed, told her that. In twin gestures—apropos, since the elderly men *were* twins— they rocked back on their heels and slid their hands into the front pockets of their khaki coveralls.

"Hi, Jed. Ed." Alessandra moved quickly along the side counter they stood behind, knowing what she was after could be found at the rear of the store.

"Alessandra." One of the old men nodded a greeting.

The other just stared behind her. "That isn't your boyfriend," he declared, his faded blue eyes narrowing.

"Of course not," she answered, keeping her feet moving and keeping her voice light. "He's just doing some work at the winery."

"Then why's he staring at your backside like that?"

Face flaming, Alessandra whipped her head over her shoulder to glare at Penn.

He lifted his hands from his sides, the picture of innocence. "Senile," he mouthed, sliding a meaningful look at the elderly twins, but the corners of his lips were twitching, as if ready to smile again. It made her want to smack him.

Which meant she would have to touch him, and instinct told her she shouldn't do that.

Instead she increased the speed of her footsteps. At the rear she found the display of work gloves. Shoving her right hand into one that was much too big, she ignored Penn as he came up beside her. "I love hardware stores like this one," he said, sounding happy. "You can still dump nails in a brown paper bag and weigh them like grapefruit."

Her second choice of handwear caught his attention. "Not those," he said, plucking the flowered pair away. "You wear that kind when cutting flowers or weeding the herb garden. I'm putting you to real work, honey."

"Don't call me that," she said. "Don't call me 'sweet thing' or 'baby' either, and don't look at my . . . my . . ."

"Ass?" he supplied, still in that happy voice. "But you have a very cute ass. I can't help myself."

She huffed out a sound, knowing he was discomfiting her on purpose, knowing that he took enjoyment from it, but unable to stifle her annoyance anyway.

"What?" He was all innocence again. "Is there some law around here against checking you out?"

"Yes," she hissed. Because there kind of was. And she liked it that way.

"No," he scoffed, picking out a pair of sturdy leather gloves and handing them to her to try. "It's just part of your game—"

"I don't play games!" Frustrated, she whirled to face him. "You don't know anything about me, about who I am, about what I—" She broke off, mortified that her frustration had morphed into a telltale sting behind her eyes. Some people were just easy criers, damn it, and she'd always been one of them.

"Here the tears come," he said. His expression hardened and he made a point of glancing at his watch. "Right on schedule."

Without answering, she stomped off again, heading for the other side of the store and the paint counter. There was a small line there and she reached toward the old-fashioned metal dispenser and took a paper number.

Thirteen. Yeah. Her lucky day.

As she queued up, the person in front of her turned. "Alessandra! Good morning."

She managed a smile for an old friend of her father's. "Morning, Rex."

"You need paint?"

"Picking some up." She felt Penn's presence and explained for him, too. "I ordered a few gallons to refresh the kitchen when I get the chance."

"Then step up, girl," Rex said. He tapped the lady in front him. "Alessandra needs to get her paint."

"Oh, but I don't want to go ahead . . ." She started to protest, but already she could tell how this would turn out. Throughout the last five years, the town's citizens had given her special treatment. She'd been determined to put a stop to it until her sister Stevie explained that it assuaged some of their grief by doing so.

"But I want you to," Rex assured her, and the woman was shuffling back and the man in front of her turned around, saw it was Alessandra, and with a gesture ushered her to his place at the start of the line.

The transaction was over in just a few minutes, but it felt much longer with Penn radiating disapproval. It didn't take a genius to guess he considered her manipulative and most likely spoiled, and this latest episode must seem like just more proof.

She could explain the kindness and consideration by telling him about what hadn't happened five years before. The wedding of Alessandra, age twenty, and Tommy, age twenty-two, had been eagerly anticipated, in part because their youth made the union so sweetly romantic. The bigger bonus, however, was it had presented an opportunity to celebrate health and vitality as only those whose livelihood depended upon farming—grape-growing was really nothing more, after all—could appreciate.

Yesterday, Liam and Seth had been a breath away from detailing at least some of that. For a second she'd wanted Penn Bennett to hear the story and see him squirm like the lowly worm he was. Then he'd be sorry, she'd thought. Then he'd be sorry for *her*. But . . .

She didn't want his sympathy. And why should she care what he thought about her anyway?

She didn't.

She wouldn't.

Back in front of Ed and Jed, she purchased the items they'd collected. Besides the paint and the gloves, Penn had picked up a new broom and a stack of disposable face masks. He tossed wooden stir sticks onto the counter and plopped a tissue-thin painter's cap on top of her hair. "If you're going to do some painting, you'll need this, too."

"Uh . . . thanks." She glanced at him, but he shifted his gaze away and busied himself stuffing change into a collection for the San Francisco Ronald McDonald House.

Jed was putting the loose items into a bag while Ed watched. Then his head snapped up. "I have something I want to tell you. I said to Jed—"

"'I have something to tell Allie,'" his brother parroted.

"Right." Ed looked at her expectantly. "So what was it?"

She laughed. "I don't know, Ed. What *was* it?"

He frowned. "It's so damned irritating this getting old—oh, I know now!" His smile beamed on. "Thinking about getting old led me straight to thinking about dying young."

Alessandra's own smile faded. She sent Penn a sidelong glance, but he was still plunking nickels and quarters into the plastic canister. "So, um, what do you have to tell me, Ed?"

"I went to visit Carlene on Friday."

"Oh." Carlene was his late wife.

"Passed by your dad. Everything looks great there."

"Good."

"But Tommy . . ."

Tommy. She saw him then, still too thin, but grinning like a fool, like someone who'd won the lottery, like someone who was marrying his love the very next day. "We're going to have such a great life," he'd whispered to her at the rehearsal dinner. Happiness had swelled like bubbles inside of her, filling with the sweet juice of expectation, just like grapes growing in a summer vineyard. How young they'd been. How big her heart.

Pressing her lips together, she forced herself back to the present. "Is there a problem at Tommy's grave?" she asked, then regretted the phrasing immediately as beside her, Penn froze. A final coin landed with a lonely plink.

"A vase was knocked over, filled with some purple spiky things."

Lavender. She'd brought them on her last visit.

"I re-righted it," Ed continued. "Tried to prop it up against the headstone. But it may fall over again."

"Okay."

"I thought about calling Sally, but with her so involved with Clare's wedding and all . . . well, I decided to wait until I saw Tommy's girl instead."

"Thanks, Ed," said Tommy's girl. Tommy's almost-bride. "Thanks."

With the purchased items stowed in the truck, there was nothing left to do but get into the cab. It was quiet inside as they drove toward Tanti Baci and a different kind of tension now thrummed between her and Penn.

Alessandra pulled in a breath and then glanced over at him. "So . . ."

He continued staring out the window as he steered. "I'm going to feel like an asshole, aren't I?"

Despite everything, she felt a smile try to take over. "Maybe."

"Then don't tell me," he said. "Don't tell me another word."

She let the smile go ahead and bloom then. It eased the sadness inside her and wrapped a little cushion around the tight kernel of her heart so that it didn't rattle quite so much in the cavern of her chest. For the first time since meeting Penn she felt relaxed. Her normal self. Alessandra Baci, the Nun of Napa.

Penn seemed comfortable, too. Or he was quiet anyway, as they parked the truck beside the cottage and unloaded their purchases. At his instruction, she tidied the cottage's floor with the new broom. He stripped off his shirt and began to move panels of Sheetrock from the porch to inside. They kept clear of each other, until her sweeping took her into the main room. She had to sidestep to give him a clear path to the bridal boudoir. Her foot found one of the white plastic bags they'd brought in from the hardware store, and it slid on the film of grit she'd yet to clean.

She slid, too, letting out a little yelp as the broom left her hand and her balance wobbled. Penn grabbed her upper arms, swinging her toward his bare chest to keep her on her feet. It was a reflex on his part, and a reflex on hers to clutch his biceps as her gaze jumped to his face.

His handsome face. His strong body so close. His bulging biceps against her palms.

Heat flushed across her skin, that prickling, sunburnheat that set fire to her nerve endings. She couldn't read the expression in his eyes, and it didn't matter, because it was all she could do to handle her own feelings—the spiking desire, that encompassing heat, the sexual rush that flooded her mind with images of skin and lips and tongues and male parts mating with female parts . . .

"Penn," she whispered. Just like that, just that quick, she wanted something from him, she needed anything—everything—he could offer with his strong body and his clever mouth. It had been so long. She pressed her body to his. "Penn."

He stared down at her.

"Please, Penn . . ." Her tongue brushed her dry lips. *"Please."*

With an inarticulate sound, he jerked away. Quick strides took him outside.

Her gaze followed his escape as mortification proved to be the backwash of that brief but intense sensual tide. She put her palms against her hot cheeks, but they were just as overheated as the rest of her. They'd been touching him. And she'd been coming on to him, no doubt about that. In the look in her eyes, the sway of her body, the desire in her voice. She knew he couldn't have mistaken what she was feeling. There was no way of pretending it hadn't happened, either.

And they had almost a month of togetherness to go.

Maybe she could wiggle her way out of working with him now, she thought. But that was the kind of thing he probably expected from her. There was Clare's upcoming wedding to consider, too. Alessandra would do what she had to, face fiery mortification and even mocking men, to get the job done for Tommy's sister.

That wedding was the important first step toward saving the winery, too.

Inhaling a breath, Alessandra followed Penn into the sunshine. He stood, facing away from her, his hands laced behind his head, elbows out, back muscles tense.

"Penn."

He didn't turn. "What?"

"Sorry about . . . about that." She gestured toward the cottage, even though he couldn't see it. "I . . ."

"You don't have to say any more."

"I do. I have to explain—"

"Don't tell me any more."

"I have to. I don't want you to think I was coming on to you because it's, well, you. It's just that it's been five years since . . ." Alessandra swallowed. "Look. You touched me, and for a second, just a second, I . . . wanted to touch back. That's all."

Penn spun to face her. There was a flush on his cheeks and a glitter in his eyes. "So that incident wasn't about me personally."

"No. It was only about the five years and about me and . . ." The words trailed off as her face heated up again.

He moved toward her.

Though her pulse went crazy once more, she forced herself to hold her ground even as she continued to babble. "It was momentary. And nothing. Less than nothing."

"Less than nothing?" He halted a foot away, his tanned chest rising and falling in counterpoint to the thick beat of her pulse. "Is that right?"

She swallowed again. "Yes."

"So, baby, you're telling me . . ." he began, his hazel eyes mesmerizing her.

She trembled, a poor little bunny hypnotized by the hungry fox. "Telling you what?" she whispered.

"That you're not interested in changing the terms of our bargain."

And she could see it: A new bargain, a different deal. Not Boss and Laborer, but Man and Woman. Lover and Lover. Limbs and tongues. Skin and sweat. Sex . . . and sin. Because as the Nun of Napa, wouldn't it be that, too?

Penn took another step closer and she flung up her hand.

Then flung out the truth.

"Five years ago I was supposed to be married," she said. "My fiancé—Tommy—he'd had cancer. He was in remission, though—we thought he'd beaten it. But then . . . then he died on our wedding day. He died fifteen minutes before we were supposed to say our vows."

4

Stretched out on the king-sized, unmade bed, Clare Knowles watched her best friend step from the bathroom into the bedroom, wrapped only in a towel.

"Pretty," Clare commented, appreciating the view.

Gil jolted, then his hands grabbed for the terrycloth sliding down his hips. Since he was six foot five and two hundred twenty-five pounds of olive skin and etched muscles, the bath sheet looked closer to a washcloth. "God, Clare, scare the hell out of me, why don't you?"

She sent the key ring he'd once given her spinning around her index finger. "Maybe you should be more careful with this."

In three long strides he was close enough to snatch the key from her. "Good advice."

"Hey." Clare sat up, hurt. "Are you really taking that away?"

"You won't be watering my plants anymore." He turned his back on her to rummage through a dresser drawer.

Then he disappeared into the bathroom again, reemerging moments later wearing a pair of buttery Levi's.

"First off," she said, watching him cover up his impressively chiseled chest with a ratty T-shirt, "you've never had any plants. But if you did, why wouldn't I be watering them anymore?"

"Clare. You're getting married in less than a month." He said it as if she was the kind of stupid girl who got her tent zipper stuck and then cried until she could be rescued by him.

Of course, she was that girl.

"I have no idea what my wedding has to do with me and you." That was a lie, of course, since the whole reason she'd ambushed him tonight had everything to do with her marriage and Gil.

He looked at her through inscrutable eyes. Dark-lashed, dark brown eyes that had made females swoon since he was five years old. Girls used to chase him around the kindergarten recess yard begging for kisses. Clare had pushed more than one of them down before Gil confessed he sort of liked it, proving that they'd always been there for each other—and that they'd always told each other the truth, too.

"Why have you been avoiding me?" she asked.

"I don't know what you're talking about."

But see, now Gil had started lying to her, too. Clare ignored the way her stomach curled inward at the thought of that. Pasting on a little smile, she patted the mattress beside her. "Then come over here."

"I don't think that's a good idea."

Now it was her turn to stare at him. They'd been two peas in a pod during childhood. Remained close friends in high school. Had been sharing their lives throughout their twenties. Last summer, they'd even spooned on a couch three nights straight, when they'd taken a road trip to visit one of her college friends. "I won't bite."

He let out a mirthless laugh, and then with a shrug of his broad shoulders threw himself down onto the mattress beside her. Shoving a pillow beneath his head, he crossed his legs at the ankles and his arms over his chest. "What is it you want, Clare?"

She frowned at him. He was going to be difficult about this, she'd known that from the start, but even before she'd voiced her request he was acting uncooperative. "Why are you so crabby?"

He glanced at her, glanced away, then released a sigh. "It was a long day, okay? The lousy economy means everybody wants to keep the scruffiest of vehicles in working order and they don't want to go more than a day without their wheels." When he pushed his black hair off his forehead, she noticed the knuckles on his right hand were split open.

She grabbed his palm to inspect the wounds, holding tight when he tried to tug it away. "What happened?"

"Banged 'em on an engine block. Occupational hazard."

Her gaze lifted to his face. "It looks like you punched a wall."

He went all inscrutable again. "Banged 'em on an engine block. Occupational hazard," he repeated.

Her huff of impatience didn't move him, so she tried a different tack. Rolling closer to his tall form, she cupped her hands over his shoulder and propped her chin on her fingers. He stiffened, tensing beneath her touch.

He'd been so darn tense around her lately.

"Gil," she said, keeping her voice soft. He smelled like the generic shampoo she knew he bought at the local big box store along with the matching brand of shaving cream and mega-packs of Hungry Man dinners. They often shopped there together, and last month, when she'd tossed a jumbo box of condoms into his cart as a joke, she'd thought he'd developed a sudden allergy. His face had turned that red.

Which looked really funny on a man who was six foot five, twice her weight, and who'd been nicknamed the Italian Stallion at twelve years old due to his daily need of a shave. From what she'd observed in the years following, when it came to women he actually lived up to the nickname.

He was looking a little red-faced now, too, strangely enough. "Gil . . ." she started again, feeling more uncertain than before. The red face, the distance, the desire to have his house key back! What was that all about . . . ?

"It's a woman!" she blurt out, the light dawning. "You found someone with an expiration date longer than your gallon of low-fat." She tweaked him about that all the time—that he lost interest in a woman faster than it took for his milk to turn into cottage cheese.

One minute she was looking into his tanned, almost-too-handsome face and the next he was presenting her with his back. He'd swung his legs over the side of the bed and now sat on its edge, his elbows on his knees, his head in his hands.

Clare gaped, unsure how to take the abrupt move. "Gil?" She scooted closer so that she could stroke her hand down the back of his shirt. When her palm ran over the bare skin revealed by a rent in the cotton fabric, he twitched like she'd burned him.

"Maybe you should go now, Clare."

And leave her best friend feeling . . . what? "Doesn't she . . . is it that the woman you're interested in isn't interested back?" Though that didn't make any sense. No one could deny that Gil was flat-out gorgeous and by any standard other than her mother's, a business success as well. That he hadn't gone to college and yet made a good living for himself and his employees by working with his hands shouldn't put off any female worthy enough to catch Gil's eye.

"Who is she?" Clare demanded, and the little green around the edges she was starting to feel was surely due to the fact that this woman was causing Gil—Clare's best friend—heartache.

He groaned. "Clare, just leave it alone."

"I won't." She kneed across the mattress in order to sit beside him. "If she doesn't appreciate you, I'm going to slap her silly."

Shaking his head, he let out another of those mirthless laughs. "Not a good idea. She doesn't deserve it, not at all."

"Huh. So she *does* like you back?"

"Yeah. She likes me fine."

Funny, how that didn't really make her feel a whole lot better. "I think I better meet this person."

"Clare—"

"Jordan will be in town on Friday night. We'll double date."

"Clare—"

"You know how stubborn I can be."

He sighed, then turned his head to send her a look. "That's how I ended up with a broken arm, if I recall."

"So not my fault! I wanted to retrieve those abandoned birds' eggs. No one made you climb the tree to get them instead of me."

"You couldn't climb a tree worth a damn."

"How can we know?" she scoffed. "You never gave me a chance, always playing white knight like you do."

"Yeah, that's me. The good guy."

There was a glimmer of a smile on his face for the first time and she grabbed the moment. "I have the perfect opportunity for you to be the good guy yet again," she said, hearing the wheedling note in her own voice.

Gil's smile died and a wary light entered his eyes. "No."

"I haven't even told you what it is," she protested.

"When you're trying to wrap me around your little finger, I know I'm in trouble."

She bumped his shoulder with hers. "C'mon. It's a pretty finger," she said, holding it up to him.

He clasped her single digit in his fist. His skin was so warm. A little tremor of . . . *something* wiggled its way up her arm and she took her hand back, shoving it under her thigh. "You're trying to distract me."

His eyes narrowed. "Is it working?"

She shook off the strange sensation still jittering across her skin. "No. I need a favor."

"I already said I'd throw the bachelor party. Please don't ask me to jump out of the cake at your bachelorette shindig."

"What? Jump out of the cake . . ." It was the farthest thing from her mind, yet now it was *in* her mind. Gil, with his olive skin and tight muscles. His white smile and snapping dark eyes. He'd jump out of her cake and then . . . and then she'd jump him. Gil could be her final fling as a single woman.

She shook herself again. Gil. Fling. Did not compute. Gil. Friend. That worked. That's what he was. The friend she wanted beside her when she stood in front of the world and pledged herself to Jordan.

"I want you to be my Man of Honor," she blurted out.

He straightened. "What?"

"Jordan's pregnant sister had to bow out of the ceremony. The doctor has her on bed rest. She was my Matron of Honor, so I need to choose someone else. And I choose you, except we'll call you the Man of Honor, okay?"

"No."

"You don't have to wear her dress or anything like that. We'll get you a tux."

He rolled his eyes. "Gee, thanks, because I don't look good in that Pepto color your bridesmaids are wearing. But the answer's still the same."

"It's not Pepto. It's a soft, flattering pink." She bit her lip. "Gil, I wanted you in that role from the very first, but—"

"But your mother wouldn't have approved," he finished for her. "And she won't like it any more now."

Clare bit her lip again. "You know I'm letting her mostly have her way."

He lifted a brow. "Mostly?"

"Okay. Nearly entirely. Almost all. But the ceremony doesn't mean much to me and it means a whole heck of a lot to Mom." Who could blame her? Sally Knowles had been over-the-moon about Tommy and Alessandra's wedding and then had been robbed of both the ceremony and her son. Because of that, Clare thought it was the least she could do to let her mother direct her daughter's event.

"But you're ready to buck her now?" Gil asked.

"Yes." Clare nodded. "On this, yes. I need you beside me on the big day. Who else will comfort me if I get a bad case of bridal nerves at the very last second? Please, Gil, forget your macho qualms and stand by the bride's side."

He softened a little. "I'm always on your side."

Her heart leaped. "Then you'll do it?"

Gil's gaze cut away and he groaned. Then he looked back at her and his big hand reached out and cupped her cheek. "Tell you what, Clare," he said, brushing this thumb over her cheekbone. "I'll think about it."

Her heart leaped again. And that weird trilling, tickling feeling was rushing over her skin. It must be a response to the near victory, she told herself. Still, she then did just what she'd been complaining Gil had been doing for months— she jumped off the bed and skittered for the doorway, putting a very healthy distance between them.

~

Inside the cottage it was as hot as an August afternoon in hell, but Penn knew it had nothing to do with the moderate June temperature outdoors. It was Alessandra's sweet little body. And his mood. It made him as mad as the devil that he was *still* turned on by her.

Everything she'd told him the day before should have squelched his response. She'd dropped the little five-years-dead-fifteen-minutes-before-the-vows bombshell just as he was about to give into the urge to grab her and plunder. She'd been begging for it, right?

Please, Penn, she'd said, her delicate frame as hot and heavy as a brand against his flesh. *Please.* Though somehow he'd managed to yank himself and his libido free and escape outside, she'd followed. Apologies, excuses, some silly babble about her coming on to him but not really coming on to *him*—none of her chatter had registered. There was only her big brown eyes and her tender-looking mouth and he'd wanted, wanted, wanted . . .

Until she'd blurted the truth that he'd only begun to guess in the hardware store.

Five years ago I was supposed to be married.

Four sentences later, he'd hightailed it back to the Bennett place and holed up for the rest of the night with the big-screen TV in the oversized bedroom they'd assigned him on the second floor. This morning, though, he'd come back to the cottage because, damn it, a man had to take a stand.

He'd promised to complete the renovation and there was Sheetrock to hang. More importantly, he refused to be hostage to his own libido and he'd figured that once her past history had a little more time to penetrate he'd be free of it. Of her.

Except that wasn't the case. Oh, no, as much as he'd been pretending to ignore her for hours as he nailed up the sheets of wallboard in the room that was designated as the bride's boudoir, he'd really been calculating exactly how long her shorts were—four modest inches below the perky curve of her ass. In that time he'd also used his years of painting experience to pin down the exact shade of lipstick on her prim yet puffy bow-shaped mouth—Sweet Melon. Worst of all, not once had he avoided the sweat-inducing sight of her cleavage—revealed all the way to the little satin bow between the cups of her deep-cut bra. Another man might have informed her of the unintended display the very moment two crucial buttons had popped open on her shirt.

Penn hadn't. Because . . . well, wouldn't the fact he'd noticed make her uncomfortable?

See. He'd been thinking of Alessandra's feelings. Yeah, that was it.

The sound of her footsteps interrupted his thoughts. He glanced over his shoulder to see her awkwardly wrangling another four foot by eight foot rectangle of Sheetrock in his direction. With a curse, he punished the head of the nail he was setting with a final blow from his hammer, then racked the tool in his belt and strode over to yank the panel away from Alessandra.

"I'll get those myself," he bit out. This close he could see the fine tendrils of damp curls around her hairline. The heat seemed to twist her hair tightly, and it released a subtle wave of her perfume, too. The scent went to his head and was almost as dizzying as the view of her breasts heaving in and out with her labored breaths.

"I can do it," she said. "They're not heavy, just awkward."

"You'll break a nail," he replied unkindly. "And I don't have time to mop up your waterworks over that."

Her jaw dropped. She even had cute teeth, small and white, and it pissed him off yet again to notice that. He wanted to run his tongue over them, to feel them bite into his chest, to experience the scratch of their edges when she—

"Hello!" a man's voice called from the front room, followed by the rap of knuckles against wood. "Allie? You in here? It's Mark and Mike about those benches you ordered."

She shot Penn a narrow-eyed look and then spun away from him.

Good riddance, he thought, moving to prop the piece of Sheetrock on the far wall. Then he remembered the open shirt barely covering her, which would allow "Mark and Mike" to ogle all that Penn should have pointed out.

He rushed for the doorway leading to the other room, dismayed to see that Mark and Mike were a couple of young dudes in their twenties and that she still hadn't discovered those unfastened buttons. The three people were all gathered close, and she had her knee propped on a box as she studied a sketch of some sort. Her pose lowered her chest and laid out her bounty practically right in the faces of the young men who . . . weren't looking.

Wearing serious, respectful expressions, they were focused entirely on the paper in her hand. One of the guys made a couple of notations in a tattered, palm-sized notebook with a stubby pencil. Penn recognized the pencil, the frayed notebook, the kind of men. He'd dealt with carpenters like these for years. Hardworking guys who perpetually had sawdust stuck to their forearms, who drank beer when they knocked off for the day, and who would never miss a chance to take an appreciative eyefull of a beautiful woman. But he'd seen carpenters look at a length of oak with more sexual interest than these two were directing toward Alessandra.

Puzzled, Penn stayed where he was, watching as the trio straightened.

She handed the sketch back to the taller man. "Looks great, Mark." There was a moment's pause, then she caught the young guy's eye. "But I was wondering . . . do you think you could deliver them three days earlier than we originally discussed?"

"Allie, um . . ." Mark seemed mesmerized for a moment. "Um . . . Maybe . . ." Then he shook himself like a wet dog and deliberately redirected his gaze. "No. I don't think . . ."

"Please, Mark," she said softly.

"But Allie . . ."

She put her hand on his arm and his gaze slowly came back to hers. "*Please.*"

Penn flashed back to the day he'd first met her. The laborers speaking together in Spanish. *Everyone knows not to look her in the eyes.*

Mark's buddy Mike made a little whining sound as the other carpenter nodded like a marionette.

"Thank you!" Obviously delighted, Alessandra grabbed one carpenter and then the other, bussing each on the cheek.

Instead of enjoying the burst of affection—and finding some way to prolong it like any normal, red-blooded male—Penn saw that the two couldn't get away from her fast enough.

"As soon as the cottage is complete," she called to their retreating backs, "I'll make you each a batch of cookies!"

Penn came up behind her as the men drove off. "Kisses and cookies," he said. "But they're still running from you like you're spreading cooties."

Her eyebrows rose. "I don't know what you mean."

"Seriously. Do you have mono or something?"

"I'm perfectly healthy," she answered, followed by a big breath that proved just how healthy she was.

Penn didn't try to hide the direction of his gaze this time.

Her glance followed his, and she bleated, her fingers immediately doing up the disobedient buttons, including one more for good measure.

"You're a dog," she fumed.

"Yeah," he agreed, shrugging. "But what I want to know is why those two men were like a pair of neutered tabbies."

Her cheeks turned pink. "I never understand a word you're saying." She made to move past him.

He caught her shoulder. Big mistake. His grip on the

fabric popped her buttons again. More dangerous, he felt her under his hand. The delicate framework of her bones, the sudden rush of heat to her skin, the shiver that quivered through her body at his touch.

His breath caught in his chest as that subtle shudder seemed to roll through his palm, across his arm, and down his own body. Desire crashed into him, washed over him, burned through his veins to race like fire in his blood. *She* did this to him, the goddamned Nun of Napa.

That he still couldn't prevent it really ticked him off. And something else had him raging, too.

"They never even look at you, do they?" he asked, his voice harsh.

She trembled but didn't move away, as if trapped by his hand. She didn't answer.

He tightened his hold. "Tell me what you haven't," he heard himself say, even though there was no reason to know the details. "Make me understand why people around here treat you like this. They're afraid to meet your eyes. They're afraid to glance at your tits."

She gasped in offense.

"Well, hell, Alessandra. They're damn good tits and you're the one laying them out there."

Her glance fell to her cleavage once again and then she jerked her shoulder from him as she buttoned up a second time.

Penn shook his head. "This just doesn't make sense. Something's not right here."

Her gaze jumped to him and there was fire in her eyes. "I hate the expression on your face," she said, and he could tell her mad mood matched his. "It's like you're trying to punch holes in my story. Do you want me to track down Tommy's obituary that ran in the paper? I have it somewhere."

Yeah, she probably did, along with a pressed flower from her wedding bouquet and the rings they'd never exchanged.

For some reason that thought only spiked his ire. Beautiful Alessandra Baci, languishing after what couldn't be. Yearning for a touch from ghostly hands.

"Well?" She slammed her arms across her chest, popping the top buttons yet again. "Why are you so suspicious of me?"

He didn't have every answer to that himself. Shaking his head again, he slid his hands in his pockets, determined to keep them to himself from now on. "Maybe it's my job. The first season of the show we had to revamp the participant application six times to get it right. Now it's fourteen pages developed by a unit of lawyers. A regiment of PIs then go about verifying every fact. The schemers we've seen—"

"I'm not a schemer!"

"You're something," he muttered. "What that is, I just don't know. Except it's weird as hell how they treat you like you're made of glass."

"That's because—" She broke off. "You wouldn't understand."

He thought he did, remembering the old guys in the hardware store. His fingers tightened into fists. "You're still Tommy's girl, is that it?"

"Look, I don't owe you any explan—"

"Give me one anyway."

She rolled those big brown eyes, but then her gaze met his. "It's just that . . . that we were always a couple. We were high school sweethearts when Tommy was diagnosed his senior year. We danced at his prom with him in a wheelchair and me on his lap. Then four years passed and everyone believed he'd beaten it—he *had* beaten it— but the drugs that helped him had damaged his heart. It gave out on the way to our wedding. So just as he'll always be the one who died too young, then, yeah, I'll always be Tommy's girl."

"Christ," he ground out, not the least bit satisfied by her answer. "You're a woman—"

"Widow," she corrected, then frowned. "Well, almost a widow."

Worse than a widow, Penn decided. A baby almost-bride who might as well be buried beside the hometown boy who'd died too young to make good. People looked at her and saw tragedy instead of a living, breathing person. Hence the acquiescence to her every request, the tremors at her every tear.

She took a step closer to him, bringing her scent that much nearer. He sucked it in, and his head spun. But his vision was clear enough to make out the thrumming beat of the pulse in her throat, and he knew his nearness affected her, too.

He saw her face flush and her pupils dilate, but she challenged him all the same, silly woman. "Satisfied now?" she asked.

Silly, silly woman. "Not even close," he answered, knowing as he did that he was no longer going to keep his hands to himself. He couldn't, not with that scent in his head and this clamoring need to show baby bride that she wasn't as cold as that corpse in her past.

As he bent his head closer to her lips, he slid his palm inside that half-opened shirt that had made him crazy all the long, damn day.

5

Alessandra saw the kiss coming. She had all the time in the world to leap away from Penn or to push at his chest and shove him back. But her feet seemed rooted to the scarred floor and it was only at the last second that she arched her spine, avoiding his mouth.

The movement pushed her chest toward his descending palm.

His callused fingers slid right between the gaping edges of her cotton blouse, to glide under the cup of her bra. Maybe he only meant to cop a quick feel over her clothes— or at least give her the scare that he was trying for one—but she'd provided him with intimate, naked contact. In instant response, her nipple tightened to a painful bud, her breasts swelled, and goose bumps broke out like prickly heat over the rest of her skin.

He was infecting her again, and she was helpless against the virus rushing through her system. It paralyzed her.

Him, too, perhaps, because they just stared at each

other, as if they were complete strangers surprised to find themselves bedmates in the quarantine ward.

"W-what are you doing?" she whispered.

His gaze dropped from her face to his hand, half-hidden by her clothes. She saw the long muscle in his arm flex. Yes. Good. He was going to pull away.

Instead, his fingertips drew toward each other, each one taking a short path until they met around her stiff nipple. The back of her neck burned, and even her watery knees couldn't put out the fire, it was just that hot. "Penn," she managed to choke out, but she didn't think he heard her.

He appeared fascinated with his hand, or maybe it was the budded center of her breast because he tested it with a tiny squeeze, his face going hard as she twitched in help-less, pleasured reaction. "You like that," he said, his voice husky. His gaze flicked to hers. "Admit it. You like me touching you."

"Don't." Not *don't*, she thought. *No.* She should say that, right? *No* was on the tip of her tongue, it was echoing in her head, but then that inner voice amended the word. *Yes, yes, yes,* it moaned instead as he tightened his fingers in a second gentle pinch.

She couldn't breathe. Her nipple was throbbing now, matching the pulse at her throat and the second one thrum-ming between her legs. It was soft there, aching, and it had been so long since she'd felt sensual pain—and it was so wrong to feel it now, with Penn Bennett, a man she didn't like—that her brain couldn't prescribe a plan of action.

"I . . ." Her voice drifted off as he applied more delicate pressure. A shudder raced down her spine.

"Alessandra, admit you like me touching you."

"Penn," she said, protesting his familiarity, his ex-pertise, the confidence in his damn demand. Her fingers closed around his wrist. She was going to remove his hand, show him the door, kick his disturbing presence out of the cottage and out of her life.

But instead she hung on as he caressed her again. This time she voiced her moan, a soft and needy sound that brought a small smile to his face.

"Yeah, that's what I'm talking about, sweetheart. You and I, we could . . . we *should* . . ."

But he didn't finish the thought. His head came up and his eyes narrowed. Something over her shoulder caught his attention and within another short breath his hand was gone and her shirt was buttoned up to her chin.

She hated her disappointment. No, damn it. She hated *him*.

Righteous indignation returning, she shoved at his chest. "You're never touching me again," she said.

He looked at her with pity. "Keep telling yourself that, baby."

"I mean it!"

His head was shaking back and forth. "We—"

"Will never be alone together after this," she spit out, furious with herself as much as she was furious at him. "You might like to play these kinds of games—" She broke off as he laid a finger over his mouth.

"It's not a game, Alessandra, it's visitors." He gestured behind her with his chin. "We've got company."

She whirled. Through the open doorway, she could see Clare and Sally climbing out of a car. "Oh, God."

"I was hoping to hear that in an entirely different context," he murmured.

A rattlesnake would have envied the venom she put into the look she sent him over her shoulder. "No way."

"Way," he replied. "Maybe not now, maybe not today, but between your history and our combined combustibility, we're not going to be able to ignore this chemistry forever."

It was too late to put him in his place, not with the other women almost over the cottage's threshold. Alessandra settled for pasting a smile on her face, and it was a genuine one, too, full of the welcome only a woman who'd been saved—partly from herself, she had to admit—could feel. "Sally! Clare! I am *so* happy to see you!"

She pretended not to hear the dark chuckle behind her.

Lucky for her, it seemed the mother-daughter pair's preoccupation with the upcoming wedding caused them to overlook her flustered state and still-burning face. At their request, she showed the bride and her mother around the cottage, describing her vision of the finished product.

They ended in the bridal boudoir, where Penn was at work again. He'd removed his T-shirt, revealing the contrast between the pale blue of his low-slung Levi's and the toasty, warm color of his skin.

Clare nudged Alessandra with an elbow. "Poor you," she whispered. "Having to work all day with a guy who looks like *that*."

Pretending she didn't notice the play of muscles in his shoulders, arms, and back, Alessandra shrugged. "The fact is Penn doesn't really need me. I'll be back to my regular work in the office tomorrow."

The hitch in his hammer stroke told her he'd heard. His backward glance touched her face, then moved on to Sally's. "Ah," he said. "But I don't think I can guarantee this place will be wedding-ready without that extra pair of hands you provide."

The instant alarm on Tommy's mother's face goaded Alessandra into stepping closer. She ignored the distracting ripple of Penn's pec muscles as he turned to face her. "Listen," she told him, "there's no doubt whatsoever—"

"We had a deal, didn't we?" he said. "And you said you had someone filling in at your desk."

The intern was nearly as good as Alessandra herself, not that she'd tell him that. "I know, but—"

"And face it," he continued. "You'll have a better chance of restarting your social life out here with me than if you're holed away in your office."

Oh, that rat.

Sally was already swinging toward Alessandra, a new distress in her expression. "Allie, are you . . . are you *dating*?"

"No." When Tommy's mother's tension didn't ease, Alessandra shot Penn a sharp look and raised her voice. "*No.*"

"My bad, Mrs. Knowles," Penn put in affably. "I can't help myself. Around my friends, I'm always the one matchmaking."

Oh, please.

He smiled at Alessandra, all pearly whites and Hollywood-style sincerity. "I see a pretty young thing like this," he pointed to her with the business end of his hammer, "and I just can't help myself from wanting to . . ."

"Wanting to what?" Sally prompted.

His glance slid to Alessandra, his eyes laughing. Her neck burned again as she relived the sensation of his fingers on her breast. *Admit you like me touching you.*

"He wants to embarrass me," she muttered.

Clare was regarding her with raised eyebrows. "I think he's right, you know I do," she murmured. "It's past time you returned to the dating circuit."

Dating wasn't what Penn had in mind, and unfortunately, Alessandra's traitorous body wasn't interested in miniature golf or a night at the movies, either. "I'm not looking for anyone."

Sally sidestepped closer and slid her arm around Alessandra's shoulders to hug her close. "Because it would be impossible to replace Tommy in her heart. Everybody knows that."

"Everybody knows that," Alessandra echoed. "So let's let Penn get back to what he was doing—"

"Not when Penn thinks it would be so easy to find a man to take my Tommy's place," Sally countered. "If you're going to be working together every day until the wedding—

and Allie, I'll only feel confident if you're right here by his side—I need to take just a minute to explain how very irreplaceable my son is."

Alessandra barely held back her groan, now neatly trapped into weeks of more togetherness with Penn.

As Sally began describing for Penn the superb athlete, student, and cancer survivor her son had been, Clare pulled Alessandra a short way from the other two.

"I really thought my wedding would give Mom a new purpose," she said in a low voice, her expression glum. "But she's still focused on Tommy."

Alessandra patted her friend's arm. "She *is* enjoying herself, Clare. And letting her make so many of the decisions has been very generous of you."

Her friend didn't look cheered. "Just trying to live up to my dead brother."

"Oh, Clare—"

"But let's not go there," the other woman replied. Her face brightened. "I want to pump you for information instead."

"About what?"

"Your cousin, Gil. Tell me everything you know about this woman he's seeing."

Alessandra frowned. "Gil's always seeing a woman. They come, they go, they—"

"Never exceed their 'best used by' date." Clare pushed her newly highlighted hair over her shoulders. "But I have a feeling this one is different."

"I don't know who she is. Anyway, you're his best friend. If he'd tell anyone, he'd tell you."

Clare was already shaking her head. "No, he's very close-mouthed around me these days."

"Interesting. But maybe there's nothing to tell. If the relationship is so new, he's probably not having sex with her yet." Alessandra met Clare's gaze.

"Nah," they said together.

"Six-foot-five, two hundred twenty-five pounds . . ." Alessandra started.

"Of sexy Italian stallion," Clare finished, then her voice turned sly. "And speaking of sexy."

Alessandra kept her gaze from even flicking toward Mr. Hollywood. "Yes? Do you need help picking out your honeymoon nightwear?"

Clare made a face, then jerked her thumb at Penn, the movement hidden from him by the angle of her body. "Allie, why not? He's delicious, and you deserve a, um, social life. Why don't you . . ."

"No." She wouldn't let her friend finish the thought. It was bad enough that she was going to have to work with Penn. Going "social" with him was completely out of the question. A dozen reasons made it a bad idea, ranging from his annoying arrogance to her sinless status in the community.

Clare didn't appear convinced. "Allie . . ."

"I mean it," she told her friend, loud enough to get her point across, she hoped. She would work with him, but that was all. "Not going there. Definitely not going there."

"But you already said yes," Sally Knowles's voice joined their conversation.

Alessandra blinked, then realized her words had been taken as part of a different discussion. "I'm sorry, Sally, I was responding to something else."

"Oh, good," Tommy's mother answered. "For a moment I thought you were backing out of the barbecue at our house tomorrow night. I invited Penn to come and I assured him that while you don't 'date,' no one will think anything about the two of you attending together."

~

For a nun, Penn thought with irritation as he followed Alessandra from her car to the Knowles's barbecue, the woman dressed too damn sexy. In Cinderella-blue, the sleeveless dress dipped squarely across her breasts and then fell in petallike folds to her knees. A skinny black belt was buckled around her narrow middle and matched the strappy sandals on her feet. Yes, it was entirely unfair for her to look so good since he'd made—yet another, but this time for good—vow to keep his hands off her.

He took his gaze from Alessandra's swaying hips and the enticing little flutter of her dress's hemline to glance around the spacious area behind the sprawling, ranch-style home. There was a long, wide deck running along the rear of the house. On one end, painted wooden steps turned toward a sparkling swimming pool. On the other, a short staircase led to sloped grass that was shaded by big oaks. At the bottom of the incline, water trickled along a narrow creek bed.

After listening to Sally Knowles eulogize her son Tommy the day before, it was impossible not to see the young man on that lush grass, sending a football spinning into the warm summer evening air. He would have crossed the wooden deck with an armful of books, preparing to ace yet another exam. And once it was dark, he would have snuggled close to his little sweetheart, their bare feet tangling in the cool creek water.

Even after he'd gone into remission, Tommy Knowles had been no slacker. He'd enrolled in college. He was getting back into sports. He'd acted as chairman for the survivor's charity ball put on by the regional chapter of the cancer society. The event had taken place three weeks before the wedding that hadn't happened.

Sally Knowles had even shown off a picture of the guy, and Penn imagined his blond, crew-cut good looks had been the perfect foil to his fiancée's sweetly exotic beauty. Alessandra's beauty.

No wonder the young woman was still devoted to the love of her life. Who was Penn to determine the limits of her grief? The only thing he'd mourned recently was the loss of his self-respect after Lana had taken him to the cleaners.

Still, he thought as Alessandra paused beside a tub of ice to fish out a beer, it was a damn shame he hadn't kissed her. Wasn't going to happen now, of course, but the sparks between them would have started one spectacular fire.

She held out a dripping bottle and he moved to take it from her. Their fingertips met and even that small brush put off heat. Her gaze flew to his and he saw it all in her bedroom eyes: the wide mattress, the soft sheets, her tight nipples, and the way her lashes would lower and her bottom lip pout as he thumbed those hard tips and insisted she tell him the truth. *Admit you like me touching you.*

She yanked her hand off the glass between them. "Stop it," she hissed. "Stop looking at me like that."

He held his hands up, away from his body. "I don't mean to do anything, sweetheart. It just happens this way sometimes."

She shot him a suspicious glance. "For you, maybe."

"With *you*, baby. But I'm officially done trying to get into the hot pants you wear beneath your habit, little nun."

"Right." More skepticism.

He used his free hand and started to sketch an *X* over his chest. "Cross my heart and—"

"Don't." Alessandra lunged for his fingers, grabbing them. "Don't finish that thought."

"Okay, okay." Hoping to die wasn't what she wanted to hear.

Remembering why, he withdrew his hand from hers. Sparks or no sparks, he was leaving her alone. Glancing around the party, he decided there had to be sixty, seventy people there, none of whom he knew from Adam. "Go off and enjoy yourself."

She hesitated, obviously torn between playing Miss Manners or protecting herself from the unwelcome sexual chemistry that bubbled between them like that science experiment he'd botched in senior year Chem.

"You good girls . . ." Penn sighed, shaking his head. "Look. You better keep moving or I'll renege on my promise and slide my hand under your short skirt to answer that eternal question: thong, boy briefs, or bikinis?"

He'd gone for outrage, and for a long, silent moment he thought he'd got it, but then she laughed. "All right, Penn, I'll let you scare me off." She turned to go, but stopped herself long enough to send him a wicked look over her shoulder. "But you forgot one other option . . ."

The Nun of Napa with the devil in her eyes sucked his breath straight from his chest. "Huh?" he managed to choke out.

"Think about it, Penn." Her voice lowered to a husky whisper. "Maybe under there I'm . . . bare."

A man with faster reflexes would have caught the saucy flutter of her hem and reeled her back. But Penn was paralyzed. He'd met Demanding Alessandra, Angry Alessandra, Vulnerable Alessandra, but Flirting Alessandra—it was a contradiction in terms. And it caused his head to spin. He stared after her retreating figure until someone jostled his elbow.

Stevie Baci was regarding him with interest, looking slim and cool in a pair of formfitting white jeans and a sleeveless tunic. "When my little sister said she'd meet me here, she didn't mention she had a date."

"Because she doesn't," he replied. "Everybody knows Alessandra doesn't date."

"Hmm," Stevie said, still studying him. "But I don't think that stops you from wishing she would."

Just then, the sister in question emerged between two nearby clusters of guests, rushing their way. Her appearance saved Penn from having to answer aloud. Inside, though, he agreed, if by "dating" Stevie meant he'd get to stroke that luscious flush of pink on Alessandra's cheeks and be the focus of the bright eyes that were right now fixed on her sister.

"Emerson is here!" she said as she came to a stop, her voice breathless. "Stevie, Emerson Platt is here."

The taller woman stilled for a moment, then she shrugged. "So what?"

"You said the next time you saw him you were going to shove him in a swimming pool. He's right over there, by the deep end."

"I threatened that because he doesn't swim well," Stevie explained, then shrugged again. "I don't care enough to murder him anymore, though."

Alessandra looked indignant. "He should pay. He was supposed to be your happy ending."

"A man who broke things off by leaving me with the impression he'd merely been slumming with me is *not* my happy ending, Allie." Stevie reached into the nearby bucket to extract a diet cola, and her chin-length dark hair slid across her cheek, hiding her expression. "I don't have a lot of faith in those anyhow."

"You don't believe in happy endings?" Alessandra echoed with a frown, then looked toward Penn, her expression an unspoken plea: *Tell her* you *believe.*

He opened his mouth, ready to cave on the instant. Then his cynical outlook reasserted itself, and he cut the words off with a snap of his teeth. *Good God*, he thought, *they were right. You shouldn't look her in the eyes.*

"Penn?" she said, once more all irresistible appeal.

He steeled himself. "Hey, don't ask me," he said. "My dear old dad made a quick deposit then boogied out of town, so I don't hold much with the ever-afters, either, honey."

Her mouth pursed, which on that pretty kisser looked more like a pout than disappointment, and he shook his head at her sentimental streak. Silly kid, clearly she was one of those daydream believers, which chalked up yet another reason to keep clear of her. Why risk tarnishing her bright fancies?

"Alessandra!" From the doorway leading into the house, Sally Knowles beckoned to the young woman.

With a last glance for her sister and Penn, the little nun headed toward the mother superior of the Convent of Saint Tommy. Penn made sure not to look after the youngest Baci this time. He'd promised himself not to indulge.

Popping the top off his beer, he smiled at Stevie. "So, what is it you do again?"

Her gaze was over his shoulder. "I own a limousine service," she said absently, her eyes narrowing. "You know, airport runs, driving people on tasting tours, that sort of thing . . ."

Her voice trailed off as she tensed. The new alertness sent a bad feeling tiptoeing down Penn's spine, but he wasn't going to turn around. It wasn't any of his business, even if the Nun of Napa was hypnotizing yet another victim or stripping down to her birthday suit.

Okay, fine. The idea of Alessandra naked—*bare!*—had him taking a quick glance back.

Nothing looked out of place. The woman was still wearing that summery blue dress, and if anything she was more covered—she held an oversized, buff-colored envelope to her breast.

"*Christ on a crutch,*" Stevie cursed.

Penn turned back to see Alessandra's sister's stricken expression. "Not again," she said.

"What?" He was a pretty laid-back guy, but her alarm sent another ice cube down his back. "What is it?"

"They arrive out of the blue," Stevie muttered. "She never sees them coming, and it's like being kicked in the stomach every time."

"*What* arrives out of the blue?"

Stevie glanced at him then grimaced. "I'm talking about letters from Tommy. When he was ill with cancer, he wrote a number of them to Allie, commemorating certain special events to let her know his thoughts in case he wasn't here to share them with her."

Penn winced. "Morbid."

"Or romantic," Stevie said with a shrug. "That's what Tommy's mom thinks anyway. Though I think Tommy's dad, Dr. Knowles, objects, Sally follows instructions and hands the damn things over to Allie. It's hard to know what my sister feels, but she can't exactly refuse to accept them."

Penn glanced back again, to see the Nun of Napa spin away from Tommy's mother and push through the crowd in the direction of the sloping grass and the oak-shaded creek. One tight fist clutched the buff envelope.

Stevie groaned. "Damn! I guess I'll have to go after her. I never know what to say."

Chivalry wasn't a quality Penn aspired to, so it came as complete surprise to hear himself murmur, "I'll do it."

"Really?" Stevie gaped. "You'll go?"

And hell, he was going, Penn thought as he actually found himself trailing in Alessandra's wake. He couldn't articulate why, not even to himself. When it came to this girl, impulse was the best explanation he had—which only underscored the problem. He wasn't an impulsive kind of man, and didn't want to become one, especially after the debacle that was Lana.

Sighing, he kept his gaze on Alessandra's retreating figure and threaded through the partygoers, brushing past them until a hand caught his sleeve.

"Penn Bennett!" a man said. "Small state and all that. Though ever since Coppola arrived, there's been plenty of entertainment industry types enjoying the fruits of the vine up here."

Penn blinked, trying to place the face of the one who'd halted his progress. "Rocky Reed." He was a game-show host, a DJ, and a notorious collector of Hollywood gossip, the juiciest of which he shared with listeners on his syndicated and very popular Top 40 radio show.

Short, blond, and fox-featured, he was practically licking his lips as he looked up at Penn. This wasn't good. Did Rocky have something on him? Little asshole.

"Have a drink with me," the other man said, tightening his hold on Penn's arm.

He shook Rocky off. "Busy," he said shortly, already striding away. "I'm after someone else."

The someone he'd explicitly vowed not to pursue, Penn remembered with a belated sigh. But there she was, standing near the creek bed, one slender, golden shoulder propped against the trunk of an oak, her head bent over the missive from beyond the grave.

Christ on a crutch, as Stevie would say. His feet came to a stop as he realized he didn't know what he could do for Alessandra, either. Maybe he should back away, even go have that requested drink with Rocky Reed. This was not Penn's problem, and he'd had his one disaster with a problematic woman.

He was commanding his feet to retreat when suddenly Alessandra looked up and he blinked in surprise at her expression. What had he expected? Tears, he supposed. But her face was flushed, not tear-stained. There was a bright, almost manic light in her eyes. Even from eight feet away he could see the slight tremble in her limbs.

"You," she said, her voice husky. "It's you."

Then she was rushing toward Penn. Without even thinking, he opened wide his arms—who wouldn't, knowing about that letter?—but when she came up against him, the comfort-hug he expected to provide didn't happen. Looking into his eyes, she rose to her tiptoes and then was kissing him.

With hot, demanding desire.

Jesus. He went hard quicker than she could thrust her tongue into his mouth and if there was desolation in the kiss he didn't taste it. He just tasted Alessandra, sweet and juicy and fresh, like an unfamiliar fruit from a just-discovered land.

At some Beverly Hills party, a drunk model/reality star/celebrity stylist had tried explaining to him the basis of physical attraction. Had she claimed pheromones? Or was it facial symmetry?

He couldn't remember. It didn't matter.

Though at some level he knew this was wrong, that surely it was a big mistake, those concerns were swamped by sensation: the softness of Alessandra's lips, the heady flavor he found between them, the strength of her arms as she clung to his body and sucked on his tongue.

She broke the kiss before he was near done. They stared at each other, chests heaving. His hands cupped her ass; hers were tangled in the hair at the back of his neck. He watched her open her mouth. This was it, he thought. They'd shared the kiss that had been in the air between them since they'd met. Now she'd kick him to the curb and he'd be glad for it.

"Penn Bennett," she said, her voice low but fierce. "I want to have an affair."

Gil Marino figured there was nothing fashionable about his lateness as he strolled into the Knowles's backyard. The air was already filled with the scent of grilled chicken and juicy bratwursts and the laughter was at the beer-and-wine-have-been-flowing-freely pitch. Maybe that was better. Clare would be peeved by his tardiness, setting the mood for the news he had to impart. No Man of Honor gig for Gil, no how.

At six foot five, he had a clear view of the guests. His gaze skipped around the crowd. There were few faces he didn't recognize. Most were old-time Edenvillians and included Stevie Baci, who was his cousin on her mother's side. Wearing a frown, she was staring off toward the creek, but Gil couldn't see what had snagged her attention in the midst of the close-growing oaks.

A soft laugh to his right had his feet moving in that direction. He'd know the sound anywhere. A knot of people shifted and Gil's feet stuttered to a halt. Clare was there, all right, but he wasn't accustomed to seeing so much of her.

The teeny tiny dress she wore was sleeveless and strapless, the material wrapping her breasts and then falling in soft gathers that ended in a poufy hem at mid-thigh. Her peach skin—so much peach skin—glowed against the whipped-cream color of the dress.

She looked delicious.

She looked like a bride. Which made sense, since she was engaged to be married.

He allowed himself fifteen more seconds to take in the sight and take in the pain, and then he forced his feet to move forward again. The sooner he told her he wouldn't be holding her bouquet as another man slipped his ring on her finger, the sooner he could leave the party and find some way to nurse the wound.

Four feet from his goal, a hand snagged his elbow with enough force to halt his forward progress. He glanced back and had to stifle a groan. Sally Knowles, never happy to see him.

"Gil! What a surprise."

Oh, hell. If he was seeking a reason to disappoint Clare, he had it now. She'd invited him to the barbecue without letting her mother know to expect him.

He grimaced, but decided to forgo any explanation. Sally would only assume it was an excuse. "Still crashing your parties, Mrs. Knowles."

How many times had he sensed just such a sentiment from her? Even when he had an invitation in hand—whether it was Barbie-embellished on Clare's sixth birthday or tiaras all the time on her sixteenth—Sally managed to make him feel like the help sneaking in the front door.

"I suppose my daughter will be happy to see you," she said, the essence of graciousness.

Not after what I have to say. He heard Clare laugh again, and his gaze was drawn her way once more. She tucked her straight, feathery hair behind her ears and he saw that she was wearing dime-sized mother-of-pearl earrings shaped like flowers, small garnets at their centers. He'd bought the pair for her two Christmases ago, before . . . better not to think of that.

She brushed at her hair again, and the diamond on her left hand caught the light. So. Jordan Wilson's ring on Clare's finger, Gil's jewelry in her ears.

Better not to think of that, either.

Squaring his shoulders, he started toward her once more, but Sally's grip on his arm tightened. "Where are you going?" she asked.

Suspicion dug a line between her arched eyebrows. Crap. The last thing he wanted was anyone guessing . . . that thing he didn't want anyone to guess. So he gave a casual shrug. "I was going to say hi to Clare, but is there something I can do for you?"

Her hand relaxed on his arm. "Actually, there is. I need to move some cases of wine and beer from the kitchen to replenish the coolers out here."

"No problem." He didn't bother pointing out that if his brawn was good enough for the bride's mother, the rest of him should be, too. What did it matter? Sally Knowles had never managed to prevent his friendship with Clare and anything else was out of the question anyway.

It didn't take long to restock the ice-filled beverage tubs. Snagging a beer for himself, he popped off the top and then fumbled the metal cap. It hit the ground and he bent to retrieve it, giving him the perfect view of a pair of slender legs on the approach.

Bow-topped white pumps, trim ankles, smooth calves. Right knee marred by a dark, shiny scar the size of a silver dollar. He stayed where he was. "You never could learn to stop on second base."

"I thought you were telling me to keep running," Clare said.

"I was, until I told you to stop running. And even then

I didn't say 'Hit the deck and grind to a halt using your palms, knees, and elbows.'"

"Don't remind me," she groused. "And I haven't forgotten how you promised that the hydrogen peroxide wouldn't sting a bit."

Grinning, Gil straightened. They'd both been members of a coed softball team until they'd reached the mutual agreement that Clare didn't have any skin left to lose. When it came to sports, she'd always had more determination than talent. Thanks to him, she was hardly ever picked last for a team—as the usual captain he'd sneak her into round six or seven—but she'd never been any good at anything athletic, even Steal the Bacon on rainy days in second grade.

That thought had his smile widening, as he pictured seven-year-old Clare with her missing teeth and scrawny body—the little girl who aced the spelling tests but ran from spiders. With that image in his head, he reconsidered his decision. He'd known her forever and she didn't ask that much of him. Would Man of Honor really be so bad?

Then twenty-nine-year-old Clare stepped closer to him. "You're laughing at me."

"Well . . ." Still thinking of her crappy batting average and her Pippi Longstocking looks put a snicker in his voice. He cut a glance at her, and his smile died. No missing teeth. No scrawny body. This was his Clare, his best friend, in her grown-up guise. Straight shiny hair, peachy skin, actual breasts.

Breasts! God, Clare wasn't supposed to have breasts. Or at least he shouldn't notice if she did, not any of her curves. But there were those three nights . . .

Shoving the memory from his head, he looked away and took a breath. Her perfume entered his lungs, and that was bad, too. It wasn't the bubble gum and strawberry lip gloss smell he'd identified with her for so long. This was sophisticated, adult. Womanly. Sexy.

Oh, shit.

He had to tell her, and he had to tell her fast. By refusing to be her Man of Honor, he'd anger her for a while, even hurt her maybe, but those feelings wouldn't last and they'd be better than the alternative.

"Look, Clare—"

"There's my girl," a voice interrupted.

All Gil's muscles tightened as his best friend's fiancé, Jordan Wilson, joined them. Brown-haired, blue-eyed, the other man always reminded Gil of the bus stop bench on the corner of Main and Fourth. That was because the bench's back was a full-face photo of some realtor type with too-perfect hair and a too-friendly smile that looked just like Jordan's. Oh, and because the bench was stiff, like Jordan, too.

And because Gil always had the urge to sit on him.

The kiss Jordan placed on his bride-to-be's cheek was perfunctory. "Hey, don't you look pretty."

She looked effing beautiful.

As if he heard the comment out loud, Jordan turned a sharp eye on Gil. "Marino," he said, holding out his hand.

By unspoken agreement, the shake was also perfunctory.

Clare looped her arm through Jordan's. "Did you get held up? You promised to be here early."

"Did I?"

Gil took a long drink of his beer, trying to cool a new flare of annoyance. Didn't the guy know that Clare got nervous around big crowds? He pictured that Sweet Sixteen birthday bash her parents had thrown for her at the Valley Ridge Resort. She'd worn a pink dress that day, with matching pink pumps and lipstick the same candy color. As she waited in an anteroom, one of her trembling hands had been pressed against her stomach and the other had clutched Gil's in an icy grip.

Her mother, whose dislike had been at its height when

he was a lanky, long-haired teenager, had been persuaded by her daughter's stark shyness into letting Gil walk her onto the dance floor when she was "presented" to the crowd of party-goers. He'd held her fingers in a warm clasp and willed confidence to run between them like a blood transfusion.

It occurred to him that her wedding day was going to be ten times worse.

Now Clare seemed comfortable, though, comfortable enough to send both men a smile. "Jordan, maybe you can persuade Gil to promise to be part of the wedding party. He's yet to agree to be the Man of Honor."

"Oh, come on," her fiancé replied, his voice impatient. "Why don't you cut the man a break, Clare? Haven't you outgrown your need for a bodyguard?"

Her face fell for a moment, then she worked up that smile again. "What are you talking about?"

"You know how people talk around Edenville," he answered. "I heard all about you and your BFF."

Clare made a shooing gesture. "Everybody knows about Gil and me. We've been best buds since we were five. What's there to talk about?"

"That your friendship was amusing when he was the tough jock and you were the girl geek."

"Amusing?" she echoed faintly. Her cheeks flushed the pink of that Sweet Sixteen dress. "Girl geek?"

Gil wanted to punch someone. Preferably Jordan. Maybe Gil had been the tough jock in high school. But Clare had never seen herself as a nerd, and whether his close friendship with her was the reason for it or not, no one had ever called her "girl geek" to her face.

"But you're out of the library now, sweetheart," Jordan added. "And past your days as the secretary of the Stamp Collecting Club and treasurer of the Science Fiction Society."

Gil's eyes narrowed. Someone had been spilling Edenville High trivia. "That was a long time ago, Wilson," he said.

"Exactly," Jordan agreed. "So you don't need him anymore," he continued, addressing Clare.

That did it. Gil stepped closer to the woman he couldn't bear to lose—or let down. Damn it, as much as he knew Clare's marriage would put a wedge between them, as much as he realized this step would be going against his own self-interest, he couldn't stop himself from committing to a pledge he'd fully intended not to make.

"She might not need me," he said, his jaw tight, "but I'll be privileged to be her Man of Honor, anyway." If only to ensure Clare's future husband knew that Gil would always and forever be watching her back.

~

Alessandra had never known a man's hands could burn. Penn's were hot fire against her bottom, lifting her into the heavy erection she could feel prodding her stomach. The fire, the heaviness, both made her shiver.

Staring at his mouth, she licked her bottom lip. "An affair with you, Penn," she clarified, desperate for him to understand—or at least comply. "I want to have an affair with you."

His fingertips tightened on her flesh. She pushed to her toes to adjust their pelvis-to-pelvis fit. He let out a soft groan, his fingers flexing again. "You shouldn't tell me that," he said.

"I'm asking you," she whispered. Her tongue caressed the stubble on his chin, then she sucked his bottom lip into her mouth.

Groaning again, he pulled away, staring down at her with glittering eyes, his chest moving quickly with labored breaths. She crowded closer, evaporating the two inches he'd tried to put between them.

"Don't," he said through gritted teeth.

But she knew he wanted her. She'd known it when he sent her away at the party—she didn't mind admitting she'd been a little disappointed by that—and she knew it now. It was in the firm grip he had on her behind, in the tense set to his muscles, in the impressive bulge that was so deliciously good to rub herself against.

She rotated her hips and he closed his eyes.

"Alessandra," he said in a warning tone. "I'm trying to find my conscience here."

"I don't want a man with a conscience," she countered. "You're perfect because I suspect you don't have any conscience whatsoever."

His eyes flashed open, their expression unreadable. Not . . . hurt?

She tried to make him understand. "I mean that in only the best way possible, Penn. You'll take what I'm offering, nothing more, nothing less."

"What you're offering because of the letter."

My Darling Allie . . .

She didn't want to think about the letter! But panic struck as she realized she'd dropped it on her dash into Penn's arms. Breaking away from him, she searched the area, then ran to pick up the fallen page and envelope.

My Darling Allie . . .

Staring down at Tommy's handwriting, she was hit by the familiar punch of dread, sadness, and longing. Sally and so many others thought Tommy's posthumous letters the ultimate symbol of romance and Alessandra understood her fiancé's intention had been to wrap her in love with them. Sweet Tommy. But . . .

She looked away from his masculine scribble and met Penn's gaze. Dread evaporated, sadness snapped, and a new sort of ache overtook her. Forget the past. She wanted this man's hands on her again.

Her feet stumbled toward Penn as she recalled his hot touch, his clever mouth, the pinch of his fingers on her nipple. He would take her away from the old memories and her now-urgent need for that had her eagerly, wantonly succumbing to their sexual attraction.

She was still a foot away when he spoke. "Tell me about the letters," Penn said.

Her steps halted. She blinked at him, then down at the paper crinkled in her fist. "What?"

"Tell me why they're driving you to an affair with a man without a conscience. I think I have a right to know."

Her pulse was still thrumming and she couldn't think beyond being in his arms again. "I—"

"Tell me."

Fine, fine, she decided. If that's what it took . . . "One was delivered on my first birthday without him," she said quickly. "Another five years after his prom. Last December it was a letter he'd written on the Christmas before he died."

Penn's gaze moved to the crumpled letter she held. "And that one?"

She wanted to touch him so badly she took another step forward. "It's the last, it says. Today is the tenth anniversary of our very first kiss."

Done. She rushed toward Penn.

His hand stopped her again. "And?" he prompted.

And . . . what? Did she have to really lay this out for him?

"Alessandra?"

Frustrated tears stung her eyes. "What else do you want to know? Do you need to know that reading tonight's letter made me realize I might never kiss anyone again? That no man has touched me or looked at me with desire since the night before my wedding day? That I haven't looked at anyone that way either until . . . until . . ."

"Until now."

Alessandra swallowed. "Until you." Then she closed the distance between them, because she so *did* want his touch, she so did need more of those kisses that he'd promised were practically inevitable.

His arms didn't close around her this time. But his mouth complied, his tongue sliding against hers. Heat spread across her body again, but now it didn't feel like a virus. It felt like spring, when the buds flowered and formed clusters on the grapevines.

Hope bloomed in her near-empty chest. She didn't expect to recover her younger, unsinkable self, but at least she could feel that someone wanted her again.

She crowded closer, sliding her right hand up Penn's chest, but the crinkle of paper surprised her eyes open. Tommy's final letter, she realized, breaking the kiss. Funny that it would get between her and Penn's heart.

And then it didn't. Lean fingers plucked the sheet away. She met Penn's eyes, supremely aware that he was removing the obstacle of her past—at least for the moment. His heartbeat thudded against her palm and her pulse took up the rhythm as he once again bent his head toward her mouth. His lips brushed hers, soft enough to tease goose bumps on her neck.

She moved her head to catch his kiss, but he eluded her to run his tongue along her jawline and down her neck. Spring was over, she thought in a sudden burst of lust. It was summer, August, September, with the sun blazing at full strength, the fruit swelling, and harvest just around the corner. He curled one arm around her waist to draw her closer to his body. She leaned into him, willing, and gasped to accept his tongue as his other hand drew up the hem of her skirt.

The material tickled like fingertips along the back of her thighs and every cell was sensitized waiting for his next move. Her fingers dug into his scalp in demand, wanting more, wanting all, wanting—

"Hell." Penn broke away. "Not here."

The skirt of her dress fell. Dazed, Alessandra blinked. "But—"

"Not here." He briefly closed his eyes. "Even I have enough of a conscience to insist on that."

"Huh?" She wasn't sure what he was talking about.

He looked at her a minute, then sighed. His big hand grasped her chin and turned her face to force her gaze uphill. She blinked again, realizing that though the thick grove of trees had hidden her and Penn, not far away was the party, the crowd, the familiar yard. "Oh."

"Yeah," he agreed. "Oh."

His hand dropped from her face to slide down her bare arm. She suppressed her shiver as their fingers entwined. "Let's get out of here," he said.

Let's get out of here and start our affair, she amended for him. Her pulse started thumping again. What would sex be like Hollywood-style? What would it be like with an experienced man like Penn?

But the thought was superseded by something else as her gaze returned to the direction of the party. There they'd find her family, her friends, her community. Penn took his first stride that way and she resisted. He glanced back, brows rising.

"Our secret," she said, expressing the single caveat.

He stilled. "Our secret?"

"Our secret affair."

For a moment, it was as if he hadn't heard her. Then he laughed, letting go of her hand at the same time. She didn't like either action.

"No offense," she said, frowning at him.

He laughed harder. "None taken. Now that I think about it, I don't want anyone to know I'm screwing you, either."

Her frown deepened. "Why's that?"

"Because I shouldn't be that dumb," he said, and still smiling, he strode back toward the barbecue.

Except the dumb one was her, she thought morosely, as she followed at a discreet distance. His insult should have cooled her eagerness, but both she and her gaze followed him as he made for the exit. Confidence oozed from his pores, and he wore sex appeal as easily as his silk shirt. Did nothing faze the man?

She hated him.

She wanted to rub up against him.

She was going to have him in her bed.

The thought caused her breath to catch in her chest. Her feet paused, then Penn paused, too, his attention caught by a short, good-looking man who looked vaguely familiar. A celebrity, she thought, though she'd have to ask Clare to place him for her.

Curious, she sidled by the two men.

"Someone's been phoning my radio show's gossip line," the other man was saying. "My screener didn't get the details the first time, but—" He stopped talking as Penn turned, apparently sensing Alessandra's presence behind him.

His expression was polite. "Can I help you with something?" he asked as if they hadn't just flamed in each other's arms. As if they hadn't just agreed to a secret affair.

Her face flushed. He made her feel like some pesky groupie and her stomach churned at the thought. Was that how he saw her? Instead of answering, she shook her head and hurried past him.

"I haven't forgotten you want my shirt," he called after her, a low laugh in his voice.

Ha ha. Everyone else would think he was talking about a piece of his *Build Me Up* gear, when he knew she knew he was referring to her wanting his shirt *off*. And everything else, too.

In answer, she flipped her hair over her shoulders and kept walking.

He pitched his voice a little louder, and that laugh

was still there. "I'll get it to you at your place as soon as possible."

Code: Go there and wait for me.

And though she was peeved by the way he teased her, it didn't stop her from wanting him still. From going home and waiting.

For the shirt—the *man*—who never arrived.

7

The temperature was in the cool sixties as Alessandra walked from the farmhouse to the winery under the umbrella of the morning overcast. Against the gray, the vines' greenery appeared even more vibrant in color, the leaves shielding the delicate flowers from the sun that would burn through the clouds later in the day and increase the temperature another twenty degrees. This daily divergence of the thermometer reading was an essential element of Napa Valley wines, creating in the grapes a unique balance of sugar and acidity.

Thanks to her appointment with a bride and her mother about siting the young woman's wedding at Tanti Baci, she had an excuse to avoid the cottage. And Penn. Not that she had any idea whether he'd be working. For all she knew he'd be a no-show today, just as he'd been a no-show at her house the night before.

And not that she had any plans for ever speaking to him again anyway.

The winery's administrative offices were located in a

stucco-and-red-tile structure adjacent to the caves, and in the small lobby Alessandra greeted the anxious-looking, very young blonde and her more composed mother. The bride, faced with her fiancé's unexpected military deployment, had decided to move her wedding up by several months if a suitable venue could be found.

Given that Alessandra needed every booking she could get to prove her plan to save the winery viable, she was determined that mother and daughter find Tanti Baci very suitable indeed. With a smile, she ushered them into her office and closed the door.

Bride-to-Be looked with mild interest around the room, her gaze zeroing in on the wooden shelves to the right of Alessandra's desk. They'd been painted the same pale peach as the plaster and held the collection of vintage wedding cake toppers that her mother had started collecting after her marriage. Some were ceramic, some were of bisque, while the oldest was from the 1920s and made of stiff paper and wire.

"Oh, Mama," the girl said, pointing to them, her expression delighted. "Look how sweet."

Mama released a tight smile. "I see."

And I *see*, Alessandra thought. The mother was going to be the much harder sell. Maybe because she didn't like the winery as a wedding site or maybe because she didn't want her darling daughter—so young, probably as young as Alessandra had been—to marry at all.

"We like to say we specialize in happy endings," Alessandra said as the two other women took their seats. She continued standing, casually leaning on the front of her desk, though nerves made her warm enough to remove the cardigan she'd worn over a short-sleeved striped cotton dress. "I recall you've been to our website, so you're aware of our special wedding wine, the bubbly *blanc de blancs,* that's made from our estate-grown chardonnay grapes."

She picked up a bottle of Bella Amore from the corner of her desk and passed it to the younger woman. The glass was clear, showing off the pale liquid inside, with the cork caged by wire but without any overwrapping foil. Labeled with a simple, small octagon, the old-fashioned illustration featured delicate grapes and leaves in pastel green and pink. "It looks exactly as the first retailed bottle did nearly fifty years ago and reflects our commitment to tradition and our belief that beautiful things last forever."

Bride-to-Be passed the wine to her mother who handed it over to Alessandra. She set it back on her desk and clasped her hands together. "Also a testament to Tanti Baci's dedication to our roots is the newly renovated cottage we'll be using for our weddings. It's where my ancestors Anne and Alonzo Baci began the winery and began their romantic and successful marriage."

"*Newly* renovated cottage?" Mama-of-the-Bride questioned, straightening in her chair. "Does that mean it's completed? If so, we'd like to take a tour."

Alessandra cleared her throat. "There are only a few details left to complete," she answered, and inside her black pumps she crossed her big toes over her second ones. "However, for reasons of safety, we can't let anyone inside until after the final inspection."

"But—"

"I have this artist's rendition to share, though," she said, plucking a cardboard-backed rectangle from the desk behind her.

Bride-to-Be went dreamy-eyed as she inspected the watercolor painting. Alessandra had commissioned it from a local student at the community college—now ever mindful of the winery's weak financial state—and the result was something not as fanciful as a Thomas Kincade or Stephen Whitney painting, but no less idealized. The cottage looked enchanted, surrounded by the vineyard and with grape vines twining the wide entry and rose petals carpeting the shallow front steps. A fairy peeking around a corner wouldn't have been out of place.

"Mama . . ." the young woman breathed, her shining gaze lifting to her mother's face.

Mama was made of sterner stuff. She shifted in her seat to focus on Alessandra. "I'm still concerned that the cottage will be available on my daughter's wedding date."

"I can promise you that the renovation will be complete," Alessandra replied without a tremor. "I'm slated to be a bridesmaid for our very first Tanti Baci wedding at the end of this month. Your date isn't until fall."

"What I mean is, will the Tanti Baci winery still be in operation by then?"

Alessandra's face froze, even as her stomach turned inside out. "I, uh, what do you mean?"

"I've heard there are financial problems," the older woman said.

Oh. Oh no. Until now, Alessandra had thought the winery's difficulties were as secret as that affair she'd wanted with Penn. But look how well *that* had turned out.

Pasting on a serene smile, she gestured to the window behind her desk, which provided a view of row after row of Tanti Baci vines. Leafy and lush, they looked in the peak of health, unlike the bottom line on the Tanti Baci financial statement. "When you're holding your breath waiting to hear your daughter pledge her life to her groom, all of us at the vineyard will be holding our breaths, too, waiting for harvest to begin. I guarantee we'll be picking grapes next autumn."

No lie whatsoever. Everyone pitched in at harvest time, and if the winery went belly-up, the entire staff would likely be signing on as a harvest assistant somewhere— including Alessandra. She was able to lift the requisite fifty pounds and could claim experience in sanitation, punch downs, and barrel prep, just to name a few of the tasks that could earn her a cellar rat's minimum wage.

Unfortunately, the older woman seemed to hear everything Alessandra didn't say. Her eyes narrowing, she hesitated, first looking at her daughter—who was back to mooning over the artist's rendition of the cottage—then at Alessandra.

Damn, damn, damn. How many in the valley were aware of the winery's financial troubles and how would that affect her chance to save it? No one liked being associated with a losing concern. Winners were much more appealing.

As if on cue, her office door burst open, and a handsome man stepped inside. Penn Bennett stopped short upon seeing mother and daughter. "Whoops," he said, his mouth curving into that celebrity smile of his. "I came at the wrong time."

Alessandra shot him a cool look, though socking him in the stomach seemed much more appealing after her sleepless night. "You can say that again."

His gaze moved from the strangers to settle on Alessandra's face and that smile turned more private. "I came at the wrong time," he repeated, his voice seductive.

She was saved from having to douse him with a bucket of ice water by Bride-to-Be, who turned in her chair. "You're Penn Bennett," the young woman said. Her eyes were round in awe. "You're famous."

Alessandra's lip curled. "He's not famous."

"Yes I am."

"Yes he is."

Penn and Mama-of-the-Bride spoke at the same time. "I'm a huge fan of his show," Mama continued.

"Oh, that's right," Alessandra murmured, barely suppressing her sneer. "*Build Up My Ego.* How could I forget?"

"*Build Me Up,*" Mama corrected. She was looking a little moony herself as she gazed on Penn, which didn't make Alessandra any happier remembering she'd practically begged the man to have an affair with her. It obviously put her squarely in the ranks of his fan-girl nation.

It was downright mortifying. She glared at him since a hole in the floor didn't open up for her to fall into. "If you'll excuse us?" she prompted, remembering too late she'd vowed never to speak to him again.

"No problem," he said, with another flash of his Hollywood bright whites. "I just wanted to let you know I'm back at work in the cottage. Got a bit of a late start this morning."

Probably because he'd found some other groupie to boff last night, she thought, shoving away the fuming feelings the thought provoked. Who cared if he'd stood her up her the night before?

"You . . ." Mama-of-the-Bride sat even straighter. "*You're* working on the Tanti Baci cottage?"

"As a special favor to Alessandra," Penn said. "I can't seem to tell her no."

"Do they have a name for men who say yes but who don't follow through?" she asked sweetly, then cursed herself for not only addressing him again but also for giving away that she even recalled the event-that-wasn't.

Penn looked at her. "Full of remorse?"

"Full of something, anyway."

Mama and Bride-to-Be had been watching their last exchange like it was a Wimbledon match. Heat warming her cheeks, Alessandra cleared her throat and returned her attention to the business at hand. "Penn, I'll have to ask you again to excuse us—"

"He's really working on the cottage renovation?" the bride interrupted, her gaze glued to the TV star. "Mama, I could be married in something built by Penn Bennett."

He straightened from his casual slouch against the doorjamb. "You're planning on having your wedding here at Tanti Baci?" he asked with another smile. "Good choice."

"That's what I'm thinking," Mama said, doing an about-face from five minutes before. "It seems like a very good choice."

Penn's smile widened as he nodded at the two bedazzled women. God, Alessandra thought. He was pumping out the charisma with the force of a fire hose. Now that she saw his effect on other females, she didn't know if she felt more or less irritated with her own reaction to him. Obviously it was entirely due to his very potent—and very practiced—sexual allure.

Jerk. She *was* never speaking to him again.

Nor was she leaving the booking of this wedding up to his facile charm. Pushing away from her desk, she walked toward the shelves of cake toppers that had earlier captured Bride-to-Be's attention. "As you can see from this collection handed down from mother to daughter here at Tanti Baci, we treasure marriage at the winery and we'll do whatever it takes to make your wedding unique and memorable."

She lifted her favorite topper from the shelf, a bisque bride and groom from the 1930s. The groom was in traditional black-and-white, and his partner's dress was highnecked and long-sleeved, painted an opalescent ivory that still glowed. A netting veil circled her head as she gazed up at the man, and tiny fabric flowers were clutched in her hand.

"It's so pretty," Bride-to-Be said.

Alessandra smiled as she returned the topper to the shelf and layered on a little more icing. "It sat atop my great-grandparents' wedding cake. They held hands like young lovers from the day they said 'I do' until the last day of their lives. They're my inspiration—and they married right here at the winery."

"Impressive," Penn put in, as if he meant it. He even sounded serious as he continued. "If I found the right woman to spend the rest of my life with, Tanti Baci would be the perfect place to make my promise to her."

Alessandra barely managed not to roll her eyes, aware he had no faith in ever-afters.

"I was concerned about the rumors I've been hearing about the winery's financial status," Mama said, her gaze on Penn. "But now that I know someone of your caliber is involved . . . well, I'm too aware of all your good works not to trust your fine judgment. If you're involved here, then I can be at ease with booking my daughter's wedding."

Maybe it was just her, but Alessandra thought Penn cooled a little at the praise of his "good works" and "fine judgment." But he was smiling now as the mother-of-the-bride wrote out the deposit check and then shook hands with Alessandra. He swept the ladies out of her office with more of his high-profile charm.

Then he shut the door, leaving the two of them facing each other, alone. His shoulders against the paneled wood, he gazed at her, his expression unreadable.

Alessandra crossed her arms over her chest and fought the urge to have a little cry. Now that she had Mama's signature on the contract, a headache was throbbing at the base of her skull. Good God, that was close. Word was out about the Tanti Baci financial problems and she'd nearly lost a booking due to the rumors.

And this infuriating man—the one she'd promised herself she'd never speak to again—wouldn't go away and stay away. "Good-bye, Penn."

"Not so fast."

Well, it had been worth a try. She sighed. "I suppose you expect me to thank you for that."

He gave her one of his happy grins—the kind he saved for nails sold in brown bags and ogling her backside. "I'm not saying I saved you, but I did help you get the gig."

"Listen, Penn," she said, steel in her voice. "Believe me when I say I don't—and won't ever—need you to save me."

His happy smile turned seductive as he pushed off the

closed door. "On the contrary, little nun," he said, gesturing at the shelves of cake toppers as he came closer. "Someone needs to save you from drowning in all this gooey 'I do' garbage and redirect your attention to what we both know you really want—getting it on."

~

As Penn approached the young beauty across the office floor, alarm crossed her exotic face. He'd never seen anyone with such an enticing combination of features: golden skin, golden-brown eyes with an alluring tilt at their outside corners, the small, yet full mouth that was doll-like in its lush prettiness. Alessandra Baci, the tragic, virtuous baby bride who inspired in him so many devilish ideas of sin.

And now he was ready to take up where they'd left off the night before.

Her voice rose as he took another step forward. "What are you doing?"

He paused, frowning. "Don't we have—"

"We have nothing."

Penn sighed. He supposed he should have known "taking up" wouldn't be easy, and the fire in her eyes confirmed it. Out of caution, he left a couple of feet between them. The Nun of Napa had a temper, he'd seen evidence of that more than once. "Look, I'm sorry about last night. The time got away from me. I had to go out for drinks with this guy I know from L.A., and once there I was hailed by a friendly group intent upon welcoming me into their 'lucky sperm' club. That was a little weird, but Liam and Seth were at the table so I thought I was safe. A few bottles later . . . well, I only know somebody's driver got us home."

She was shaking her head. "A night out with the lucky spermers."

His sperm wasn't feeling too lucky at the moment, not with that mutinous lower lip of hers in such evidence. "I didn't really get it," he admitted.

"It's a reference to the generations in the valley who didn't actually earn their wealth, just inherited it. You're fortunate offspring."

He bristled. "I've worked plenty damn hard in my life. Nobody ever gave me anything."

"That was before . . . now, you're lucky."

The notion pissed him off, and the look on Alessandra's face and the vestiges of a mild hangover didn't help his mood. "You, too."

She shook her head again. "The Bacis have no wealth to pass on. We're cash poor. Sure, we could sell off what's been in our family for a hundred years, but then we couldn't afford to pay our debts and start over anywhere near Edenville."

Penn rolled his shoulders, as much uncomfortable with the idea of the Baci sisters giving up their legacy as his new status as someone "lucky." He took another step forward, determined again to pick up where they'd left off. "I don't want to talk right now."

She threw up a hand. "We're certainly not doing anything other *than* talk."

Catching her fingers, he softened his voice. "Conversation is not on our agenda, honey."

"Neither is anything else." She tried tugging her fingers free of his.

He held them tighter. "C'mon." It was no surprise that she was pissed at him, but it wasn't as if he'd intended last evening to go as it had. On his way out of the party, Rocky Reed had dropped Lana's name and Penn had been obligated to exercise a little damage control in the form of Johnny Walker Black on ice. It had been necessary to convince the little prick that the woman calling into his radio show about her relationship with Penn was better ignored.

Christ Almighty, but the alternative made him break out in a cold sweat. He'd put up with a lot in his life but he couldn't imagine anything worse than looking like a fool in public.

"Penn . . ." the Nun of Napa said, warning in her voice.

"Alessandra," he mimicked, drawing her closer to him, even as she still resisted. Fire sparked between their bodies, and it put thoughts of everything else out of his head. Last night they'd been a dozen yards from a crowded party and he'd been so lost in lust he'd nearly had her naked. Remembering how it was, the material of her dress bunched in his fists and the sweet, fruity taste of her in his mouth, his blood slowed to a thick chug through his veins.

Her body brushed against him and desire coiled in his belly. Already his balls were drawing tight. "We have unfinished business." He drew a jerky breath into his lungs and even that felt hot. It was time to taste her, touch her, let the combustion he'd been barely controlling explode. "Honey, let's not waste time with you being mad."

"I'm not one of your groupies," she said hotly, but the anger in her voice was belied by the sudden shine of tears in her eyes. "You stood me up."

Penn froze, her words echoing in his head. *You stood me up.*

He wasn't the only one who didn't appreciate feeling the fool, he realized. Alessandra wasn't so much angry as she was hurt because she thought he'd rejected her. That he'd found her . . . what? Forgettable?

A wash of unfamiliar tenderness cooled the burn of his blood. It was foreign enough to unsettle him, but still he dropped her hand to curve his palms around her small face. The kiss he placed on her forehead was more uncle-to-niece than lover-to-lover. "I'm an ass."

"I thought we established that several days ago."

Even hurt, she could administer a sting. "Ouch." He placed another kiss on her forehead.

She broke from his hold to glare at him from two feet

away. "Listen, Daddy Warbucks, Little Orphan Annie doesn't need any more of your generosity."

Huffing out a sigh, he glared back. No doubt about it, he sucked at this tenderness thing. "You're a pain, do you know that?"

"An inconvenience to you, anyway," she said, snotty as all get-out. "Do I have to say it again? Go away, Penn."

He took a step forward. "That's not what you were telling me last night. Then I think it was," he lowered his voice to a husky whisper, " 'Do me, Penn. Please, Penn. I've got to have your hands all over me, Penn.' "

Outrage washed color over her face. "I said no such thing, you egotistical moron."

"That's egotistical-moron-I-want-to-have-a-secret-affair-with to you," he shot back, realizing that the "secret" aspect of the whole thing was still grating on him. Maybe there *was* a reason besides Rocky and the lucky spermers that he hadn't made it to Alessandra's place the night before.

Not that he was backing down now. He stepped forward again, reaching for her at the same moment.

Her hand came up and back and he recognized a girly slap when he saw one coming. Tenderness evaporated. He caught her wrist just as the momentum of her swinging arm brought her toward him. Their bodies slammed together.

Their mouths fused.

Her taste burst against his tongue as he thrust inside her lips. She was slick and sweet and they moaned together, a sound both frustrated and needy. Her arms twined his neck. He slid his hands down her back and then up again, his touch eager, his need insatiable.

He had to feel her, feed on her, find satisfaction. *Now. Now. Now.*

Some sensible part of his brain applauded his actions. Yes, it urged. Get this eruption out of the way and then there'd be no need for an affair, secret or otherwise. Surely this once would burn the want right out of them.

His right hand palmed her breast while his other drew up the back of her warm thigh. Her hem rode high with his wrist and as he slanted his mouth over hers, his fingertips breached the waistband of her panties.

Bikinis. Slinky, silky, bikinis.

His hand squeezed the cheek of her ass as her nipple pebbled against his other palm. Alessandra was crowding closer, the soft pad of her mons riding the ridge of his hard cock, and he grunted at the goodness of it.

This would do it. This would have to do it.

Something that felt this incendiary was too dangerous to risk a second time, let alone for longer term.

Her small hand was yanking up the tail of his shirt. Then it was branding the skin of his belly, causing goose bumps to break out across his ribs. For the first time in memory, he felt his own nipples tighten into hard points as a hot shudder crawled down his back.

Even this one time might kill him.

He shoved down her panties, then he boosted her up, her naked little ass in the palm of his hand. Still rubbing his tongue against hers, he opened his eyes so he could find her desk. He perched her there, almost coming in his pants as he watched her bright white bikinis slide down her legs to catch on her ankles above her businesslike high heels.

Breaking the kiss, he lifted his head. Her eyes were closed, feathery lashes against her flushed cheeks, her swollen and pink mouth raising toward his. He sucked on her upper lip as he pushed up the front of her skirt.

His heaving chest seized. *Holy Mother of . . .* The Nun of Napa was rated X where it counted, her female folds completely exposed to his gaze. "Bare," she'd teased him at the party, and that's what she was. Bare and swollen. So pretty. He lightly traced the line between those naked lips with his forefinger, opening them to release a slick wetness that made a hot shudder roll once again down his spine.

"Alessandra," he said against her mouth, the syllables like a succession of kisses. He pushed his hand against her inner thighs, widening them, preparing her for a deeper touch. Then he gave her a harder kiss at the same time as his thumb rolled over her clitoris and his middle finger found the snug wet pocket of her body.

She stiffened.

Penn made a sound at the back of his throat that was supposed to be soothing, even as he hardened the kiss. Reaching deeper inside her, he stroked in and out and then nudged her clitoris again. Her tense body tightened, he kissed, he stroked, he nudged once more, and then . . .

Her hips jerked once and her eyes flew open.

Holy Mother, he thought again. She took off, just with that, her body bowing, her inner muscles gripping his finger in an unmistakable rhythm.

His mouth lifted from hers as she came against his hand in silent pleasure, her body releasing only small, stiff tremors. Stunned, Penn watched her ride through the last of her orgasm. He'd never known a woman to come with such quiet or with such agonizing restraint.

That tender feeling washed over him again—and it scared the hell out of him.

He backed away the instant her tiny shudders abated, gritting his teeth against the pain of leaving her wet inner clasp. His cock clamored for its release, but a wise voice inside told him that finding his own little death wouldn't be the ending he was seeking to this.

"I . . ." He lifted his hand, scenting the air with Alessandra's arousal. It made him take another hasty step back before he did something stupid like fall to his knees between hers in order to taste the flavor of that sweet perfume.

On her desk, her phone rang.

She jolted, blinking, and he realized she was yet to come

out of her post-orgasmic state. That weird tenderness welled inside him again and he quickly helped her off the desk and then drew up her panties.

The phone pealed insistently.

He went all Daddy Warbucks once more and kissed her forehead before lifting the receiver and putting it in her hand. Then he made a casual spin and left her office, whistling "The sun'll come out tomorrow," despite the sudden sense that the forecast for his own near future was gloomy, with a chance of trouble ahead.

Penn returned to the Bennett home that afternoon sweaty, dirty, and feeling downright mean. Alessandra had never showed up at the cottage—good—but he couldn't get her out of his mind—bad, very bad.

He didn't know what the hell he was doing with her.

And as he climbed the steps to the Bennett villa, he didn't know what the hell he was doing here, either. He ran into the housekeeper, Charlene, in the spacious foyer. She mentioned something about the dinner she was leaving in the kitchen for them and also that Liam and Seth were both out in the vineyard acres adjoining the house. There were other acres owned by the family in different parts of the valley, places Penn had yet to visit.

That he'd never visit, he decided, as he started the shower in the granite-and-mirrors bathroom. The tub was a sunken affair, something a Roman might appreciate, but Christ, Penn was a kid from a one-bedroom apartment in the San Fernando Valley. This wasn't his place.

To paraphrase The Beatles, it was time for Penn to get back to where he belonged.

Clean, and in jeans, a T-shirt, and flip-flops, he hurried downstairs to give the news to Liam and Seth. Yeah, he hadn't finished the Baci cottage, and yeah, there were things left incomplete between himself and his father's legitimate sons, but he didn't owe a thing to anybody. Not really. That was the upside to the situation. He was the bastard, right? He might as well go right ahead and act like one.

The huge house was empty, though. The housekeeper had left for the evening but his brothers hadn't come in from the vines. He stood in the opulent game room for a moment, shaking his head at how different it was from his beachside place in Malibu, and his need to escape deepened. He headed back outside.

The temperature was still warm, the lowering sun turning the afternoon light the pale gold of chardonnay. The earth held onto the daytime heat with a greedy grasp and it seeped through the leather soles of his sandals as he headed for the barn behind the house. There, one of the workers directed Penn to an all-terrain vehicle that was used to travel through the vines and pointed to where he'd likely find the other two men.

The sooner he told Liam and Seth, the sooner he could start for southern California. Alessandra's face popped into his head, but he refused to feel guilty—or think about breaking the news to her. Let the Bennett brothers tell her he'd let her down.

Something told him she wouldn't be surprised.

He refused to feel bad about that, either.

A short ride on the ATV lifted his mood some. He was a guy, wasn't he, and four fat wheels plus thrumming engine plus the straight, narrow tracks between the grapevines equaled boyish fun. Seth seemed to agree as Penn came to a halt behind the younger man in a similar vehicle. His grin was wide, even through the dust cloud created by Penn's sudden stop.

"Bro!" he called out.

Penn pretended he didn't hear the familial greeting. Probably every guy was a "bro" in Seth's book, anyway. "Where's Liam?" he asked. He only wanted to go through this one time.

"Right here." The older Bennett was crouching to inspect something on a nearby vine. "What's up?" he asked, straightening.

Seth snapped his fingers before Penn could reply. "I've been meaning to get some info from you. You have a lawyer, right?"

"Yeah," he answered, but cautiously. He didn't like the look on Seth's face. While Penn had a lawyer, an agent, and an accountant, all supposed to be looking out for him, recent experience told him that no one truly stood between him and stupid-ass mistakes. "What do you want her for?"

"I assume your attorney will be handling the inheritance issues for you," Seth said.

Yeah, Penn really didn't like where this was going. "Look, let's be clear about something. I don't want anything from Calvin Bennett. I never have."

Liam and Seth didn't say a word.

Penn pushed his hands through his hair, then sighed, his gaze roaming the vines arranged like disciplined rows of soldiers ordered to stand with arms outstretched. They extended forever, it seemed—a startling view for an urban kid more familiar with houses arranged shoulder to shoulder and cars idling bumper to bumper.

"This isn't my place," he said, trying to explain.

"Of course it is," Liam replied, his voice mild. "You're a Bennett."

"I didn't want to be," he confessed. "I couldn't understand why my last name was different than my mother's and I would have changed it, except," Christ, this sounded stupid, but it was true, "Penn Penn was ridiculous."

Seth's mouth twitched. "Penn is your mother's last name, I take it."

"Yeah." And he could have changed that, too, he supposed, renamed himself Miles Smith or Reginald Jones, but that would have been like erasing Debbie Penn from his life and she'd been a nice woman. A loving mother. A person sucked in by a good sob story, but who was Penn to criticize that? "She had the proverbial heart of gold."

When the other two men didn't say anything, he found himself getting defensive. "Look, your father apparently was a temporary regular at the bar where she worked. I suppose he gave her the usual 'unfulfilled before now,' and 'never felt like this before,' what-have-you. When she found out she was pregnant, he stuck around for a few more months. Long enough to get his name on the birth certificate, though he was gone by the time she could go back to cocktail waitressing."

"And she didn't hear from him again," Liam put in, his expression giving nothing away.

"Not until I was getting ready to graduate from high school and he presented her with a college fund that he didn't want me to know came from him." At Cal Bennett's insistence, his mother had given it to Penn as if it was something she'd saved herself. She'd swallowed her pride and acquiesced to her former lover's demand, even though that meant facing Penn's teen anger. "She said she'd been pinching pennies all those years and I believed her—too young and stupid to realize she couldn't have saved that much in seven lifetimes. I was so damn angry. I took the money but barely spoke to her for the next four years."

The brothers exchanged a glance that didn't give away their thoughts, but Penn could guess them all the same. He ran his fingers through his hair again, frustrated, angry, ashamed. But hell, why should he be ashamed? He wasn't the one who'd been sitting in that posh house among these vast acres that were the source of a glamorous luxury product.

"When the Tooth Fairy first slipped a buck under my pillow, I was what? Six, seven years old?" His voice sounded harsh, but so were the memories. "Even then I knew we needed every dime. I would sneak the money back into my mom's wallet. If I got a gift for my birthday or Christmas that I could take back, I did that, too, and slipped the cash into her purse."

"You remembered all that when she showed up with your big fat college fund," Liam said.

"Yeah." He looked out over the vineyard, the vastness underscoring the miserly way he'd treated his mother. "And I continued remembering all that until she confessed where the money came from on graduation day. Four years after that, she had a massive stroke and died." But at least he'd spent those four years trying his best to make it up to her. He thought at least she'd understood.

Again, Liam and Seth were silent. Which meant there was more silence than Penn had ever experienced before. Here, in between the vines, there wasn't the background noise of rushing cars, overhead airplanes, or the constant pulse of surf that he was accustomed to. The lack of clamor made his thoughts too loud in his head—and made even more imperative his need to go south.

"Listen," he started. "I—"

"He said he was taking a solo backpack trip to Yosemite the week that I finished law school so he missed the ceremony and the big party my mom threw," Seth said. "I found out later he spent seven days with my ex-girlfriend at a private resort in Kauai. Oh, yeah, and she got a pretty BMW convertible out of it, too."

Penn blinked. "Jesus."

The younger man grimaced. "Not exactly what I said, but yeah."

Liam climbed into the first ATV. Though he sat calmly, with his elbows on his knees, Penn drew closer, sensing the older man had something to say, too. "You have a story as well?"

"A long time ago I had a girl . . ."

Penn stared. "Christ, he had her, too?"

"No, no." Liam shook his head. "I don't . . . I can't . . . Let's just say he ruined things between us forever."

"He screwed us all, you're saying." Penn looked between the two brothers, a little angry at them, a lot frustrated. Where were they going with these confessions?

"I guess he did," Liam agreed, still with his characteristic cool.

It frustrated Penn even more. "Then why did you stay when he was alive?" he asked, first to Liam and then to Seth. "Why the hell are you still here?"

Liam shrugged. "Because this is our place. Our land. Our town. Our friends."

"Cal Bennett isn't this," Seth added, lifting his arms to indicate the surrounding vines. "*We* are. I didn't and I won't let him chase me away from my family . . . from my brothers."

Brothers.

Jesus.

But they were his brothers, Penn couldn't deny it. They looked like him, with their dark blond hair and their rangy bodies. Liam's sober exterior and Seth's quick smile were both part of Penn's makeup, too. They might have grown up with more material things, but their lives had been just as affected by Calvin Bennett's failings as his had been.

I'm not letting him chase me away from my family . . . from my brothers.

Was that why Penn wanted to run back to Malibu? Was he looking to escape from ties that he'd never had?

He opened his mouth, not yet sure what might come out, but shut it as he saw Liam stand, shading his eyes with his hand. Penn turned to see a cloud of dust rising in the wake of yet another ATV.

One mad-eyed Italian girl was behind the wheel. For a second he thought it was Alessandra and his gut churned, but then he realized it was Giuliana Baci and her crackling temper—if her gaze was any indication—was focused on Liam.

"*You*," she seethed as she braked the vehicle.

He crossed his arms over his chest and looked down his nose at her. Penn could have told him that an exhibition of nonchalance would not sit well with one of the badass Baci women.

And he would have been right.

She was out of her seat and had hold of the tail of Liam's shirt in the blink of an eye. "Can't you keep your mouth shut?" she demanded.

Since the oldest Bennett was one of the most close-mouthed men Penn had ever met, he thought this was an odd criticism. So did Liam, who made a long show of extricating his clothing from the woman's fist. "Jules, I thought it is my lack of—how did you term it?—'emotional candor and sharing'—that is one of the things you abhor most about me?"

Penn looked over to meet Seth's gaze. They exchanged a rueful smile, brothers in sympathy for their older brother. Brothers. Once again, there was that word. Penn's gut took another tumble, but this time because he realized he was trapped. No, not trapped, but attached. Already attached.

Hell, how had this happened? Because they'd traded confidences in a fertile field? Because they shared a similar appearance? Or was it that their matching halves of DNA had some sort of magnetic property?

For whatever reason, he was part of a tribe now. From this moment on, he was connected. Penn sighed. Since there was no chance of walking away now, he decided to step up. Literally.

"Is there a problem I could help you with, Giuliana?" he asked.

She spun toward him, a little poof of dust flying into the air from the soles of her shoes. Her eyes sparked just like Alessandra's when she was angry. "Did *you* tell anyone there are financial problems at Tanti Baci? Because it appears the word is out."

He shook his head. "That word didn't come from me."

She gazed on him a moment longer, possibly assessing the truth, possibly plotting his dismemberment, then gave a little nod. "Fine. So I'll only ask that you promise on your own grave that you'll have the cottage ready for the weddings on time."

Seth bumped his shoulder as he came to stand beside him. "I'll kill him myself, Jules, if he doesn't come through."

Penn turned to stare at the younger man. So much for brotherhood, he thought.

Seth shot him an unrepentant grin. And when Penn found himself reluctantly grinning back, he had the moment's thought that the brotherhood connection might not be bad, might not be bad at all.

~

Clare turned toward the office entrance of Gil's auto service, Edenville Motor Repair, because the metal doors covering the service bays were already down for the night. It was after seven, but she was relieved to find the office open, indicating the boss still hadn't left for the day. She had to see him.

The chair behind his desk was empty, but the door leading to the service area was ajar. She cleared her throat as she approached it, surprised at how hard her heart was hammering. This was her best friend she was here for, no one scary.

"Gil?" It came out puny-sounding, so she cleared her

throat again and forced herself to say the name louder. "Gil?"

"Here," she heard the word echo in the cavernous room that smelled of grease and gasoline. "The Mercedes."

She found the car and stared at it, recognizing the sleek vehicle. "That's my mother's," she said.

A muffled laugh sounded from beneath it. "Hey, she's a woman who wants only the best, and when it comes to taking care of her automobile, she knows that's me."

Clare walked around the back bumper to see a pair of legs in coveralls sticking out. Gil's legs, of course. No one else could claim the long length. She frowned at them, because she'd come here to talk to *him*, not his ankles.

"Why'd you stop by?" he asked.

Thinking of her reasons, she felt herself flush and was glad, maybe, that they weren't yet face-to-face. "Can't a woman drop in on her best buddy?"

In response, he made a noncommittal grunt that only reminded her again of that distance that had cropped up between them in the last several months. She couldn't put her finger on when it happened . . . before she'd become engaged to Jordan, she knew that.

Clare needed her best friend—the Man of Honor—as her wedding crept closer, though. She had the usual bridal jitters that only someone as close as Gil could help her manage. Would she break out on the morning of her ceremony? Would her mother send her over the bend before the honeymoon? Was it normal to have such vivid dreams starring someone other than her husband-to-be every night?

"I can hear your wheels turning from under here," Gil called out. "What is it this time? I've already agreed to be part of the wedding party. Do I have to wear a pink dress after all?"

"No." She laughed at the thought, picturing her Italian Stallion in organza and flowers in his hair. The image was so wrong that she immediately mentally undressed him . . .

Oh, God.

Right there was the trouble she'd been having for the last several days, ever since he'd confessed to the new woman in his life. It had sounded serious, and the only woman that Gil had ever been faithful to for any length of time was . . . her.

But what kind of friend was jealous of her buddy's lover?

"You like Jordan, don't you?" she said to Gil, though it wasn't really a question. He'd never hinted at anything less, and it ate at her that she couldn't welcome Gil's new interest with the same kind of open acceptance that he'd shown her fiancé.

"Why would you ask that?" he said. "If you want to marry the guy, it shouldn't matter what I think."

Clare stilled. Yeah, she sucked at softball, and though the "girl geek" label Jordan used had stung, she knew she *was* smart. Meaning Gil's nonanswer answer was wreathed in flashing neon and whistling alarms.

Frowning at the rubber soles of her best friend's black work boots, she drew up a folding chair and sat near his feet. "You told me you thought I was ready for marriage."

"When did I say that?"

"When we went on our trip. When we drove to Colorado last summer and stayed with my friend Daphne."

"Oh, yeah. That trip."

More lights were flashing and she thought back to those seven days the previous July. Gil had agreed to go on a road trip, and they'd ended up staying in the tiny apartment of her friend from college. On the two days there and back, she and Gil had taken separate rooms at modest motels, but they'd shared the living room at Daphne's place.

As she recalled, it had been three nights of friendship and laughter. They'd brought a case of Napa wine with them, and she, Daphne, and Gil had stayed up into the early morning hours, drinking, reminiscing, planning their futures.

It was all a bit hazy, thanks to that case of wine, but two things were indelibly etched in her brain: One, that she and Gil had slept together each night, spooned, on Daphne's narrow couch; and two, on the way back to Napa she'd asked Gil if he thought she was ready to be a wife.

He'd said yes, damn it!

She'd just started dating Jordan and upon her return home—and with her mother's overwhelming approval—they'd quickly started talking marriage. A month later, she'd accepted his proposal.

Hadn't Gil shaken Jordan's hand in congratulation when he'd learned the news?

Wasn't it her cheek Gil had kissed?

And at that she could feel it, the touch of his lips to her skin. Her face burned, and she pressed her fingers to the spot, trying to rub the sensation away.

But it wasn't a kiss that innocent she'd been dreaming about.

For the last few nights Clare had been coming awake in her bride-to-be bed, tangled in her sheets and panting at a dream in which Gil—her best buddy Gil!—touched and undressed her. Then he kissed her, kissed her with the kind of sexual intent that her mother had always warned teenage Clare of when she talked about young men and what they wanted from young women. Then, Sally Knowles had probably feared that kind of stark sexuality might rub off Gil and onto her darling daughter . . . and now, all these years later, Clare was worried it finally had.

She dropped her head into her hands, wishing she didn't remember the dreams. In them Gil was behind her, spooned like they'd been on Daphne's couch, and though she couldn't see his face, she knew it was him. The size of him, the familiar scent of him were impossible to mistake.

"Clare? What's going on?"

"I'm going nuts," she muttered.

But he heard it, even from his position under the Mercedes. "Your mother?" he asked, voice full of sympathy. "What now?"

There was that, too, making her crazy. "She wants to insert a moment of silence in my wedding ceremony to honor Tommy. A special lighting of candles, too."

"Good God, Clare."

"Not so good to me," she said. "And if Tommy's the angel that my mother believes, then he should be doing something from up there to stop all this."

"You can stop it. You can tell her no."

"Oh, don't go rational on me, please. I'm in no mood for it."

"Clare . . ."

"How can I, Gil? Losing my brother messed up our family, and if this is what it takes to make Mom feel better, why should I complain?"

"What's the 'this' you're referring to, Clare? The moment of silence or the marriage itself?"

She squeezed her eyes shut, as if she could lose herself in the darkness.

"Clare. Honey . . ."

Her lids popped open to see Gil hunkered in front of her. When she hadn't been looking, he'd slid from beneath the car. There was a streak of grease on his whiskered cheek and she ached to scrub it away, but she didn't feel free to touch him like she would have in the past.

"You look like hell," he said.

She made a face. "Just what any almost-bride wants to hear."

"You been staying up late reading the dictionary again?"

"I should have never told you that," she complained. No matter that it was true at the time of her confession—ninth grade if she recalled correctly—that she'd made a plan to get through the entire *Webster's Collegiate* by the end of the school year.

Gil, already wearing a varsity letter on his jacket for football, hadn't laughed his butt off. Instead, he'd only smiled and advised her to keep the goal to herself. How kind he'd been, she realized, another flush of awkwardness rolling over her skin. "I *was* a girl geek. You *were* my bodyguard."

He shrugged. "Went both ways."

"You were never a geek."

"But you were my bodyguard, too. Remember kindergarten?" When she started to protest, he put his hand on her bare knee, right over her softball scar.

The shivery response of her skin shocked her into silence. She just stared at him.

"And remember when my mom got sick? You were there for me, Clare. And when Anita Lopez dumped me, too."

"Anita Lopez was afraid her father would find out she was dating the bad boy of Edenville and lock her up for life. That's the only reason she passed you that 'Dear John' note."

He shrugged again. "So you say. I only know that when I've been down, you've been there for me every time."

"That's not going to change," she declared, her chest aching right over her heart. That's what she didn't want to change, despite these weird dreams that were messing with her head.

His smile was sad. "I don't know, Clare. You being another guy's wife might alter things between us."

"It won't! You'll see!" She hated how he was expecting— and accepting—that their friendship would take a permanent hit with her wedding. "You're still my best friend, Gil," she announced, her voice fierce.

He glanced at her. "Okay."

Clearly he still had doubts. "I haven't been sleeping," she said, to prove to him she would tell him little things as she always had.

"I can see that."

Oh, yeah, the "look like hell" thing. "I've been having these dreams."

"What kind?"

"What kind?" She hadn't planned on getting specific. She'd just planned on coming here tonight, and fixing things by seeing Gil as her good ol' buddy, her BFF, instead of her erotic dream lover. "About kissing." The words burst out.

He looked over again. He looked at *her mouth*.

Her skin heated once more, and she felt a pulse start to throb everywhere she'd put on perfume before coming to the shop—something she'd never done before.

Gil's gaze dropped. "One of my cousins said that before she got married she dreamed of every boy she'd ever kissed. First to last. Is it like that?"

Clare grabbed at the idea. "Yeah. Like that." She swallowed. "Exactly like that."

"Then you must be dreaming of me."

"Huh?" She jolted back. How had he guessed? Her fascination with him must be written all over her face. "What are you talking about?"

"Silly woman. You've forgotten I gave you your first kiss?"

Oh, God. She had. At fifteen she'd begged him one slow summer afternoon to show her what it was like, certain she was the only teenager in America at risk of making it to sixteen without a single kiss. After much eye-rolling, he'd finally complied with a pretty boring laying on of lips to lips.

Recalling the moment, she frowned at him. "Wait a minute. I paid you ten bucks for that and only had a twenty. I think you still owe me the change."

He froze, then spoke slowly. "Or maybe I just owe you another kiss."

9

Edenville's sidewalks were crowded on Thursday late afternoons. Tourists and Edenvillians gathered alike for "Market Day" when local wineries, restaurants, farms, and other businesses set up booths in and around the town square. Handmade soap was available to sniff then buy, as well as fresh bunches of basil and clusters of cut flowers. Small cheese squares anchored toothpicks, Overpriced Ollie's offered up samples of their crème brûlée in tablespoons, and behind the booth headlined with the Tanti Baci logo, Alessandra smiled as she and her sisters poured tastes of their chardonnay and cabernet sauvignon.

Stevie sent her a sidelong look. "What's with the smile? You get lucky or something?"

Alessandra's stream of wine faltered, and some splashed onto the tablecloth instead of into the glass. "Oops," she said, then nudged the wine toward the woman wearing an I BRAKE FOR GRAPES T-shirt. Still wearing her beaming grin, she spoke through her teeth and under her breath. "I'm projecting financial stability." It was the whole point of having the sisters pour today, rather than the interns and cellar rats who usually manned the booth. They'd decided Edenville needed to see the sisters out in force, united and strong under the Tanti Baci banner.

"Financial stability with a touch of senility thrown in," Giuliana added. "Really, Allie, you look a bit loony."

"I'm still thinking lucky," Stevie said.

Allie poured a smidge of cab into a clean glass and sipped. The dark plum flavor burst on her tongue, changing to blueberry as she swallowed it down. Fortified, she glanced from the jewel-colored liquid to her sisters. "Lucky to have you both beside me," she told them honestly. "I've missed this."

"The Three Mousketeers," Stevie said. "Remember when we'd run around with our Disneyland ears on and Mom's aprons or tablecloths tied around our necks like capes?"

Giuliana looked away, and if Alessandra didn't hold the position as family crier, she might have thought her usually strong sister was on the verge of tears. She reached out to touch one slender shoulder. "We should go through the linens, Jules. We'll split them up and you can take your share back with you to L.A. You can make your place feel more like home that way."

"Or you can just stay home," Stevie said, uncorking another bottle with expert moves. "You're working in the wine business down south when you should be doing your thing here, near to us."

Giuliana stared across the street, as if the display window at the deli held a special fascination. "Near to other people as well."

Their taller sister groaned. "I swear to God, I can't believe how long you hold a grudge. What's it been? How many years since you and Liam went to Tuscany together for the summer and came home bitter enemies?"

"Ten. And I can hold a grudge until the day I die."

Yeeks. Alessandra and Stevie shared a look. Alessandra knew she could be temperamental and Stevie's mad came on like a wildfire, but Giuliana's anger burned with a blue-white eternal flame.

"Jules . . ." she ventured. "Liam . . . he didn't, you know, actually hurt you, did he?" Their sister had always remained mum about the source of their feud.

Giuliana's straight, silky hair swished around her shoulders as she shook her head. "Liam will never hurt me."

Never *again*, Alessandra thought to herself.

"Then move back home," Stevie urged, "instead of hiding from the man."

Alessandra took a hasty step back, thinking once again of Giuliana's icy temper. "She's not hiding," she hurried to say. "She—"

"Even agreed to meet him tonight," Giuliana finished. "All of us are going to be there . . . a partners' meeting at the farmhouse."

Alessandra's house. "All of us?" she echoed, dismayed. Please, that wouldn't mean—

"The three of us," Giuliana clarified. "Then Liam, Seth, and Penn, of course."

"Of course," Alessandra repeated, her mouth drying. This was going to be awkward. She'd never made it to the cottage yesterday after their, uh, encounter in her office. Today, she'd busied herself elsewhere with a thousand tasks that didn't really need doing.

Penn hadn't come looking for her.

She'd been glad about it, she'd told herself. It made it easier not to recall what had happened on her desk. She didn't want to think about that, or him, because the whole episode had not only been scandalous—her office! her desk!—but it had also been one-sided.

Which made it more embarrassing, more confusing, and put Alessandra more completely out of her element. She wasn't practiced at how to handle a situation like this—or a man like Penn who had barreled right through her defenses. One minute she'd been annoyed with him, and the next . . .

A broad chest covered with a blue shirt bearing the words *Build Me Up!* walked into Alessandra's line of sight. Oh, God, *Penn*. Her stomach jumped and heat blossomed on her nape as her gaze leaped to the man who . . .

. . . wasn't the one she expected.

"Kohl," she said in relief. It was the Tanti Baci vineyard manager, dark and silent Kohl Friday, a veteran of the Iraq War. His somber expression usually spooked her a little, but today she found herself giddy to see him. She'd rather face a dozen taciturn ex-soldiers than the man who'd made her come with hardly more than a kiss.

She hastily closed down the screen of her memory and sent him a smile. "Is there something you need?" she asked.

He grunted in answer, standing in the position of parade rest in jeans, battered straw cowboy hat, and that T-shirt. Handsome, huge, and nearly wordless. The silence between them strung out.

"Are you a fan of the show?" she asked finally, gesturing to the big *Build Me Up!*

"Fan of Penn," Kohl said.

Stevie's elbow poked her ribs. She looked over at her sister, eyebrows raised. They shared the silent thought that Kohl had never appeared to be the fan of anything besides bar brawls and busty women.

"Does work with a vet organization," Kohl continued. "For amputees. Revamps their homes. Ramps, resizes countertops. You know."

"Uh, sure." It was the most she'd ever heard the man speak at one time, though she didn't know if his usual quiet was due to his time as a soldier or because of childhood misery. It couldn't have been easy growing up with the name his hippie parents had given him—Kohlrabi. His sisters, Marigold and Zinnia, had fared only slightly better. "Penn's a real prince."

Stevie passed behind Alessandra, whispering. "Get Kohl out of here. He's scaring the customers away."

Peeking around his big shoulders, Alessandra saw her sister was right. Though the large man was good-looking, people were hanging back, as if he might be a ticking explosive. That wasn't the impression they wanted to project. Tanti Baci was a stable, family winery, not something ready to blow apart.

With quick footsteps, she came around the corner of the booth and delivered to Kohl her most winning smile. "Hey, shall we tour a bit and see what the competition's doing?"

Frowning, he shuffled his feet. "I don't know . . ."

Lifting her chin, she stared into his eyes and lowered her voice. "Please, Kohl."

His harsh expression softened around the edges. "Uh . . . okay."

She heard Stevie's snicker as they started off. "Bad little sister," she called after them.

Alessandra pretended not to hear, chatting with the near-silent Kohl as they walked among the booths and tables, pausing to sample a wine or two. They even ventured down a couple of side streets, where people were selling homemade jewelry and hawking cellophane-wrapped baked goods. The short block of Fir Street dead-ended, but a crowd was gathered there. As they neared, a big splash sounded and the audience roared.

Alessandra glanced at Kohl, who was tall enough to see over everyone's heads.

"Penn," he said.

"Huh?" She wanted to avoid that man, but how could she avoid this? Curious, she hurried forward to discover that the kids from the high school marching band had set up a dunking booth for the afternoon, complete with a celebrity climbing into the hot seat. He'd obviously fallen into the tank at least once before.

Could Penn sense her presence? Because as he settled onto the platform, hair dripping, shirt—another *Build Me Up!* of course—plastered to his body, his gaze found her at the back of the crowd. One brow lifted in challenge.

And just like that, her skin flamed with lust.

Which ignited her temper, too. A single look from him could set her simmering, a feeling she was wholly unprepared to handle, particularly since he hadn't been breaking down her door to get his share of the heat. As a matter of fact, yesterday he'd practically raced out of her office.

"Build me up!" a woman yelled from somewhere at the core of the crowd. A teeny tank top was thrown high into the air.

From the throng, another roar. She saw Penn's attention shift away from Alessandra and a devilish grin take over his mouth. A kid ran to the dunking booth, tossed Penn one of the TV show's promotional T-shirts, and he balled it between his hands, all the while obviously appreciating the charms of some half-naked bimbo out of Alessandra's view. Some half-naked bimbo who given the opportunity would, not unlike her, beg him for just what he'd delivered in Alessandra's office.

Mortified all over again, Alessandra retreated down Fir, leaving Kohl behind. She and Penn were better off staying apart, something his absence said he'd decided, too. She wasn't going to succumb to his appeal again.

Dusk was falling, and she wandered, not yet ready to go back to the Tanti Baci booth. Deep breaths of still warm air and the familiar streets brought her some comfort, just as the semidarkness gave her anonymity. It was going to be all right, she told herself. The Three Mouseketeers had poured wine together today, just as her father had always wanted. They'd find a way to keep Tanti Baci going. They had to.

Minutes slipped by and she only felt more certain that

they would pull it off. Tanti Baci would survive and that would be happy ending enough for Alessandra.

Old-fashioned street lights blinked on, their low wattage lending only ambience, not true illumination. She sighed, feeling like she'd stepped back in time. Not centuries, just a few short years ago. Any minute now she'd turn a corner and Tommy would be there.

My Darling Allie . . .

Her smile died, her buoyant mood sank as she turned onto Cedar—and then walked straight into the arms of a tall, hard, man. Her mind short-circuited. Her will fled.

She clung to him.

He held her tight.

As their mouths met, she realized he was still wet. And, now, so was she.

Bad little sister, indeed. Because she just couldn't keep her promises about steering clear. And particularly because if anyone saw the carnal manner in which her arms and mouth were clinging to Penn Bennett, her saintly image would be shot to hell.

~

Gil fingered the ten dollar bill in his pocket as he waited for Clare on a bench in the Edenville town square. It was Market Day, and downtown at dusk was crowded, but he refused to use that as an excuse to put off coming clean with her. Though they had reservations for four at a nearby bistro in sixty minutes' time, he'd phoned and asked that she meet him alone first.

The number one item on his agenda was giving her the ten bucks he owed her. The shock—horror?—that had overtaken her face when he'd suggested a kiss as payment made clear what she thought about being mouth-to-mouth with him. Then, he'd backpedaled like crazy, laughing like it was a big joke. Now, he was going to give her the money and also give her the truth: he hadn't been kidding.

Not only that, he was also going to tell her there was no other woman he was seeing, no woman he wanted to date. Not when he was in love with her.

With the lies between them out of the way, she'd understand exactly why he needed distance from her. She'd free him from his Man of Honor promise; he'd be free to be miserable from across town on the day of her wedding.

"Hey!" Suddenly she was there in front of him, standing out in the near-dark in a short lacy skirt and a top that had small fabric roses edging the neckline. Both ivory-colored, making her look bridal again.

His chest hurt.

A little kid riding a toddler-sized two-wheeler wobbled behind her. Every Edenvillian took their training wheels off in the square for the first time, and just like all before, this rider took a tumble. Clare spun, her skirt rising, and bent to rescue the bicyclist. The floating hem kept moving upward, affording Gil a brief glance at the curves of her bare bottom, revealed by a blue thong.

His cock hurt.

Maybe he groaned, because she spun back, her hands clamping the skirt at her sides. "You didn't see anything, did you?"

Incapable of speech, he shook his head. Clare's butt had started this whole thing. His geek girl, his buddy-of-the-female-persuasion, hadn't been on his radar as a woman until the fateful trip to visit her friend. Then, a little drunk in Daphne's living room, they'd decided there was no reason to play rochambeau for the hard floor. He should have insisted on rock-paper-scissors anyway, though, because nothing was harder, he discovered, than his cock the moment that Clare snuggled her little ass into the curve of his groin.

Murmuring some bullshit about back pain, he'd put a tiny throw pillow between them, but it had been no help. For the rest of that night—and the next and the next—he'd been both tortured and pleasured by the closeness of his BFF's slender body.

On their long trip home, when she'd asked him if he thought she was ready for marriage, he'd said yes, but that was before he'd considered whether *he* was actually willing to marry her.

Not soon after, he'd decided the answer to that second question was no. And so he'd said nothing about his feelings when she engaged herself to Jordan Wilson.

She eyed him now, suspicion bringing her brows together. "Are you sure I didn't flash you?"

"Yeah." He cleared his throat. "No flash." It would only embarrass her otherwise and . . . God, he was going back on his promise to himself already. But wait, it hadn't been a "flash" had it? His feelings for Clare had snuck up on him instead, after years of companionship and a camaraderie that his other friends never understood but that he hadn't examined in any depth until she'd snuggled up beside him.

As close as she was now, he thought, when she plopped next to him on the bench. "What's up?"

"I . . ." Her thigh was pressed to his, setting his brain to Spin again. Jumping to his feet, he didn't even risk a glance at her. "Let's walk."

"Okay," she agreed, even as he took off at a quick stride. Then he felt her small hand at the crook of his elbow. "Hold on. Wait up."

Neither was acceptable. He wanted to hold on to her and their friendship so damn bad, but Clare Knowles as Mrs. Jordan Wilson would cut at him if he stayed too close. As for "waiting up," it had taken him months to get this far. He could no longer put off the truth.

He stopped on the sidewalk, noticing where they were. The "far" side of town, which was only four blocks from the center. Small frame bungalows with tiny lawns marched down both sides of the street, while around the corner were metal buildings housing more commercial enterprises like a mom-and-pop flooring center and an upholstery business.

They were alone, except for the people he could see moving behind the lit windows of the little houses. He inhaled a deep breath.

"I told a whopper today," Clare said, before his own confession could formulate on his tongue.

He blinked. "What . . . ?"

"I'm feeling really bad, but I didn't want to get into it with Jordan's grandmother."

"Clare . . ."

She rubbed the heel of her hand against her forehead, exactly as she had when she was nine years old and the fourteens times table wouldn't stay put in her memory. "Maybe I'm not cut out for this wedding stuff."

He frowned. Surely she didn't mean what he wanted her to mean? "That could be a problem, considering that at the end of the month you're—"

"Oh, nothing will get in the way of the 'I-dos,' Mom would kill me if I put any kind of hitch in her plans—even if it's merely changing the color of the ink in the guest book pen."

She looked so frustrated that Gil had to smile. He let himself run a hand over her hair. "Kid," he said, to keep it all light and easy, "you need to stand up to your mother."

"As soon as I figure out a way to bring my brother back to life," Clare said with a sigh.

He let himself caress her hair one last time. She caught his fingers before his hand could fall back to his side. "Absolve me, please, for the lie I told today."

Shaking his head, he tried to retrieve his hand but she wasn't letting go. "So what exact lie was it?"

"You know Jordan's very stuffy, very upright grandmother."

Gil winced just at the mention of the woman. Old San Francisco society, she wore pastel suits and diamond earrings as big as lug nuts. At the engagement party, she'd told him that he reminded her of the Italians she used to know, the ones who "barely made a living, yet made a lot of fat babies."

"I hope you told her you were planning on a huge family of rug rats, all of whom plan to squeak by working with their hands."

"And break the Wilson tradition of surgeons, stock-brokers, and CEOs?" Clare shuddered. "She asked me if we were planning on serving any alcohol at our afternoon reception. Apparently she finds it gauche at events sched-uled before five o'clock."

He stared. "Did you explain this is *Napa*? That you're holding your wedding at a *winery*?" As for him, he planned on starting with the hard stuff first thing in the morning on her big day.

"I told her of course we wouldn't be gauche, even though I know darn well that we're having an open bar and plan-ning on toasting with the Tanti Baci wedding wine. What's she going to think?"

"Let Jordan handle it," Gil advised. "It's his wedding, too."

"Not that you'd know it," she mumbled. "I already brought it up and he said it was my fib and that I should deal with the fallout."

Gil's free hand curled into a fist. Even if Jordan wasn't marrying Clare, Gil thought he'd hate the guy. Didn't he know the smallest thing about his bride? The sweet girl geek detested confrontation and she needed backup in a situation like this one. That's what a partner did. That's how good relationships worked. When it came to facing down new small business regulations, say, he could always count on Clare to help him through the details. In turn, he handled all her minor building repairs.

Give and take. Take and give.

Without thinking, he lifted her hand and kissed the back

of her knuckles. "Thanks, buddy." He didn't say what for. He didn't know if he needed to.

She looked away. "You know all I thought of during the conversation with Grandmère?"

"That she chose a pretentious, stupid-ass nickname for her grandkids to call her?"

She laughed, and he could feel a little of her tension seep away. "No. I thought of that *Star Trek* episode, the one where Spock tells Bones that Vulcans don't feel the 'dubious' effects of alcohol."

Gil's chest ached again. His Trekkie girl geek. "And then the good doctor says something like 'Now I understand why they were conquered.'"

She laughed again. "You love that episode, too."

No. He didn't actually enjoy that episode or love anything about the please-why-so-long series except that Clare had a passion for it. So he knew about tribbles and Red Shirts and Vulcan psychology, God help him.

He pressed a kiss to her knuckles a second time. "Yeah. Love that episode, too." Only this time he didn't feel bad about lying again. He was fast losing his resolve to be the bearer of bad news.

She started chattering about yet another booze-related Bones and Spock moment and he was listening, really he was, until his gaze caught on the big picture window of a bungalow behind Clare's back. A pair was embracing, indulging in a hell of a kiss. It made him envious, damn it, to see this other couple indulging in what he wanted to share with Clare.

Then the man broke away from the woman, and Gil recognized them both.

Jordan Wilson. Jesus. Jesus Christ.

The woman was Tori Merrick, who'd gone to high school with him and Clare. Ah. No doubt the source of the girl geek and her bodyguard comment. If he remembered right, Tori poured at one of the several tasting rooms set up in Edenville's downtown.

And she was having an affair with Clare's groom-to-be, that was obvious, as Gil watched her reel the other man in for another sloppy, intimate kiss. Cold washed over him as he shifted his gaze from the clandestine couple to Clare's animated face.

It was going to kill her. It was going to suck any joy right out of her, and if he told her about his feelings now, he wouldn't be there to help her pick up the pieces. "Clare . . ."

She stopped in mid-Trek monologue. "What?" Her eyes narrowed. "What's the matter?"

With all the fervency he had in him, he willed her to turn her head. But she didn't. She just kept on looking at him. "Gil? What *is* it?"

He opened his mouth. "Nothing," came out of it. "Except we should probably get to the restaurant. Did I mention my date couldn't make it?" he continued as he hurried her in the opposite direction of the two people in the window using their tongues and wandering hands to say their prolonged good-byes.

He listened to her professed disappointment with half an ear. "I think I'll skip dinner myself and go check on her," he added when Clare paused. "My, uh, friend wasn't feeling well."

Not only would it make *him* sick if he had to look at Jordan's face over a dinner table, but Gil couldn't bear to tell the woman he loved any of the truths he should, not yet, anyway. It was going to require more thinking, which meant he was still being dishonest with Clare—and now he was also keeping quiet about another man's lies.

10

The only time Penn had fully cooperated with her since they'd met was now, Alessandra decided, when he was so capably kindling something inside her besides desire. In dry clothes, including yet another *Build Me Up!* T-shirt, he sprawled on a chair pulled up to the farmhouse table in her dining room, looking as if he had no memory of the steamy kiss they'd shared an hour before on the streets of Edenville.

That he could dismiss that—dismiss her—so easily heated her temper and totally turned her off. One moment they'd been pressed as close as label to glass, and the next he'd pushed her away, to grab her wrist and tow her in the direction of the town square. "Your sisters are looking for you. We all have a meeting to get to."

This meeting. She hadn't appreciated the reminder then, and she didn't appreciate the reality of it now. Liam and Seth were seated at the table, too, as well as Giuliana and Stevie. Everyone but Penn was looking at her with a peculiar light in their eyes.

A chill washed over her. This was not good.

"Sit down, Allie," her oldest sister said, nudging out the chair beside hers.

"We need beverages," she countered, scurrying toward the built-in buffet at the back of the room. She pulled wine-glasses from an upper cabinet. Three stems in each hand, she walked back to the table, her shaky nerves causing the glass bowls to click against each other like chattering teeth.

Penn shot up and grabbed the glasses from her, his warm fingers brushing over her cold ones. Back in his seat, he played Wild West saloonkeeper and passed the goblets by sliding them along the polished table.

"Pinot noir," Alessandra decided aloud. She drew a couple of bottles from the wine rack on the buffet. "Russian River Valley." That particular wine-growing region in nearby Sonoma County was known for producing the light-bodied red with its subtle fruity-spicy taste.

When the others remained silent, her nerves jumped again, and she fumbled with the wine opener. Penn rose once more. "I've got that," he said. She watched him remove the corks and set the bottles on the table.

Next, he steered her toward the free chair beside his. Resisting occurred to her, but she decided his seat choice was safer than the one next to Giuliana. The serious expression on her sister's face was not reassuring. It caused her to reach for the nearest bottle the minute she settled. Wine glugged into her glass and then she tossed back a mouthful.

Penn shifted closer as he reached for the pinot himself. "Wow, little nun, you're in a rush for all kinds of . . . rushes." His voice was soft.

Her face burned. Damn the man for reminding her of how quickly she'd reacted to him in her office. Sending him a barbed look, she took another swallow of wine.

He laughed, the rumble rolling down her back and stretching her already-taut nerves. Just like that, the stupid, silly craving for him was back. Damn the man. She put her glass very carefully on the table, and just as carefully didn't look at him again, ignoring his second laugh.

When everyone else had wine in their glasses, Seth cleared his throat, causing Alessandra to brace herself. When the lawyer was going to take the floor, it couldn't be good news. "I've taken a thorough look at Tanti Baci's books," he said.

"We already know there's problems, mostly due to the outlay for the caves four years ago," Alessandra put in, desperate to get this part over with. "But the new plans—"

"I've taken a thorough look at those, too, Allie." Seth hesitated.

She stared back at him. Another handsome Bennett, but at the moment he didn't have the smooth assurance that epitomized Penn. This man wasn't happy about whatever he had to say, and that was enough to put an ache in her throat and the sting of tears in her eyes.

"Shit," Seth muttered, then lifted his wine and took a long drink. "Can't I just go find some puppies to kick, people?"

Penn slammed down his own glass, drawing startled looks from around the table. "For God's sake! Look, Alessandra's not fragile and she's not a child. Take the gloves off and treat her like a grown woman."

Alessandra glared at him, incipient tears evaporating. "You look, Mr. Hard-Ass. Not everyone has your lack of consideration."

"Oh, come now, little nun. You know that I can be quite considerate in the right setting . . . say, in an office?"

That cemented it. She really did detest the man. While she felt awkward and . . . okay, aroused . . . in his company, he appeared unperturbed. It wasn't fair and it wasn't right and she was going to prove somehow, some way, that she could be just as unflappable as him.

But this meeting came first. She directed her attention

to the other end of the table. "What is it, Seth?" she demanded. "What is it you're trying to say?"

He hesitated again.

"Go ahead," she urged.

"I can't see this wedding business saving the day," Seth answered bluntly.

Her breath caught, but she didn't let that stop her from arguing. "It's not meant to be the sole means of digging us out of the hole. The intent is to get our cash flow up, to renew interest in our wedding wine, and to convince the bank to extend our line of credit in the fall . . ." Her voice trailed off as she noticed Giuliana was shaking her head.

"We won't achieve that with just a few weddings between now and harvest," her oldest sister said. "And I talked to the Latisse twins tonight. They've decided to do their double wedding in Maui instead of at Tanti Baci."

Alessandra drooped in her chair. "I was sure they would decide to book with us." The defection meant they'd lost a double site fee in one fell swoop.

With a shrug, Giuliana drew her wineglass closer. "They never had any taste. They've decided to dress as sea sirens and get married in the surf in Maui."

They all took a moment to contemplate that, then Penn glanced at Liam. "Which means an interesting wedding night, don't you think? I've always wondered how you make it with a mermaid. Think about it . . . the tail's in the way of the good stuff."

Liam, usually so somber, released a bark of sudden laughter. "Jesus, Penn."

The other man's infectious grin blinked on. He brought his wineglass to his mouth again. "Just sayin'."

His "just sayin'" seemed to release the strain at the table. For a few minutes everyone enjoyed their wine and debated whether the "sea siren" theme also meant the tone-deaf Larisse twins were going to sing. Even Liam and Giuliana exchanged a few nonbarbed remarks.

As the warm glow of the wine slid into her belly, Alessandra relaxed. Hope was still alive.

Until Liam turned to her. The oldest of them all, he was the one whose opinion would hold the most sway with the rest. She braced again, unable to blame her dry mouth on the pinot's tannin.

"Allie," he said, his voice kind, "in a nutshell, we don't think that your talk of legends and love stories can garner enough attention and enough bookings to achieve what the winery needs to stay afloat."

Her hand tightened on the stem of her glass. "Again, I don't expect it to—"

Under the table, a warm palm clamped her thigh. She jumped, the ruby liquid in her glass rising like a tsunami. Sexual heat shot over her skin.

"I think you're not giving Alessandra enough credit," Penn said. "I've seen her at work, sharing her vision of what a Tanti Baci wedding can offer."

Stevie made a face. "I don't know, Penn."

"But *I* know," he answered. "This is what I do, create an image, make it appealing, make people believe."

Alessandra twitched again as Penn's words sank in. He was siding with her! Pleading her case!

"And it's all the more compelling," he added, his hand stroking her leg beneath the table, "because Alessandra herself believes. I watched her nail down a booking simply by sharing her faith in happy endings."

Well, she'd actually thought it was the power of his sex appeal that had done that, but she kept it to herself. Through the shield of her eyelashes, she watched the expressions of the five others gathered around the table. From the oldest Bennett to Stevie, they all—including Penn—gazed on her like she was a sweet six-year-old who still believed in Santa. But she'd hang her stocking every Christmas Eve if it meant they'd support her plan and continue to give Tanti Baci the chance of recovery.

Then Liam cut his eyes away. "Allie . . ."

Her belly quivered. His opinion was the one that mattered most. Unless . . . She lifted her chin, turning her face toward Giuliana. Maybe her sister's feud with Big Brother Bennett would work here. In most instances, if Liam said "black," Giuliana would snap "white."

Except Jules didn't appear to be paying attention to Liam or anything else right now. Her gaze was absently trained on the wine in her glass, as if she was already back in L.A., the family land gone forever.

"No," Alessandra whispered, her body stiffening.

Penn caressed her again, but if it was meant to be soothing, she was too sensitized to his touch. She shivered and detested herself for it. "No," she said again, this time looking at him. Her hand reached for his, but he caught her fingers before she could move his away.

His touch firm, he entwined their fingers and rested them on her thigh. "I have an idea. I think it will capitalize on everything Alessandra has established so far—and maybe take it to the next level. Do you know the new cable show *Wedding Fever*? It's getting a lot of buzz."

Five minutes later, Alessandra was as giddy as if she'd swilled both bottles of pinot all by herself. A debut-season sensation, each episode of *Wedding Fever* followed the real-life nuptials of one or two couples.

"A good friend is a producer of the show," Penn said. "Someone who used to work on *Build Me Up*. I know they insert short pieces featuring a new trend or exotic wedding locale each week. If I call in a favor, I think we can get something on Tanti Baci slipped into an upcoming episode."

Exhilarated by the possibility, her fingers squeezed Penn's. "Do you . . . do you really believe you could make that happen?"

"As much as you believe in forever and ever, amen," he promised.

With hope surging again, she looked back at the others. Seth took the lead once more, his gaze shifting to each face. Finally, he caught Alessandra's eye, and nodded. "Okay. We'll give it some more time." Then he let out a long breath of air and grinned. "Whew, I feel like that time I dropped the Christmas angel from the top of the ladder, only to find out it bounced instead of broke."

Christmas Angel, Nun of Napa, she didn't care what anyone called her at the moment. Grinning too, she jumped from her seat to dole out a round of hugs: Stevie, Giuliana, Liam, Seth . . . Penn.

Who copped a feel of her bottom.

Even that couldn't dim her mood.

"Who's up for more wine?" she asked. And though her sisters and Liam and Seth begged off, she was still smiling as she showed everyone to the door and closed it behind them.

That's when she realized Penn hadn't headed out like everyone else. With an unpleasant bump, she fell from cloud nine back to planet earth. What did he want *now*?

Her shoulders against the door, she eyed him with sudden distrust. A person had to have doubts about a man who could kiss so hot and then turn so cool.

"What?" she asked. "You were just stringing me along, is that it? Getting my hopes up. You don't know anyone at *Wedding Fever*. You can't get Tanti Baci on that show."

He blinked. "What? I wouldn't do that. Christ, Alessandra. As a matter of fact, I already called my buddy earlier in the week and he's trying to free up a few days ASAP."

Then he shook his head. "What kind of man do you think I am?"

Egotistical came to mind. Too beautiful for his own good. A playboy, a player, someone who'd stood her up then sexed her good. But he seemed to be serious now. Sincere. He really thought he could get Tanti Baci some air time.

But that didn't make sense—not for the so-casual man she was certain had no conscience. And yet he was the one who had . . . who had . . .

Who had actually just given her—and Tanti Baci—a second chance—a real chance. She believed that now. And he'd done it for no other reason she could fathom except that he was—

Her hands came up to cover her mouth. "Oh my God," she exclaimed, her eyes rounding in surprise. "Penn Bennett, you fraud."

No wonder she never seemed to keep hold of her dislike for him. Because despite the front he put up, the truth was . . . "You're nice. I just figured out that you're a really nice man."

~

"Nice?" Penn echoed. The word irritated him, especially the way the pretty little nun was looking when she said it. In a flippy hot pink skirt and a pale pink sleeveless top, she looked like she should be on her way to ballet lessons. That outfit and that word—*nice!*—made him want to put her on the back of the Harley he'd left garaged in L.A. He'd drive her to a biker bar he knew, where he'd make her quake by threatening to share her with his buddies in the motorcycle gang. Then she'd know what kind of man he was.

"Yep," she said, nodding as if her diagnosis was confirmed. "Nice."

It sounded like a taunt coming from her puffy, prim little doll-mouth. The baby bride didn't understand who the hell she was teasing. "Stop."

"Ni-ice," she sang.

No, nice was some other man. Nice was Saint Tommy, the man Alessandra pined for, and the idea of her ghostly groom only made Penn more surly. "Take it back," he ordered.

"Or what?" With one hand on her hip, she was taunting

for real now, as if she didn't care that she was toying with fire.

Maybe she didn't smell the same smoke he did. Maybe she didn't realize she'd had him at a frustrating smolder for days, made only worse after that morning in her office. Since he'd watched her stifle her orgasm like a good girl stifles a sneeze. He'd walked away then, but by God, he couldn't walk away with her thinking he was *nice*. "Or what is that I'm going to make you do things that will curl you hair," he threatened.

Gaze not leaving his, she lifted a lock of her long hair and wagged the wavy stuff back and forth. "Already curly."

He took a step toward her, heat rushing up his back. "I'm not kidding around."

Her eyes sparkled. "Fine, then. Nice is off the table. How about considerate, though? Is that better? Or there's kind. Caring works, too."

All making him sound like some gullible fool—just what Lana Lang had taken him for. What Penn's father had considered Debbie Penn, cocktail waitress with the heart of gold that he'd knocked up and then left. He strode forward again, his chest meeting the tips of Alessandra's breasts. Her sharp intake of breath gratified him. The little smile continuing to hover at her mouth did not.

She thought this was a game, but oh, baby, he didn't feel the least bit playful. Placing one hand on the door above her head, he leaned into her, more of his weight pressing against her torso. His other hand slid under her short skirt to travel up her warm leg. As close as he was, she couldn't hide her shiver even though he was sure she tried to control the response.

"So inhibited," he murmured, then lifted his brows. "Or wouldn't a considerate man point that out?"

They both knew the answer to that. A considerate man wouldn't have his mouth a half-inch from hers and his fingertips the same distance from her pussy. A considerate man wouldn't be sending sexual signals to the Nun of Napa, no matter that she'd begged him for a secret affair just a few days before.

That was another damned word—*secret*. He pressed closer to her as her breaths soughed fast against his cheek and her brown eyes deepened to the darkest chocolate.

With deliberate strokes, he brushed the silky fabric at the apex of her thighs with the backs of his fingers. She twitched, the movement quickly suppressed, and he let his mouth curve in wicked intent. The bottled-up baby bride wasn't going to hold back from him this time. He wasn't nice enough, not considerate or kind or caring enough to allow her to hide from him what he did to her.

Sex was driving him now, not common sense, but he was allowing it to take the lead. This time he was going to have it all—hear it, feel it, taste it. Take it from her.

"You owe me," he said, brushing his knuckles against her panties again. She was bare under there, he remembered, another flash of heat streaking along his spine.

She swallowed, and he saw the pulse in her neck was fluttering. "Owe you what?"

"All your sugar, sweetheart." He slid one finger under the elastic band of her panties, found smooth, baby-soft skin and then her wetness. His hand braced on the door curled into a fist. They hadn't even kissed and she already was . . .

"Sticky," he whispered, stroking his finger into her flowering folds. He withdrew his hand, put it to his mouth and sucked the moisture away. "Sweet."

Her body went rigid against his. The flash of heat was from her skin this time, and he felt it on her cheek as he drew his damp finger down that soft curve. Reaching her chin, he angled it upward to position her lips for his kiss.

He pushed inside her mouth, aware that over the lingering fruity notes of the pinot she couldn't miss her own taste on his tongue. Another delicate twitch, and he knew she'd registered the new flavor. Her dead boyfriend couldn't offer her that.

Snaking his arm around her waist, he drew her into the cradle of his hips. Her head dropped back, the kiss deepening, the flames around them leaping higher. Lifting his head, his hand caressed her pretty round ass over her skirt. "Take me upstairs," he said, then kissed her cheek, her chin, the side of her neck. He sucked there, then harder, until she bowed against his body.

"Penn," she whispered.

"Alessandra," he whispered back.

She buried her face against his shoulder, and he pushed her hair off her neck to press another burning kiss to her nape. Her shudder was more detectable this time and his happy, hard cock throbbed against his belly. No more hiding, he thought, not behind nun reputations, dead-and-gone grooms, or good-girl expectations. He was going to make a screamer out of this one if it took all night. Then she'd know the real kind of man he was. "C'mon, sweetheart. Take me to your room."

Cheeks flushed bright, her eyes in that dazed-by-desire state, she took his hand and edged toward the staircase. At the bottom, she glanced back at him over her shoulder, and those big brown eyes and prim little mouth had him smiling at her in reassurance before he could think about it. Nice Guy reassuring a new lover.

Which defeated the whole purpose . . . Shit.

Inspiration struck as she placed a foot on the first step. He squeezed her shoulder with his free hand to halt her. Though he could feel her gaze again, he didn't meet her eyes. Instead, he reached beneath her skirt and yanked her panties to her ankles.

"Keep moving," he said, urging her to step out of her underwear and move up to the next tread.

As she did, he grabbed the hem of her skirt and tucked it into the waistband. *Bare.*

She froze, her delectable bottom framed by the sides of her skirt. He caressed the sweet curve with his callused palm, then swatted the round flesh. Her spine went rigid.

He watched pale pink blossom and fade on her creamy skin. "No Mr. Nice Guy, get that?"

That thawed her, though the Nun of Napa didn't respond verbally. Instead, she continued up the stairs, a new, saucy swing to her hips and her naked ass. Still holding her own, the little witch, he thought, rolling in his tongue as he trailed her up the rest of the stairs.

No matter. He was going to be on top—and come out on top—in the bedroom. She'd be sighing and shaking and crying out hosannas and he'd lap it all up in the name of sin.

The bedroom was as he'd expected: bare wooden floors, oval rag rug, pastel walls, all dimly lit by the glow of a lamp on the dresser. He looked for a crucifix hanging over the four-poster bed, but instead saw a framed photo of Alessandra and her sisters standing before the ruin that was once the cottage. It was what she worshipped, anyway, family and the winery.

Then his eye caught on a smaller photo on the bedside table: Tommy.

Under the dead man's gaze, he took Alessandra's shoulders in his hands and drew her back against him, her naked bottom to the front of his jeans. His palms slid over her arms to cup her breasts. "I didn't get to play with these like I wanted last time," he said, weighing the mounds and rolling his thumbs over the tips.

Her head lolled against his shoulder and her hips pushed into him, his erection pillowed by her soft flesh. He groaned, the pressure so good. His hands grasped her shirt and yanked it over her head.

Her little yelp of surprise was muffled by the material but she didn't make another sound when his fingers unlatched the front clasp of her bra. It was he that sighed as they spilled into his hands. Hot flesh, silky and firm, with nipples already a tight pinky-plum. He plucked at the tips, absorbing the tiny jerks of her reaction into his body.

She was still holding out on him, but two could play the control game. "Get on the bed," he rasped out.

"You first."

Damn it, for a woman who claimed to need an affair—a *secret* affair—she was still too much in charge of herself. Hyperaware of Saint Tommy's unwavering gaze, Penn picked up the burr in his side and tossed her onto the mattress . . . then followed her down, because there was no trusting the woman would stay still to take her medicine.

"I'm going to make you crazy," he promised, then laid his mouth against the hot skin of her neck to blaze a trail with his tongue to her nipple.

Her back arched, the hard nub brushing his lower lip. He caught it in his mouth, sucking strongly as her fingers found his hair. His gaze lifted to her face as he suckled, noting that while her neck was arched, her expression was set, showing nothing—no urgency, no ecstasy.

"Damn you," he whispered, but he was talking to Tommy's photograph and not the sexy woman who quivered with ruthless restraint. Moving to her other breast, he plumped it with his hand and sucked the sweet cherry on top of the mound. Her light perfume steamed from her skin, rising around him, making him dizzy as he touched and tasted the bounty of her flesh.

He crawled up her body for another deep kiss and her mouth opened, her tongue dueling with his as he found the fastening of her skirt and pushed it off her legs. He sat back on his knees, his heart hammering at the sight of her golden skin uncovered for his eyes.

Hers were drowsy, her mouth swollen. "Build me up," she whispered.

"Huh?" Then he realized he was wearing one of the show's promo T-shirts. Smiling, he drew it off, and instead of tossing it to her—as if he'd let her hide now—he held it above her breasts and dragged the soft fabric across her nipples.

Her skin flushed, and he held the shirt higher from her body. "Penn . . ." her bottom lip pushed out in a sexy pout.

He lowered his arm, trailing the fabric over her again . . . and then again lifted it an inch. This time, she followed the teasing touch, her heels digging into the bedclothes in order to arch up toward the cotton.

"God, that's hot," he heard himself murmur. Between her parted thighs he could see the wetness glazing her swollen folds. She could swallow her sighs and moans and erase the need from her expression, but she couldn't conceal this from him.

He tossed the shirt over the side of the bed and slid down to his elbow beside her. Sure she was ready enough, he tucked his hand between her legs and slid two fingers inside her.

Eyes closing, he reveled at the hot snug fit.

"Aaaah." The sound riveted him . . . until he realized it was his own voice groaning at the goodness of her. But there were telltale signs of how it affected her, too. She was bowing into his touch, taking a deeper penetration, even as her top teeth held her bottom lip closed. So subdued.

And still that way, even as he started a slow and steady rhythm, his thumb nudging her clitoris on each thrust. He bent down and sucked her nearest nipple, and still she didn't do anything more than breathe heavily.

"Little nun, silence isn't a virtue in the bedroom," he said, plunging into her body and then holding there, his thumb pressing the hard button at the top of her sex. "Talk to me."

Scream, baby.

Her gaze found his face. She let go her lower lip and it sprang back, red and swollen. He groaned aloud, heat prickling over his body, and then her mouth opened.

"Yeah," he cajoled. "Tell me, Alessandra."

"Take off your pants, Penn." She paused. "*Now*."

Shy, beautiful, bossy. She was all those things, but it didn't matter because he wanted nothing more than to be naked beside her. As he shucked his pants his wet fingers— wet from her—trailed dampness along his hip, causing his cock to go even harder. It made donning a condom quick, torturous work.

Their next kiss was luscious, delicious, tasting of ripe fruit and the piquant tang of wine. She widened her thighs and he took his place there, the head of his erection catching in the crease between her leg and groin.

He groaned again, because even that small pressure sent pleasure shooting toward his heart. It made him crazy with the need for more, so he edged back to his knees and aimed—"*Aaaah*"—straight for the center of her body. Breaching her inch by inch, he worked into the soft slick clasp of her.

The idea of holding back, going slow, torturing her with bliss was at the forefront of his mind, but when she lifted her knees to slide her satiny inner thighs around his hips, impulse took over and he thrust to the hilt. Rocked back. Thrust again.

This wasn't going to last as long as he'd dreamed. But he wasn't going down alone, he promised himself. The tension in her body beneath his told him she was getting close, too.

He focused on her face, determined to see and hear her break. Their gazes met, held, and he slid one hand between their bodies to fondle her clitoris in time with each stroke into her clasping, hot hold.

Her muscles gripped him tighter. Her body shook with the most subtle of tremors.

Almost there . . . almost there, he chanted to himself, determined that Mr. Not Nice Guy would bear witness to her sexual explosion. One of her small hands lifted from the mattress. It cupped his ass.

Pleasure shot like a starburst from the touch. His rhythm hitched, then restarted with a frenzy, feeling the frantic onset of orgasm just in the offing.

Hold on . . . hold on . . .

Hold . . .

Her fingers squeezed, and she was going over, her inner muscles clutching his cock, the goodness of it launching his own orgasm.

As the bliss hit, Penn's eyes squeezed closed and his ears rang with only the sounds of his own loud groans of release.

He collapsed to the pillow beside her. Minutes passed before he had the strength to open his eyes.

Only to find the Nun of Napa staring back at him, all signs of stupendous orgasm already absent from her face. "Wow," she remarked, "You're, um, loud."

A screamer, she meant. Oh, hell, the screamer was him.

11

Insistent raps pulled Alessandra out of the depths of sleep. "Allie," her sister Stevie's voice called from the other side of her bedroom door. "Are you decent?"

Hmm, she mused as drowsy memories of the night before flooded her mind. Was what she'd done last night with Penn "decent"? But before she could answer, her sisters came barreling through the now-open doorway.

"Hey," she protested, yanking the covers to the neckline of her old cotton nightgown with one hand while the other swept the empty space beside hers, assuring herself he was gone.

"Hey, what?" Giuliana asked, crossing to the windows to pull up the shade.

Alessandra squinted as pale morning light brightened the room. That's when she saw it, Penn's T-shirt bunched on the floor on the far side of the bed. If her sisters realized what had happened last night, how would she explain it to them?

They'd want answers besides "I was horny and couldn't help myself."

Like always with him, it had felt beyond her control from his first touch. They kept colliding like magnets, opposites attracting, the small-town girl body-slamming with the big-city bad boy. Inevitable and hard to regret, though now that she was awake there was a vague disquiet hanging over her head.

"Coffee?" Stevie asked, then lifted Alessandra's limp hand and wrapped her fingers around a cardboard cup.

"You brought me coffee," she exclaimed, bringing it to her mouth. Her first sip brought more clarity to her brain and she looked at her sisters with suspicion. "You brought me coffee . . . why?"

Stevie shrugged. "I have some clients to pick up out this way. But since the tasting rooms don't open until 10:30 at the earliest, I thought I'd kill some time with you."

Alessandra switched her gaze to her oldest sister. Giuliana shrugged, too. "Um, I work here, remember?" Her job was at the winery offices, where she'd taken over the administrative tasks that had been their father's, though she lived in town instead of at their family home.

"Your room is just down the hall," Alessandra felt compelled to mention.

Stevie snorted. "Rapunzel's afraid of what—who— might come crawling through her window."

Alessandra blinked. "Huh?"

The middle Baci sister was looking in Giuliana's direction, while Giuliana herself was playing with the comb and brush set on the dresser, as if she wasn't the subject of the conversation. "Allie," Stevie said, "haven't you ever wondered what wore that path between our house and the Bennetts'?"

"I know what wore that path," Alessandra retorted. "Liam and Jules . . . oh." *Oh.*

At only fourteen when her oldest sister swore eternal enmity on Liam Bennett, Alessandra had never known what had seeded such passion. And now she realized that it was . . . passion. That meant Giuliana herself had only been eighteen, but you didn't need to tell Alessandra about her sister's ability to hold a grudge—or about the intensity of first love.

"Oh," she said again.

"You can't trust them," Giuliana pronounced.

Bennetts? Men in general?

"We have to remember that, Allie," she continued. "That's why I came this morning. To warn you not to get your hopes up."

"About Penn?" Alessandra scooted higher on the pillows. "Don't worry, I have no expectations whatsoever about him." She tried pushing away the hovering uneasiness. No way could he claim a heart as hard and small as hers.

Frowning, Stevie wandered toward the window. "He's not going to call his friend from *Wedding Fever*?"

"Of course he's going to call—" Alessandra broke off, realizing she'd been having a different discussion. She waved her hand to erase the past few sentences. "Let's start over. I'm certain Penn can get Tanti Baci on that show. He'd already contacted his friend when he told us about it last night."

Giuliana didn't look placated. "Still . . ."

"Hey." Stevie's attention was riveted by the view outside. "Come look at this."

Eager to move on to something new, Alessandra climbed from the covers. Her foot brushed cotton as she crossed the floor, and she took the opportunity to swipe up Penn's shirt and hold it to her chest. Inside out, the telling logo was hidden, but she could still smell him on it.

Her nipples tightened as she clutched it closer to her body. Memories of their encounter flowered in her head. His strong shoulders under her hands. The thrust of his hips. The hot suction of his mouth on her breast.

Stevie's voice interrupted the replay. "I forget about this sometimes."

Alessandra shook her head to clear her thoughts, then joined her sisters at the window. Beyond the glass, it was nothing special. At least not anything she couldn't see any morning she chose. The sun was just cresting the eastern mountains. Their ragged outline was etched in gold and that same warm light infused the fog with tawny sparkles that looked like champagne bubbles rising from the rows of leafy grapevines. A view that had been in the family for over one hundred years.

Her arms tightened on Penn's shirt. Thanks to him, they had a shot at keeping the legacy alive. What was there to worry about when she was better off this morning than any other morning since their father died? All because of one arrogant, sexy, confident, charming man.

No wonder she couldn't think of him without a thrill goosing her stomach. Without a smile playing at her mouth. It shouldn't be such a surprise that she had a little crush on the man.

Was that the source of her uneasiness? She'd never had a crush before. When other girls were swooning over a boy band or their best friend's big brother, she'd been in love with Tommy . . . and Tommy had loved her back. With a crush, though, there was no requisite for reciprocal feelings.

And Penn was too cool to crush.

Stevie and Giuliana were staring at her. "What?" she said.

"Why are you mumbling about the crush?" Stevie asked. "We're not even to harvest yet."

"Uh . . . I know," she answered, casting about for some way to put them off the scent. "I was, uh, just thinking about . . . thinking about when we were kids. When Papa would put grapes in our little play pool and let us stomp them."

Giuliana laughed. "Mom used to scold about our stained feet, but she never insisted that we stop."

Alessandra had forgotten that. The memory rose in her mind, the squishy, warm feel of ripe grapes between her toes, the pungent, sugary smell of the split fruit, the firm grasp of her mother's hand as she kept her steady. Their handsome, dark-haired father had stood nearby, exhorting his girls to dance like gypsies in order to add magic to the flavor of the grapes.

The magic hadn't been in the dance, but in that moment of togetherness. All the moments of togetherness their family and their family's ancestors had experienced at Tanti Baci. She draped Penn's shirt over her shoulder and wrapped an arm around each of her sisters. "I couldn't bear to lose any of this," she said. She couldn't bear to lose one square foot of where all that had happened. Where her heart had once been so full.

If Penn's plan worked, she wouldn't have to.

At the thought, the sun breached the mountaintops and its bright rays burned away the last of the lingering fog. Her apprehension evaporated with it. The sun was out early today, and it would bring sweetness to the fruit just as her days ahead looked to be very sweet, too.

Maybe she was crushing a little on Penn, but she also believed in him—more than she'd believed in anything in a very long time. Her hold on her sisters tightened. "It's going to be okay," she said, vehement. "I think it's going to turn out all right."

The phone on her bedside pealed. All three sisters turned in its direction, but Alessandra reached it first. The voice on the other end made her jump, but what Penn said before he hung up had her leaping for the bedroom door.

She glanced over her shoulder at her sisters. "Something happened at the cottage."

~

Both hands occupied with cardboard cups of steaming coffee, Gil used his elbow to push open the door to the

Wagon Train, one of Clare's small chain of boutiques located throughout the wine country. Instead of a bell, the opening notes of the *Star Trek* theme signaled his entry. Clare looked up from where she stood at the back of the shop, unpacking new inventory.

He stopped, taking in her slender form in denim overalls and a colorfully embroidered white top. She looked a little funky and a lot geeky, surrounded as she was by the collectibles that were sold in her stores named for Gene Roddenberry's original pitch of the classic *Star Trek* series—"A Wagon Train to the Stars." Action figures, chess sets, plates, playing cards, posters, glassware, all devoted to pop culture icons such as *Star Trek*, *Star Wars*, and *Batman* filled the shelves. New to the scene, but with its own entire corner, was memorabilia from the *Twilight* books and movies. It looked like that sparkly Edward was going to make Gil's best friend a boatload of money in lunchboxes alone.

She smiled, clearly happy to see him, and he took that in, too, his heart aching because it might be the last sight he'd have of it for a while.

Last night he'd walked away from Clare, keeping his secrets as well as those of her fiancé.

This morning he was walking back to her, determined to tell the bride-to-be that the man she was planning to marry was cheating on her. His own confession would wait, he'd decided, until their world re-steadied after that explosion.

"What are you doing here?" she asked as he handed her a soy latte.

He ducked the question by taking a sip of his own cup of house blend, no sugar, because it was certain to be a dark and bitter day. "I didn't expect your front door to be open."

She shrugged. "I couldn't sleep, so I came in early and did all my backroom chores. Shelves need stocking next, which I won't complain about, considering the slow economy."

Money concerns had hit the wine country just like everywhere else, but Clare's business was surviving better
than many. Tourists from the Silicon Valley—a staple of
the wine country clientele—loved their geek-souvenirs,
and if they could afford a weekend away to taste wines
and buy bottles that started at twenty dollars a pop and
skyrocketed from there, they had the ready cash for their
Barbie and Ken *Star Trek* gift set, official Yoda light saber,
or sparkly Edward thermos—though what women saw in a
guy who drank blood, he just didn't get.

Clare caught the direction of his gaze. "I've told you
and told you. It's because he's waited for you all his long,
long life and will love you for eternity."

It made him grin, the way she could read his mind. Then
his smile died, knowing her ESP wouldn't pick up the vital
information he'd come here to impart. He'd have to tell her
that. Out loud. In words.

"Clare . . ." He couldn't stop himself from tucking a
strand of her highlighted hair behind her ear. The new look
was pretty, but the best part was that she'd gone against her
mother's wishes to get it. Sally Knowles had a definite way
she wanted things done, whether it came to her daughter's
hair or her daughter's wedding.

Another woman heading for a painful fall.

Clare's brow puckered. "What's wrong?"

Love was hell, wasn't it? The knowledge that Clare
wouldn't be marrying cheating Jordan should make him
happy, but the idea of being the delivery guy of the bad
news was making Gil sick. "I'm all right."

She set down her cup and went on tiptoe to put her palm
to his forehead. "You have a fever."

Really, how could someone so smart be so dumb? He
circled her wrist and pulled her hand from his face. "Sweet
Clare, you've just been holding a hot cup of coffee."

"Oh." She laughed at herself a little, then lifted up
again, this time using her left hand to gauge his temper-

ature. Their faces were just inches apart and he couldn't miss the quizzical expression in her big blue eyes. "You've never called me sweet before."

"No?" This close, he also couldn't miss the light floral scent of her. Feminine, and it had him thinking of the places a woman put perfume, at her ears, on her wrists, behind her knees, between her breasts. His gaze dropped and there they were—Clare's breasts. Or rather, a slight hint of cleavage revealed by the droopy bib of her overalls and the low dip of her cotton blouse.

It rose on a quick breath, and he hastily jerked his eyes back to hers. There was a new flush across her cheekbones, obscuring the light golden freckles that had been fascinating him since those three fateful nights on Daphne's couch.

"W-what are you doing?" Clare asked, her voice uncertain.

"Thinking of your friend Daphne," he said, starting on the road toward honesty. "How is she, by the way?"

"Daphne?" Clare shuffled back and picked up her coffee, giving him a little glare over the cup. "You're not planning to hit on her at the wedding, are you?"

"No." A promise he could make since there wasn't going to *be* a wedding.

"Oh, that's right," she said, still looking annoyed with him. "You have that new woman of yours."

Her disgruntled tone surprised him. He narrowed his eyes, trying to figure out what was making her angry— even *before* he ruptured her bridal dreams. "What's got your nose out of joint?"

She picked up a Princess Leia action figure, fussing with the doll's hair as she sent him a sidelong look. "I couldn't care less who you date."

He blinked. *Hello.* Non sequitur. "Clare?"

Instead of elucidating, she jammed the tiny woman back onto her display stand, nearly causing fatal injury in the process. He winced, glad the figure survived, since it was likely worth more than the price of a Super Bowl ticket, God only knew why.

"Fine, I'll admit it," Gil's best friend finally muttered. "I don't think I like her."

But she'd never met the woman.

Wait—there was no woman.

He shook his head, trying to figure this out. "Clare?" When she wouldn't even look at him, he turned her to face him with a hand on her shoulder. "What . . . what don't you like about her?"

Her mouth pursed. He focused on her lips, soft and pink, soft and pink and now wet, her tongue darting out to moisten them. His shoulders tensed, his gut, his thighs, every muscle everywhere going hard at the sight of the very same tongue that Clare used to stick out at him when he teased her.

Now he wanted to tease *it*.

Swallowing a groan, he forced himself to look away. On a shelf at his right, Spock stared at him from the side of a mug, one of his Vulcan eyebrows raised in that mocking manner of his. *Yeah*, Gil responded silently to the Starfleet science officer, *emotional attachments are a pain in the ass*.

And definitely not logical.

He heard Clare's sigh. She put her hand on his forearm and he felt the light touch all the way to his marrow. "I find myself . . ." she started.

Spock couldn't keep Gil's interest, not when he heard such confusion in his best friend's voice. When he looked her way again, it was to find another flush on her face. "We've always been honest with each other, right?" she said.

Guilt shouldn't pierce so deep. He was going to tell her the piece of news he'd been sitting on. Any minute. Though he'd decided—and not without some relief—that it wasn't his own truth he would tell today, but Jordan's.

"Yeah," he answered, while guilt poked him again. "We're honest." Mostly.

"I've been thinking of your new woman and you and . . ." She trailed off, then looked away from him and out the plate-glass window. "And I've been thinking of you kissing me."

It came out so low and so rushed, he thought he'd imagined it. "What?"

She still wasn't looking at him, but she spoke more clearly. "I've been thinking about you kissing me."

His heart bonged in his chest, like the first strike of the grandfather clock in his parents' living room. It reverberated in his body, making his muscles tingle and his brain quiver. This wasn't like when she was fifteen and willing to pay for an experiment. This was a woman talking . . . no, he knew enough about the gender to know this was a woman *asking*.

Oh, God. This morning wasn't supposed to be about him and Clare. It was supposed to be about Clare and Jordan. Gil's heart bonged again, a knell signifying something. He wasn't prepared. He hadn't thought he'd be honest today about this . . .

But a kiss, he told himself. A kiss was a whole other way of communicating. He leaned close . . .

The blasted *Star Trek* notes sang out again. Gil jerked straight, Clare stumbled back, Jordan Wilson walked in.

Gil cursed, then backed away from Clare as the other man approached. The interruption meant his original plan was best. Get Jordan out of her life, then address changing Gil's relationship with his BFF. Breakup first. Kissing Clare second.

Relief, frustration, and an urge to kill had Gil concocting a quick excuse to leave the shop. He'd be back, he promised himself, and he'd tell her about Jordan's betrayal then. God knew she deserved the truth.

He was only as far as the corner when he heard his name. Turning, he was forced to confront the fiancé who didn't deserve Gil's best friend. "What the hell do you want?" he asked, crossing his arms over his chest.

Jordan grimaced. "Damn, I had a feeling . . . You know, right?"

"That you're lower than a worm? Yeah, I know."

"I'm going to tell her about the woman," Jordan hastened to say. "I've just got to find the right time and place. You'll give me the chance to do that, right?"

Gil should have said wrong! But he didn't, because . . . because it was Jordan's failing, damn it. And Gil was not so eager—if he was honest with himself—to rush into heart-to-hearts with Clare. With the wedding off the table, Gil could wait for his own right moment to make his confession to her.

It was only later, when he was elbows deep in grimy car engine that an even dirtier thought occurred to him. Jordan said he'd tell Clare about the other woman. But he hadn't mentioned anything about ending the engagement—only about admitting to the affair.

12

Braced against the exterior wall of the cottage, Penn shoved his hands through his hair, his gaze on the road leading to Alessandra's farmhouse. Waiting for her . . . again.

Last night he'd been attempting that, too. Waiting for her to break, for that restrained façade to shatter and release a wild passion. He'd assumed she'd have no defense against his expertise.

She'd shattered him and his ego instead.

Quite the wake-up call for a confident man, and the fact that it bugged the bleepin' hell out of him had set off yet another alarm. He shouldn't be so concerned with one little nun who lived like an enchanted princess in her forest of grapevines.

So this morning, rising from his bed in the Bennett brothers' home—he'd not lingered long with Alessandra— he'd determined his next step. And that was getting the cottage buttoned up and then getting himself back to his real life in L.A.

He'd rushed to the Baci vineyards . . . and run into trouble.

Now three dark-haired beauties were flying toward him. He didn't focus on any particular face, but instead turned his back on them as they breached the porch steps in order to lead the way inside the cottage. There, he gestured with his hand at the gouges and holes in the newly installed and taped sheets of drywall that had been waiting for paint. "This room, the bride's boudoir, the groom's waiting alcove—all the same," he said. "Someone vandalized the place."

Giuliana's head was tipped up.

"Yeah," Penn confirmed. "The ceilings, too."

Alessandra made a little sound of frustration—more noise, Penn noted despite himself, than she'd let loose last night in his arms. Without looking at her, he said, "Yeah, it sucks. Worries me, too." Understatement.

"Worries you?" Stevie echoed, sounding surprised.

"Well, sure." The princess slept alone while a mere quarter-mile away crowbars or something very similar had created this destruction. He should have nailed plywood over the front entrance, but he'd been expecting the new doors to be delivered any day.

"I've called the cops already. Can you think of anyone who'd want to trash the cottage? And why?"

"You didn't hear anything last night, Allie?" Giuliana asked.

He didn't dare look her way. A guilty flush would piss him off, a careless shrug even more. Her quiet in the sack made him nuts . . . if she maintained it the morning after he might give everything away. Blow their goddamned secret.

"I guess I slept too well," she said. "I must have been worn out."

The thought of that only slightly mollified him. "Back to my question—who and why?"

"That's easy," Stevie said, without a trace of doubt in her voice. "The why is the treasure."

Giuliana groaned. "Not the treasure," the oldest Baci girl went on to plead. "Please don't bring up the treasure."

Stevie struck a stubborn pose, her arms crossed over her chest. "I didn't say it was real, I just said somebody believes in it enough to be looking for it."

Looking from pretty face to pretty face to pretty face didn't provide Penn answers to a slew of new questions. "What treasure are you talking about? And why the cottage? I know the locals have used it as some sort of trysting place . . ."

"I blame Stevie for that, too," Giuliana said. "She and her little friends used to sleep out here at night and they made up stories they told all their other little friends that—"

"Lovers came to the cottage even before I was born," Stevie protested.

"Yes," Giuliana agreed, "but in greater numbers after you and your goofy group circulated the story that if the one you kissed at the cottage was your 'True Love' "—she air-quoted the two words—"then the ghosts of Anne and Alonzo would appear in approval."

"Papa told us that story," Alessandra said. "He swore it was true."

Penn snorted. "Ghosts. True Love. You guys gotta be kidding me."

"Visitors eat it up," Alessandra added.

But she didn't say she didn't believe it. Though he had to admit the ghosts-love thing *did* have a commercial appeal. "Sorta *The Bachelor* meets *The Blair Witch Project*," he mused aloud. "We should tell the *Wedding Fever* people . . . Wait, wait, wait. I'm getting off track. *Treasure*?"

"It's a twist on the Tanti Baci legend," Alessandra said. "While we know that the original owners, Alonzo and Liam, had a falling out over Anne, there are those who say that argument was aggravated by some silver that went missing—the last load from their mine."

"Raw ore?" he asked.

"Maybe," Stevie replied.

Giuliana shrugged. "Or it could be that Liam had it made into a silver tea service for Anne in expectation of their marriage—a set then stolen by Alonzo."

"I prefer the jewelry version," Alessandra put in. "In this one, the silver was used to create a stunning silver-and-gold pendant, brooch, and earrings that Liam gave Anne as an engagement gift. They disappeared before she could return them after she and Alonzo eloped."

"Okay." Penn frowned. "So you think treasure hunters thought the silver—in some form—might be hidden here?"

"It's happened before," Stevie said. "Every few years someone tears into the cottage or starts digging holes in the hill property behind the vineyard. Some kids probably figured with the new construction this might be their last chance to discover their fortune."

Shaking his head, Penn wandered into the bride's boudoir and from there to the large arched window that overlooked the rows of vines that stopped at the bottom of a craggy hillside. The Baci-Bennett one-hundred-year-old legacy included rumored treasure and a legendary, ghostly romance. Who could resist? Even a hardened cynic like himself wasn't immune to the mystique. Throw in some bubbly wedding wine, a ruby red cabernet, not to mention three beautiful Italian sisters, and Tanti Baci was a honey-baited romance trap.

Or an attractive nuisance, he thought, the hair on the back of his neck rising as he felt a presence come up behind him. Like an unfenced swimming pool or an open pit that entices children but also endangers their safety, the winery was proving to hold a dangerous allure for Penn.

Yeah, he needed to get back to his real life in L.A.

"I'll go into town and get some more wallboard today," he said to Alessandra, because there was no mistaking that the now-debauched Nun of Napa was standing close enough to breathe on his shirtsleeve. He knew her scent. "Maybe I can convince Liam to give me a hand so we can get back up to speed."

"I'll put my workboots and gloves back on," she said.

An acknowledgement that she'd been shirking her duties—and ducking her part of their deal—at the cottage for the past couple of days. He should encourage the shirking and ducking, because she was proving to be yet another hazardous attraction, but the quicker the wedding cottage was finished, the quicker he'd be done with his duty here.

He glanced back, taking in her ankle-length yoga pants and faded sweatshirt. She was staring at him, a little frown marring the smooth skin of her forehead. Without thinking, he tried thumbing it away, then jerked back his hand as if he'd been burned. *Ouch.* The beaker was still bubbling; their volatile chemical combination had yet to stabilize.

She didn't seem to notice his movement, instead tilting her head to study him some more. Her long hair slid behind her back to reveal the alluring curve where her neck met her shoulder. He remembered smoothing his mouth over that very spot, licking a line across her heated, scented skin. *Mind*, he instructed, *don't go there. You've got things to do—as in doing the rest of the job on the cottage, not doing Alessandra.*

But she was still staring. He shifted his feet, crossed his arms over his chest, shifted his feet again. "What?" he demanded. "Did I miss a spot shaving?"

"I was just wondering about your earring."

"I don't wear an earring."

"I know. I thought all blond Hollywood guys had a tattoo and an earring. It's like a rule."

She seemed sort of put out and he found it so damn cute it killed him. "Darlin'," he said, leaning closer, "you ever hear of a Prince Albert? An ear is not the only place a guy can get pierced."

The immediate horror on her face made him bust out laughing. "You should see your expression."

Her eyes remained rounded. "But . . . but . . ."

He nudged her with a gentle elbow and lowered his voice to an intimate whisper. "Alessandra, you know I'm bare down there . . . but, uh, speaking of bare . . ."

Color suffused her face. "Don't," she protested.

"Hey, I'm only curious." And turned on by thinking of it again. All that sweet soft skin, every curve and petal naked to his sight like a flesh and blood Georgia O'Keefe painting.

She looked away and spoke from the side of her mouth, her blush reaching from throat to hairline. "I have a friend who works in a spa. She needed someone to try it out on . . . I never expected anyone to see . . ."

"Well, what I saw I liked," he assured her, then to ease her embarrassment, he nudged her again. "So can I sit in on the next practice session?"

"No!" Then she caught his overdone leer and pushed him back, her hands to his chest. "You're a rat."

Laughing again, he caught her wrists and yanked her close. Their body heat mingled and he breathed in her sweet scent and remembered all her naked parts next to his naked parts. All her very bare naked parts giving way to his touch, his fingers, his cock. Flames flared again and his gaze focused on her mouth. It wasn't sane, it wasn't what he wanted to feel, but he wanted more of her. More of her fruity taste, more soft skin.

"My sisters . . ." she warned in a murmur, obviously reading his intent.

Yeah, her sisters. In the very next room. But with Alessandra in his arms he couldn't think of anything beyond the need to hold her close, to have her smiling like she was now, melting against him like butter on toast. There were pressing issues that should stymie him, but they were nothing compared to the press of her against his body. He slid one hand down to her butt, pushing her groin against his.

The urgency to get away from Napa, to get back to his real life was nothing compared to the urgency his sex was clamoring for. His mouth brushed hers.

Her breath caught, causing a sweet little sound in her throat. He could live on these kisses, those muffled sounds, the heavy silk of her hair tangled around his fingers.

"Penn!" A voice sounded from far away. "Penn!"

Blinking, he lifted his head, realizing it was his name, Alessandra's sister Stevie's voice, some kind of summons. "Huh?"

"People to see you," Stevie sang out again from the room next door.

Alessandra stumbled back from his embrace. He scraped his hands over his face, trying to refocus on reality. Grateful would come later, he guessed, but he should feel it, because more fooling around with the nun would only delay his return to L.A. and to his real life.

Yanking his T-shirt lower, he stepped back to the main room.

Where, to his shock, he came face-to-face with that real life he thought was waiting down south. Instead, it had found him here, in the guise of his buddy, Roger, which shouldn't have been such a surprise, since the other man was the *Wedding Fever* producer Penn had made contact with four days before. The shock came from who was clinging to Roger's arm.

Lana Lang.

~

"What's wrong?" Alessandra whispered to Penn as they trailed her sisters and the Hollywood duo across the gravel parking lot toward the wine caves. "You've gone all wooden Indian." There was a funky little market on Highway 128 between Napa and Sonoma counties that had an old life-sized statue of a Native American on its front porch, right next to the vintage Coke machine and the freezer of locally produced, hand-churned ice cream. Its stance was mirrored in Penn's tight muscles and forbidding expression.

The instant he'd glimpsed his producer friend and the female assistant with him, his mood had changed. One moment he'd been teasing her about sexual things, even dragging her close for a kiss though her sisters were just a wall away, and the next he'd turned tense and grim.

Penn didn't *do* tense and grim. His signature temperament was a balanced mix of confidence and charm. Half "I'm beautiful" and half "you're fascinating." Heady stuff, she knew, and it reminded her to keep their bout of sex in her bed in perspective. It was a body-to-body experience only, no emotions involved, and that was fine with her.

Still, he was a partner in the winery and had called in a favor for the Baci family. It was only good manners to inquire about this sudden reversal. "Penn?" When he didn't respond, her concern deepened and she slid her palm against the crook of his elbow and tugged to slow him a little. "You can tell me."

He didn't spare her a glance. "I don't know what you're talking about."

"Your friend doesn't seem bothered by the couple of days' delay until the cottage is repaired."

As a matter of fact, Roger—the *Wedding Fever* guy—had been intrigued by the treasure legend they suspected was the cause of the damage. He'd seemed perfectly willing to explore the wine country until they could put the wedding venue to rights and then complete the final touches that would make it ready for filming.

"The show's not in full-steam production yet," he'd said. "I wanted to put this together with a little impromptu vacation, anyway. Lana and I will do our wine tasting before rather than after we film."

Stevie had suggested they start with a tour of the Tanti Baci wine caves and so here they all were, shepherding Penn's pal and his coworker across the parking lot. Roger, tall and lanky, in jeans and leather flip-flops, wore gold-rimmed glasses and a shy smile. It didn't surprise Alessandra that he spent his showbiz time behind the scenes. On the other hand, Lana Lang flashed, from the trendy stacks of rings on her fingers to the salon-straightened and shined blond of her hair. She teetered on her high heels as the pea gravel slid beneath the soles of her Rodeo Drive sandals.

"Eek," Alessandra murmured. "If she falls in that outfit we'll all get an eyeful." The other woman's tight skirt was just that short.

"It's nothing that would rate a second glance in Beverly Hills," Penn answered, sounding defensive.

"Sorry." Alessandra looked down at her own loose clothes, suddenly embarrassed by her sloppiness. Had she bothered to brush her hair before rushing to the cottage? Teeth she remembered, but . . . With hasty fingers she tried combing through the mass that was sex-tousled and sleep-mussed. What must Penn think of her in comparison to the Hollywood honey by Roger's side?

It took the slap of the cave-cooled air to bring her to her senses. As she followed the group to the tasting area, she let her hands fall to her sides and slowed her pace. Penn's mind-set—about her, about anything that wasn't winery-related—was not her problem.

For their guests, Giuliana went into a little spiel about the caves themselves. Two visiting couples wandered in and joined the knot of people. Her older sister assured everyone that the caves were entirely safe and not nearing their one hundredth birthday like the vineyard itself.

Constructed like an upside-down swimming pool, with rebar and gunite, they'd only been carved into the hillside four years before.

At great expense, Alessandra thought to herself. A decision her father had made, to dire consequences. There was a plus side to the caves though, she mused. The wine business was changing, and while in the past they'd sold most of their product through distributors that in turn dealt with stores and restaurants, small wineries were having trouble holding the attention of those middlemen. The big wine companies were monopolizing that relationship, so wineries like Tanti Baci were turning more and more to building personal bonds with their customers.

Get them to the winery as a destination for a wedding or a weekend getaway. Sell them the wine through the tasting room and sign them up to the wine club—direct sales generated more profit for the product's producers. At the very least, the idea was you sent consumers back home where they'd ask for their favorite wines at their local stores and restaurants.

The caves, the weddings, the Tanti Baci legends could do all that if they got the right kind of attention and then had enough time to make it work.

Wedding Fever and the producer, Roger, was their big opportunity. Her eye on him, she watched him leave Lana Skirt-Too-Short and sidle around the edge of the small crowd to engage Penn in low-voiced conversation. Alessandra sidled that way, too, telling herself that eavesdropping was a savvy business move.

They weren't talking about business.

"I didn't get a chance to tell you about Lana and me when we talked on the phone a few days ago," Roger was saying. He laughed self-consciously. "Well, I wasn't even sure there was a Lana and me at the time, but things have happened pretty fast."

"Looks like it," Penn answered.

"I should thank you, though."

Penn shoved his hands in his pockets. "Roger, I—"

"You were the one who introduced us, remember? At your barbecue in Malibu."

The man sounded smitten. Glancing at the woman in question, Alessandra conceded Lana was beautiful in a polished, salon-perfected way. Suddenly self-conscious herself, Alessandra hitched up her sagging pants and retied the cord around her hips, reminding herself she had some perfectly nice clothes, too. And didn't she go to the salon? She'd even submitted to a Brazilian wax process—and now that she remembered, her friend had called the whole bare thing the "Hollywood version."

Their small group was on the move again, including yet another couple they'd picked up from the tasting room. Though they had interns who were regular tour guides, Giuliana retained that role as she led them deeper into the caves. There she explained about the process of winemaking, from harvest to crush to fermentation to maturation. As it was June, with harvest only some short weeks away, the time had come to bottle in order to clear room in the barrels and tanks for the result of this year's yield.

As she explained the process of making their cabernet sauvignon and then the more complicated manner of the wedding *blanc de blancs,* Alessandra paused behind Penn and Roger again. The producer was speaking in low tones, though it was obvious he was excited about his subject.

"She's great, you know? Funny and smart as a whip."

"Maybe too smart," Penn put in.

"What? Nah. When she called about a job, I figured you didn't have an opening on *Build Me Up.* So I took her on as my assistant. I'm showing her the ropes here since we'll be doing this quick and dirty. I'll man the camera and show Lana how to handle the sound. Good, huh?"

Penn looked away. "Sure."

"I feel like I've known her forever," Roger enthused. "And the way she's just made herself at home in my place . . . I can't tell you how great it is that we're living together now."

Alessandra smiled as he waxed poetic about Lana and

all her charms. Obviously he'd been struck by Cupid, and couldn't help but bleed admiration and accolades. A rare combination of beauty and brains, he said. A woman with talents, many of which he'd yet to tap. When the subject of all this talk turned to look back at the two men, Alessandra smiled at her. Of course Lana Lang had a striking appearance, but surely she must be just as lovely inside to engender all this high regard from the adorable Roger.

"Be careful," Penn was saying to the man. "Don't get in over your head. Sex is just that, pal. Sex."

Alessandra winced at the bald sentiment. Not that she disagreed, but didn't he notice Roger's crestfallen expression?

Still, Penn continued, his voice urgent. "Don't go leaping before—"

Alessandra stopped him mid-warning. "Hey," she said, stepping up to take each man by the arm. "We're all moving on. You two don't want to miss my sister revealing the secrets of sparkling wines, which include the second fermentation, the flash-freezing of the lees . . ."

Her sunny smile didn't budge Penn's feet. She leaned around his stiff body to look into his eyes. "C'mon, Penn, we're all moving ahead."

After a moment he let out a sigh. "Yeah. Sure. I guess so."

Roger strode away to catch up to Lana. Alessandra saw him slide a hand down the back of her arm, then entwine her fingers with his. She was the one sighing now, as the producer lifted their joined hands to his mouth. "Aaah," she whispered.

"Ah, shit," Penn replied.

Her head whipped toward him, and that's when Alessandra realized he wasn't replying to her. He was commenting again, his eyes focused on his friend's new girlfriend. As if she felt his stare, Lana glanced over her shoulder and the clash of her gaze with Penn's sent a jolt through Alessandra.

His body hummed with tension. Something sparkled in the blue depths of the blonde's eyes.

Oh. My. God.

Penn and Lana. Lana and Penn.

There was no doubt about it . . . and from that shared look she'd just witnessed, "it" wasn't completely over. At least not on his side. Clearly, Penn Bennett had feelings for a woman who was now with another man.

Poor Penn, she hastened to tell herself. She should feel sorry for poor Penn.

Except it wasn't pity she was feeling, she realized, unless pity felt a little hot and a lot interested in kicking him in the back of the knees. Because face facts: "Poor Penn" had gone to bed with her when he was emotionally involved with someone else!

Though Alessandra shouldn't care about that, right?

Sex was just sex, so it should mean nothing to her that he had unrequited feelings for some blond bimbo who wore her skirt way too short—no matter what the good folks from Beverly Hills would think or not think about that. The hot feeling crackling under Alessandra's skin, the ball of ire in her belly, was due to lack of sleep or something. Dropping her hold on Penn, she inched away.

He glanced down at her. "What's wrong?"

"Nothing," she replied, because the lack-of-sleep excuse wasn't worth mouthing to the man who'd been the partner in her brief-now-over affair.

Alessandra acted as bait, but it was Stevie's idea to kidnap Gil. One minute he was locking the office door of Edenville Motor Repair, and the next he was responding to her voice warbling through the open door of one of the Napa Princess Limousine's fleet. "Gil . . . Gil, can you give me a hand in here?"

Gentleman to the marrow, he hastened toward the sedan and then eight pairs of female hands reeled the Italian Stallion into the dark leather interior. Stevie, acting as chauffeur, snapped closed the locks once the door was shut behind him.

Gil blinked at the legion of young women in cocktail dresses. Then he grinned. "All right, I'll go along quietly, sweethearts, as long as you promise there'll be handcuffs later."

Alessandra shook her head. Her cousin's easy way with women reminded her of Penn—but she wasn't thinking of Penn tonight. This was a girls' night—Gil really didn't count in this particular instance—and she was determined to keep her focus on something other than Pining Penn and the Hollywood hottie he couldn't forget.

Stevie pulled out of the parking lot and onto the street as she called through the open privacy panel. "Sorry, bud, this celebration's not for you . . . it's Clare's bachelorette party."

"Oh no," he said, a look of panic crossing his face. "Don't make me—"

"You're the Man of Honor," Giuliana reminded him. "It's your job to be there."

"Nobody told me, and if they had I wouldn't have—"

"Exactly," she continued. "That's why we decided to make it a surprise for you . . . as well as for Clare."

"She doesn't know about this."

"Nope. Another limo is kidnapping her, too."

Alessandra didn't understand the look of dread on her cousin's handsome face. "How bad can it be, Gil? You know you love the ladies."

"Yeah. Love 'em." He closed his eyes. "Is there a beer lurking in that fridge?"

Two of the single girls cheered, and then a double-fist of longnecks were passed down the row. Gil took them both, hammering down one, then the other. He wiped the back of his hand across his mouth and said just a single word more. "Again."

A two hundred twenty-five pound man could pack away a lot of alcohol to little effect, Alessandra discovered as they made their way into the small restaurant they'd rented for the evening on the outskirts of Edenville. It was a mom-and-pop place that was usually open only for breakfast and lunch, but was available for special evening events. The bridesmaids had decorated with flowers and streamers and paper wedding bells. Alessandra's added touch was a R2-D2 dressed as a bride and C-3PO in groom-wear.

When she set them on the table they'd designated as the bar at the rear of the room, Gil appeared woozy for the first time. He grabbed another beer from the ice bucket and rocked back on his feet as he stared at the Star Wars robots. "Those are wrong," he muttered. "Some pairings are just not meant to be."

Alessandra frowned. "Is it some sort of geek sacrilege? I don't know all the rules."

"Me neither," Gil muttered. He threw himself into a chair at a nearby table. "For example, I thought these kind of parties were man-free zones."

"Except for those men willing to striptease," Stevie said, striding up to them.

Gil jumped from his chair. "I'm not—"

"Kidding, big boy." Stevie pushed him back into his seat. "We nixed the nude dancers because we figured Clare's mother and in-laws-to-be would faint from the fun of it."

Gil drained his latest beer. "Don't tell me they're going to be here, too."

Commotion at the doorway drew their attention. Another contingent of women had arrived, including Clare, her mother, and some of Jordan's female family members. "Great," Gil said. Standing up, he reached for another beer, then started toward the newcomers. "Better get this over with."

Giuliana brushed past him on her way to join Alessandra and Stevie. Her eyebrows rose in question. "What's with the death march? Gil looks like he has an appointment with Madame Guillotine."

Stevie fished a bottle of water from the ice. "I never waste my time trying to figure out men."

Stepping closer, Giuliana tapped her plastic glass of wine against Stevie's beverage. "A woman after my own heart."

"Uh-oh," Alessandra said. Her sisters sat down at the table Gil had vacated and she took a third chair. They were in an out-of-the-way corner, far from the celebrating crowd, but she lowered her voice, anyway. "Jules, does this mean it's definitely over between you and that guy from Redondo Beach . . . Dusty?"

"Dustin." She studied the wine in her glass. "He started talking the whole shebang. Living together. Marriage."

"And you weren't ready," Stevie supplied.

"I know I'll never be ready for what he wants. He's crazy for kids."

Alessandra's gaze jumped to meet Stevie's over their older sister's head. They exchanged an unspoken, *Huh?*

"You, um," Alessandra cleared her throat, "like kids."

"I like kids, I just don't want them," Giuliana said, her tone flat. "So Dustin and I broke up. What was the point?"

A breakup, a no-babies decree, where to start? "Well."

Stevie drummed her fingers against the tabletop for several moments, then spoke. "All right, I'll just spit it out—and you can say I'm taking this wrong, but I can't keep quiet. When you say you don't want kids, Jules, it feels like you're rejecting what we had. That somehow our family, that me, that Allie . . . that you don't value us."

Giuliana didn't look up, didn't reply, and Alessandra jumped into the silence. "A woman isn't required to want kids, for goodness' sake. You know that, Stevie. We all know that. As a matter of fact—"

"Don't tell me you don't yearn for little fat-cheeked *bambinos*, Allie," Stevie interjected. "You're the most traditional of the three of us."

"You say that because I was going to be married at twenty. But have you ever thought that maybe I was too young to make that kind of decision? Maybe it was a mistake and nobody saw that through the romance of it all . . ." Her voice drifted off as she registered the shock on both her sisters' faces.

Where had that come from? Why had she spoken aloud private musings that only showed up in the middle of deep, dark nights? Heat flooded her face. "Anyway, how is the

Nun of Napa going to make any of those fat-cheeked bambinos you're talking about? Immaculate Conception?"

Pity supplanted the surprise on Stevie's face. "Okay, I'll
give you that. Your sex life is arguably the worst of anyone's in this room. Maybe in the entire valley."

Alessandra sniffed, ignoring the guilty image of a naked
Penn Bennett beside her in bed. He was out of her mind,
remember? "Thank you." Then she frowned. "I think."

Giuliana suddenly grabbed her hand. Then Stevie's.
"You've got it wrong," their sister said in a fierce whisper. "I value you, insults and nosiness included. I *cherish*
you."

Tears stung Alessandra's eyes. She looked over, to see
Stevie suffering the same. "Then stay," their middle sister
said. "Allie wants to make a go of the winery, and we can't
do that without you."

"I can't guarantee that will happen if I move back," Giuliana said. "If we survive the summer—and that's a big 'if'
right there—that's just the beginning."

Alessandra squeezed her sister's fingers, her throat tight.
"If we survive the summer, then we set the next goal. Making
it to New Year's, then making it to the one hundredth birthday next June. I'm sure we can do it, Jules. Say you'll stay."

A small smile curved Giuliana's mouth, then she
shrugged. "I already gave my notice. Since I've been on a
leave of absence since March, they weren't surprised."

Stevie's jaw dropped, then she cuffed her big sister on
the side of the head.

"Ow!"

"When were you planning on telling us?" she demanded.

"I only made the call today. With *Wedding Fever* giving
us the promo . . . I decided to take a page from Allie's book
and have some faith in happy endings."

Stevie beamed Alessandra's way. "Gotta love the little
sap."

"Hey." Alessandra's glare softened as she turned her gaze on her oldest sister. "But are you sure, Jules? What about . . . are you okay about being so near, um, Liam?"

Her sister's gaze dropped, but her voice held firm. "Of course."

Alessandra took her at her word. She knew she was smiling, because this was great, the Mouseketeers were a trio again and it was the kind of distraction that would keep her from thinking of Him-Who-Was-Heartbroken. "Then let's tell everyone!"

Giuliana laughed. "This is Clare's big night. And I'm not sure 'everyone' will really care."

"At least let's tell Gil." Getting the news outside their small circle of sisters would make it feel more real. "He's going to be so happy for us."

Their three heads turned toward him.

Alessandra's exuberance dipped. Clare stood at the front of the room, surrounded by other women. Her face was flushed, and she had a near-empty glass of wine in her hand. From the looks of things, it wasn't the first she'd drained. The usually reserved Clare was chatting away, making large gestures with her free hand.

One wild motion almost cold-cocked Gil, who sat on top of a table behind her, staring at the bride-to-be.

"Eek," Alessandra said, expressing what she guessed they were all thinking. "The look on his face says . . ."

"Misery," Stevie put in.

"Heartbreak," Giuliana added.

Oh, crap, not Gil, too? "He's in love with her," Alessandra pronounced, then groaned.

Unrequited love. It was wrenching to watch. It was painful to contemplate. It was all around her.

And then Penn was in her head again, just like he shouldn't be. The damn man never stayed banished for long. She recalled the tension in his arm, the tick in his jaw, the trampy tart for whom he still carried a torch.

Geez, but he had lousy taste in lovers. Present company excepted.

"What should we do?" Stevie asked.

Giuliana shrugged. "What can we do?"

"Just be there for him," Alessandra mused. "Provide comfort, distraction . . ." *Sex.*

Oops, there she went thinking about Penn again.

But the man hovered in her mind, even as presents were opened, appetizers eaten, a sugary cake consumed. He was still there as she played a few silly shower games, "winning" a plethora of gag gifts, including a pair of velvet handcuffs that she tried to pawn off on Gil, but somehow ended up back in her possession. As Stevie commented, quite the haul for the woman with the worst sex life in the county.

And who couldn't put from her mind a man preoccupied by someone else.

~

Gil figured nothing short of a direct lightning strike would rouse Clare—a long shot since she was passed out in the back of Stevie's limo. The driver met his gaze in the rearview mirror as she pulled in front of his half of the duplex they shared.

"Will you be all right with her?" she asked. "It might take me a while to get back . . ."

"Sure." There were five other young women slumped in the passenger area under varying influences of alcohol, sugar, and risqué party games. Instead of making the duplex the last stop, however, they'd decided it should be first. If Clare came around during the miles of winding road ahead, the outcome might require a full interior detailing of Stevie's fancy vehicle.

Better to get Clare stationary—and close to the facilities—sooner than later.

To that end, he took her up in his arms and carried her

from the car to his front door. One of the departing young ladies managed an admiring—if drowsy—*yeehaw!* of admiration. Clare herself didn't stir until he placed her gently on his couch. Then, just as he was drawing a blanket over her, she sat up, looking as bright-eyed as morning.

"Hey!" She glanced around, her expression puzzled. She pushed the woven fabric aside, revealing the red dress she was wearing. It had drawn his gaze all night, the color as sweet as a cherry Popsicle, the low cut and short skirt something that had made him sweat beneath his calm façade.

"Is the party over?" she asked.

In more ways than one, he thought, dress going out of his head as he damned Jordan Wilson for his continued silence. When Clare broke it off with her fiancé after she heard the truth, she'd have yet another pre-wedding ritual to regret. "We popped the cork on the last bottle of champagne an hour ago," Gil told her.

She pouted, an action so un-Clare that he couldn't help but smile. "You had fun," he said. It was hard to be angry about that.

"I like champagne." Then she frowned, her fingers going to her head. "Is it the bubbles or the ugly truth? Did I really see R2-D2 and C-3PO in wedding wear?"

He dropped next to her, now grinning. "Alessandra said they were bride and groom wine bottle covers that she altered for tonight's event."

"Poor robots," she said, but it was accompanied by a goofy smile.

He shook his head. "Poor Clare. You're going to have a hell of a hangover tomorrow."

Her cheek landed on his shoulder. "But for now I feel sooo wonderful."

Sliding a hand around her, he tried adjusting her position, which only led her boneless body to half-sprawl over him. That goofy smile lit up her face again as she gazed up. "You wanna hear a secret?"

No, and he didn't want to tell one right now, either. This wasn't the time. "First rule of over-imbibing: Do not drunk-dial, drunk-text, or drunk-tell."

"I'm not drunk!"

Bombed, then. "Okay, baby, whatever you say."

Her smile turned smug. "I love the way you call me baby." She sang the phrase as a catchy little tune.

His heart jolted. "You do?"

"It's from a Gap commercial." Her eyes closed. "In my favorite ones, the people dance. In khakis, I think. You look scrumptious in khakis."

" 'Scrumptious'?" He laughed, because it was a word he'd never imagined in Clare's vocabulary. "You really are toasted."

She jerked straight, then put her hand to her head as if it was spinning. "The toast! Your toast. I didn't imagine that either, did I?"

He shifted on the cushions. "I don't know what you mean. Yeah, I gave a toast. Someone told me I had to, being I'm the Man of Honor." And even knowing everything he knew, he hadn't been able to find a way out of it.

"Say it all again," Clare demanded.

"No." When she continued staring at him, he shook his head. "No. I don't even remember—"

"I'll help." Her voice lowered in a terrible imitation of his own. " 'To the girl on the playground . . .' "

He groaned. "Clare . . ."

She grabbed one of his hands in both of hers. "Please. If you love me, you'll say it again."

If you love me . . .

He closed his eyes to savor her touch. "To the girl on the playground, to the girl at the prom. To my friend, to my fellow on this road, to the female in my life who makes me laugh and think and slay all her spiders." Opening his eyes, he took a breath and then drew the back of his free hand against her warm cheek. "Be happy. Be healthy. And most of all, be yourself."

Clare let go of his hand and fell back against the cushions in a mock swoon. "You're amazing. Every woman in the room must have fallen to her knees following that little speech. I can't believe it didn't get you laid tonight."

"Maybe I still have hopes."

She froze.

Damn! Hell! Crap! What had made him say that, and say it in the voice he usually saved for when he had something by Marvin Gaye oozing through the air or his favorite seduction song of all time, "Cyprus Avenue."

Her gaze drifted to one of the silent speakers in the corner of the room. "What? No Van Morrison?"

He laughed. *Whew.* "We've been friends too long if you know all my moves. You find them humdrum."

She rolled her head on the cushion to look at him, her blue eyes a little sleepy now. "I don't know about that. When I was considering who could be my last single girl fling, the only one who came to mind was you."

It was his turn to freeze. "Come again?"

"Last. Single. Girl. Fling." A pause. "You."

Reserved, quiet Clare wouldn't dream of a last single girl fling. But if she did, wouldn't she wish for a fling with . . .

Her best friend. The Man of Honor.

Of course she would.

He was the one whose refusal she counted upon. His Clare could be daring if she had that safety net in place. She'd insisted on climbing a tree knowing he'd do it for her. Her decision to go camping came with the full expectation that he'd never make her face the wild beasts of the night alone. Yep, her safety net. That's all he was to her. That's how she saw him.

And it was starting to piss him off.

He'd smiled, sacrificed, stayed silent for so effing long.

There'd been dozens of women in his life—the Italian Stallion loved women—but this one, this particular woman thought she had him pegged.

Clare presumed she could thrill herself by throwing out the word *fling* because it wasn't dangerous. Not when her best bud would let her play with matches without ever letting a single one catch fire.

Bullshit.

"It's that damn red dress," he murmured, then he reached out and hauled her against him. A squeak of surprise came from her mouth, but he muffled any further sounds with his lips. Hers opened beneath his, and then his tongue stroked into her mouth, and he could taste the tart bubbles of the night's champagne . . . and the strawberry lip gloss of her teenage years, the chocolate of their hundreds of shared Milky Ways—her half always larger—even the graham crackers and milk that were a kindergarten snack.

One of her hands landed on his thigh and it was his brain revolving in a drunken spin. He slanted his mouth to take the kiss deeper, his heart slamming like a piston. His inner works needed a mechanic, he thought, pulling Clare into his lap, and she was here, the fix he craved.

Her free arm curled around his neck and he stilled, just reveling in the feel of her light weight against his groin, the side of her breast against the wall of his chest. She squirmed, her ass against his hard-on, and he groaned at the goodness of it, and slid his hand up her thigh, over her belly, to cup the mound of her breast.

They both shuddered.

"Clare," he breathed, breaking the kiss, only to run his mouth along the line of her jaw to her ear. He slid his cheek against the skin of hers, knowing his beard was already heavy enough to mark her, but that's what he wanted.

She's mine. She's always been mine. She'll always be mine.

Her hand left his thigh and went to the buttons of his shirt. He stiffened, agonized by the slow flick of each unfastening. Clare was undressing him. Clare was pushing the plackets to the side. Clare was running her small, warm palm over his belly, up toward his throat, down to caress one pectoral.

He couldn't move, he couldn't breathe as the edge of her thumb caught the hard point of his nipple. Groaning, he dropped his head back and she took the opportunity to draw a line along his throat with the tip of her tongue. Her touch was tortured pleasure, the now-tight fit of his pants was exquisite anguish, the couch was much too narrow for how he wanted to ease all this distress.

"Clare. Baby." Somehow he had to get them from the living room to his bed. But he didn't want to break the beautiful flow. He slid his hand down her spine and she turned in to him, her mouth now on his chest. His arm was long enough to reach the end of that short skirt, which he brushed aside in order to write messages on the skin of her upper thigh.

Sweet. At last. Finally.

Fling.

His fingers checked, his heart arrested, his brain iced over. Was that what this was to her? Was that what Jordan was doing with Tori Merrick and because of this, Clare would be all right with that?

With the truth out, would there be no broken engagement . . . only Gil's broken heart?

He slid out from under her, setting her on the cushions beside him and instantly putting distance between himself and further temptation by rising to his feet. His hands tore through his hair.

"Clare . . ." Shit. He couldn't look at her. "Clare—"

Knocks sounded on his door. He knew who it was, and he found himself so damn glad for the interruption. Stevie stood on his small porch, her gaze immediately going past him to find the bachelorette. "How's she doing?" she asked. "Can you walk over to my place?"

It was just next door. "Yeah."

When he turned back, however, it was to see her passed out again. It meant he'd have to carry her once more. She didn't rouse until he placed her flat on Stevie's couch. Her drowsy voice called his name as he opened the door to leave.

"Yeah?" he asked. From the look of her, he wouldn't be surprised if by morning she didn't remember a thing that had happened from mid-party on.

"Why?" she croaked.

He thought he knew what she was asking, and his mouth twisted. "Why stop?"

She was already shaking her head. "Why start?"

"A good question to ask yourself," he advised, then slipped out and shut the door.

On the way home from the bridal shower, Alessandra decided the only prescription for her own unhealthy preoccupation with Penn was a good night's sleep. But that plan got off the rails almost immediately. Climbing the steps to the farmhouse's front door, she noticed a dim glow coming from the cottage. "Damn it," she muttered, immediately reversing direction.

Whoever was in there—lovers or treasure seekers—she was in a mood to escort them out with a good swift kick to the butt. Upon reaching the cottage's porch, she noticed the yellow hazard tape crisscrossing the open doorway—obviously an ineffectual barrier. Damn kids, she thought again, preparing to step over. Then caution asserted itself.

She couldn't be sure the intruders were harmless, could she? So instead of marching straight inside, she opted for a more wary approach. With quiet footsteps, she walked around the outside of the structure toward the windows of the bridal boudoir. The light was coming from that room. She peeked through the glass, then swallowed her groan.

Why hadn't she guessed? The man who'd been trespassing through her mind all evening was now at her winery without her permission.

Through the window she saw Penn lying on a thick sleeping bag, his hands behind his head, a small camp lantern emitting a pale yellow beam that barely penetrated the gloom. It washed color across his face, the masculine angles of it creating deep shadows that gave away his mood.

Somber. Sad, even.

When she'd spied that exact same expression on Gil earlier in the evening, an empathetic ache had filled her chest. But now, seeing Penn in a similar state, it wasn't compassion that was surging inside her. Because to start, couldn't he have seen just by looking at her blond perfection and scant hemline that Lana Lang was a bad bet? And second, what kind of man told another woman their horizontal tango was inevitable when he was really in love with someone else?

He wasn't merely a rat. He was a dog. A dog who should pay for all the baloney he'd thrown her way, she decided, shifting as an itch of annoyance crawled over her skin. The sole of her shoe slipped on the soft dirt at the edge of the cottage and she had to catch herself against the rough adobe, producing a muted thump that caught Penn's attention.

He jackknifed up, peering into the darkness around him as if he was looking for . . . ghosts.

Which gave her an idea. Though it might not settle the score between them, it just might be enough to settle her mood so she could go back to her bed and get that good night's sleep.

As silently as she could, Alessandra tiptoed toward the cottage's entrance. Stacked on the porch were some old sheets she'd brought down from the house to use as drop cloths. Still clutching her purse, she ducked between the hazard tape then yanked a sheet inside after her.

She hesitated a moment. Okay, maybe her intention was a bit silly, but if it caused Penn a momentary jolt, she'd be satisfied. After all, he *had* scoffed at the Anne and Alonzo story.

The sheet covered her from head to ankles, but through the worn material she could see a glimmer of the light in the bridal boudoir. Crossing the floor of the main room, she headed toward it, jiggling her purse instead of rattling a spectral chain.

Sudden laughter welled up inside her. It might be the dumbest idea she ever had, but this small taste of revenge was going to go down very sweet. Breathless with anticipation of his frightened reaction, she stretched her free hand forward—and was swept off her feet from behind.

She shrieked.

A dark voice edged with irony spoke against her sheet-covered ear. "*Now* she screams."

Air passed below her dangling shoes for another moment, and then she was on her behind on Penn's pallet. He flipped the sheet over her head and gazed down at her. "What the hell are you doing?" he inquired, clearly displeased.

Huh? *He* was displeased? That rankled even more, though she was almost as mad at herself for finding him still so damn attractive. Shirtless, with his jeans slung low on his belly, the lantern shadowed the ridges of his hard abs. She ran her gaze over his muscled arms and wondered why it thrilled her to recall how effortlessly he'd picked her up. *Good God*, she thought, *I'm easy.*

"Well? What are you doing here?" he repeated.

"I could ask you the same thing," she said, knowing she sounded sulky.

His brows rose at her tone. "I stopped by the farmhouse to let you know, but I guess you were out."

"I had a date." With twenty-five women and her cousin. He shrugged, as if he couldn't care less with whom she spent her evenings. "Since the doors are still a no-show, I thought I better stay here until we can secure this place."

Her displeasure upped a notch. Why couldn't he have some nefarious purpose? Now she supposed he expected her appreciation—which good manners predicated she should feel, unless . . . Her gaze narrowed at him. "Or are you here to meet someone?"

Think about it. He could easily have made an assignation with ex-lover Lana.

"Huh?" Penn seemed surprised. "What are you talking about?"

"It doesn't matter," she said, feeling huffy all over again. She got to her feet, fumbling with her purse. It crashed to the ground, the latch popping so that the contents spilled across the floor and sleeping bag. She glared at Penn, aware placing the blame on him wasn't fair. "Look what you made me do," she said anyway.

He was staring at the items on the floor. Then his gaze lifted to hers. "You have handcuffs?"

She made a face. The gag gifts from the shower were strewn about. She bent down to swipe up the soft pair. "These little ol' things?" she said, tossing her hair behind her back. "Just something I carry for emergencies."

He was pointing at something else. "And is that . . . ? No. No, no, no."

Hah. Here was the jolt she'd been hoping for. Holding back her smile, she retrieved the next item. "A gift from . . . a friend." Which was the truth, right? "Anatomical candy."

"Your friend gave you . . ."

"Let's see." She half-bent toward the lantern so she could read the label on the plastic-wrapped treat. "It says it's a 'Pecker Sucker.'"

He just stared as she stowed it back in her purse.

The next object she picked up had attached leather strips that she waved in the air. "And then there's this whip keychain." She contemplated it for a moment. "Hey, it might actually be practical. It could be a deterrent, you know, like pepper spray or something, if a bad guy comes up to me on a dark street and—"

"No," Penn choked out. "Thinking of you and a flogger . . . not a deterrent."

Flogger? She shot him her own surprised look—what else did he know that she didn't? Then she dumped the rest of her haul back in her purse one by one: the glow-in-the-dark massage lotion, the edible body paint, the vibrating lipstick.

"What kind of thanks did you give your 'friend' for that stuff?" he asked, his voice suddenly gritty.

Ignoring the question, she slung her purse's strap over her shoulder. "I'm going to bed now." Finally. For that good night's sleep.

As she moved past him, he caught her arm. "What the hell is that in your hair?"

Oh, sheesh. She'd forgotten one of the party favors, something that Stevie had experimented with at the end of the night. Clare had insisted she try them, announcing to all in her slightly drunken state that the ornament matched Alessandra's nude-colored slip dress.

Now her fingers went to work on the elastic band, the ponytail holder no different than what they'd had as kids, except instead of winding the elastic band around plastic flowers or colored balls, this had two thumb-sized rubber penises. Tacky, true, but the bachelorettes had laughed until some cried and others ran to the bathroom.

Penn didn't appear to find anything funny about it. "You were out with a 'friend' with that in your hair?"

"All night long," she lied. She pulled the elastic band free and combed her fingers through the wavy mass, pretending a nonchalance she didn't feel. Her insides were jittering.

Because that weird chemistry thing was back, this time

floating in the air between them like smoke. It was thick and hot and it tickled her skin. She felt roughed up a little, like a cat with its fur stroked in the wrong direction.

"I should get going," she said. Her feet didn't move.

Penn wrapped his other hand around her free arm. "You didn't answer my question. How did you thank your friend?"

It was a ridiculous question and she didn't know why he asked it in that harsh tone of voice. Easygoing Penn was gone, but it didn't change one whit of his appeal. Nor her need not to fall prey to it again.

She flung her hair behind her shoulder. "Maybe it was how my friend thanked *me*."

His nostrils flared as he pulled her closer, until her body was a breath from his. One inhale and he'd feel her hard nipples against his bare chest. "How was that then? How did your friend thank you?"

She and Karen, the bridesmaid in charge of party favors, had bussed each other on the cheek at the end of the evening. Alessandra curled her fingers into her palms, trying to resist the temptation to tease the man who smelled, as always, like delicious sin. She stared at his throat, at the pulse pounding there, then jerked up her chin, her gaze going only as high as his mouth. Her belly clenched, her womb, too, as a shiver skittered down both thighs.

Don't, she told herself. *Don't say it.*

"A kiss," she heard herself whisper.

His mouth descended—as she'd known it would—and her muscles tightened to the point of pain. Her skin tingled in aching anticipation.

His lips touched down. She controlled the sudden twitch of her body. His hands moved from her arms to her hips and he yanked her against him as his tongue plunged inside her mouth. Oh. *Oh.* Heat flushed over her as she swallowed down a moan.

Penn jerked back from her mouth. "Damn it," he said, his voice thick. "You don't do this right."

Embarrassment followed the same path as the sexual heat. She remembered Stevie. *Your sex life is the worst in the entire valley.* She'd had very little practice.

As she tried to shuffle back, he hung on. "I don't know what you mean," she said, her mind tumbling. "Is it the way I kiss? Is it the bare . . ." The words died and she did a little, too.

"I *love* the bare." He gave her a little shake. "I hate that you're so damn quiet. Like you're in church, for God's sake. You're not really a nun, you know."

Is that what was bothering him? A giddy laugh escaped her. "I—" Then another. "I was a teenager the last time I was . . . *with* someone. Quiet was kind of SOP."

"Not standard operating procedure for adults, honey. We get to be loud. Passionate."

Penn ran his mouth over her cheek, down her throat, and chill bumps chased the hot tingle. Her head fell back, leaving herself open to the burn of his mouth, the warm wet stroke of his tongue, the scrape of his teeth. She shuddered and released the tiniest of moans.

"Yeah. Like that." He bit her again.

The sting made her shake. "Penn . . ." There was something she was supposed to be remembering. Some reason not to surrender to the inferno inside her belly and the sensual smoke teasing over her flesh.

He was in love with someone else.

That's right. She should stop all this. Men might be able to compartmentalize, especially men like Penn, who were charming and playful and who were wanted by hundreds of women.

But Alessandra Baci, the Nun of Napa . . .

"I should go," she said, even as she shuddered against the thumb teasing her breast. "I should go to bed."

"Yeah," Penn said. "I definitely think it's time for bed, too."

~

Alessandra found herself on the soft sleeping bag, Penn's mouth still exploring her skin, his body weight a pleasure against her. Damn him. Damn her traitorous bones for jellifying just when she needed them.

"You don't want to do this," she murmured to herself.

"Oh, yes I do," Penn answered, leaning on his elbows to look down at her. "All night long."

The promise shivered across her skin like another touch. *All night long.*

"But . . . but . . ." There were reasons, good reasons. "It's late."

"Adults don't have curfews, honey." Penn's hand slid up the outside of her thigh, under the chiffon material of her dress. "We get to stay up all night making love."

Adults got to stay up late and make passionate noise. His fingers curled around the elastic waist of her bikinis and his callused fingertips caused her belly muscles to spasm, her womb contracting along with them. Oh, God, how could she, knowing his heart was with someone else?

The fact was, she'd used up her shallow well of sexual sangfroid when he'd tucked her skirt in her waistband and made her walk up the stairs in front of him. All her daring had been exhausted when she'd ordered him onto the bed, out of his clothes, and then into her body that night in her room.

Yet he was already drawing down her panties!

But maybe that's what adults got to do as well . . . it wasn't a man thing, but an adult thing, that compartmentalizing. Sensation out in the open and in-the-moment. Emotions separate and locked safely away.

"Oh, God," she whispered as he tossed her underwear over his shoulder.

Moving lower, Penn pushed her hemline higher. Then he eased between her legs and wrapped her calves with his warm palms to push up her knees.

Oh, God.

His gaze fixed on her . . . *there* . . . his thumbs slid up and down her cleft, opening her, exposing her. Who knew she could be even more bare?

Heat rushed up her neck and flooded her face. "Penn. No one's ever . . . I . . . This is so . . ."

His gaze flicked to her face and she thought he knew what she meant. "Intimate?"

She bobbed a little nod, even as he continued stroking her in that confident, carnal manner. "We, uh, I, well, it was mostly kind of furtive," she said, her face burning again, as she considered how gauche she must seem to him. Before Penn, her only experiences had been as one of two rookies groping in the backseat or under a blanket.

"Most teenage boys suck at sex," Penn replied.

She relaxed, thinking he understood that this was moving too fast, too intimately for her. Her legs tried drawing together, but then he was lowered between them, his shoulders keeping her knees parted.

"Adult males on the other hand," he added, his smile wicked, "we just suck."

And then he did that! Right there!

Alessandra's eyes rolled back in her head. It was a good thing she'd stuffed her feelings in that secure compartment, else she might feel mortified about now.

Instead, she was electrified.

Oh. My. God.

His mouth eased up, and his tongue lapped at her, teasing little licks that made her hips lift in entreaty.

He laughed. "You taste good," he said, and then ran a finger down her pulsing skin to slide inside her. He pulled free to paint her own wetness over her bottom lip. "See?"

Her tongue reached for his finger and she tasted the

creaminess of her own body. Another burn washed over her skin, and beneath her bra her nipples furled tighter, the lace of her bra rasping against the sensitive flesh. She wanted to be naked.

Only, oh wow, how arousing it was to be mostly dressed, and with a half-naked Penn Bennett between her thighs. She felt the silky ends of his hair caress the skin at the inside of her hipbones and then he was kissing her there, too, sucking again, little stinging kisses that made her jerk and shudder. It hurt, it didn't. She wanted him to stop. She wanted him never to stop.

"Penn," she whispered, closing her eyes.

"A little louder, honey," he said.

But she'd given him so much already. Given him more of herself—like this, anyway—than she'd given anyone. To hang on to what little power she had in this circumstance—where he had all the moves and she had only the helpless reactions—then she was going to have to keep them as subdued as she could.

Just another security measure.

She opened her eyes to catch him watching her face. There was knowledge in his expression, another example of his expertise, and she could tell he thought he could break her. Make her beg, plead, show her passion with her voice. Be shattered by an orgasm.

His fingertip circled her clitoris. She caught her breath, caught the moan that wanted to break free, and hung on to her senses, even as he tried to make her release them with his mouth, his fingers, his intimate kisses that had her throbbing, pulsing, tingling. Everywhere.

She almost lost the game when he lifted his head, his beautiful mouth wet. His thumb rolled along the edge of his bottom lip and then he licked the moisture off it, as if to savor more of her taste. Her belly clenched. A moan welled in her throat.

Still watching her, he ran his tongue over his two longest fingers and slid them inside her body. Still silent, she bowed up and clenched hard on the delicious intrusion. Penn groaned.

"You're killing me, baby," he said.

She was the one dying. Any minute now he was going to break her self-imposed chains and then he'd know . . . he'd know . . .

There was nothing to know! She was an adult. This was sensual, sexual, not emotional and even the rookie could win the contest sometimes.

His fingers moved out, pushed in. She tried breathing with the rhythm, letting the pleasure roll over her in controlled waves. He slid deep, held, then drew his fingers out again, curling them to touch her in a new spot. An expert touch, one that had the climax waiting to pounce curling tighter and tighter, even as her restraint was raveling.

He was watching again . . . waiting to pounce, too, the minute her passion overtook her. When she gave voice to it, he'd win.

He couldn't win. Alessandra reached for her neckline. She yanked on her dress, the skinny straps sliding down her arms so she could pull the bodice and strapless bra beneath her breasts. The bunched material plumped them high, her hard nipples standing hard. Penn froze.

She didn't. Hoping he couldn't see her that her fingers were trembling, she ran them over her hot skin, then cupped her palms around her flesh and thumbed her nipples. Under Penn's fascinated stare, she pinched them as he had that night in her bedroom. The sensation arrowed down her body and she clenched tighter on Penn's fingers.

"Oh, no, you don't." He shook his head, as if shaking himself awake. His fingers glided free of her and then he crawled up her body, pushing her hands away so that he could cup her breasts in his own.

She bit her lip. It was so much better to feel his workingman's rough skin against her. He plumped them in his palms, then brought them closer together, to lick the top of one nipple and then the other. She writhed against the sleeping bag, and he threw a leg on top of her. The side of his jean-clad knee pressed against her mound, giving her a delicious weight to wiggle against.

Penn tightened his hands on her breasts, the touch firm as he brought both of them closer together. His shaggy hair tickled her flesh and she slid her fingers through it. He groaned, his knee pushing harder against her, just as he pushed her nipples closer toward her center and took both in his mouth. Sucked.

Her fingers bit into his scalp and every muscle in her body stiffened. Her hips pushed up, fighting the weight of his leg. He didn't release it.

Or release her. Instead, his hands grew more insistent, cupping her harder even as the suction on her nipples increased. She felt the edge of his teeth at the base of the hard nubs and her breath held in her chest.

Her legs widened, his knee slid against her center and he pushed there, firm. The gentle bite on the base of her nipples sharpened, and then his tongue rubbed over their tips.

Her hips rose, her bare folds brushed the rough-soft denim, and she pushed against the steady pressure of his leg and . . .

Came.

Surprise stole her voice, her breath, her thoughts. She rode through the waves of bliss in spontaneous silence, not trying to win a contest, just trying to survive the sweet agony of it.

From far away she heard Penn curse. Then he was naked, over her, in her, his erection stretching her contracting inner muscles and giving her another wave of pleasure as they found something to wrap tight.

"Alessandra. Good. God, so good." Penn was chanting as he drove inside the clasp of her body. She tilted her hips, and he rubbed against that special inner spot on every thrust. She was still quivering around him when he climaxed, again groaning her name.

He collapsed half-on, half-off her body, his cheek against her fanned hair. Pinning her, she thought with a smile.

Penning her in. *Ha. Funny me.*

She opened her mouth to share with him the pun, then the thought froze in her brain.

No, no. He hadn't penned her. Not at all. After too many years, the Nun of Napa's *passion* was free. *Emotions* were caught, but stored safely away from him.

Alessandra was safe, wasn't she?

Her pulse was pounding with anxiety as her lover drew up on one elbow. He stared down at her, his gaze benign, then his eyes narrowed and his head tilted, as if he could read her apprehension on her face.

She swallowed, her vulnerability bringing her to the edge of tears.

Penn's expression cleared. Grinning, he tweaked her nose between his thumb and forefinger. His smile turned more wicked as he raised his gaze skyward. "I'm blessed, for I have sinned with the best damned fuck in the universe."

Oh, the rat. She shoved him off her, pretending to be mad as her pulse stuttered, steadied. *The best damned fuck in the universe.* Wouldn't you know that Penn Bennett would be intuitive enough, and yes, raunchy enough, to say the right thing in the right moment.

A woman with a real heart might fall in love with him for that.

15

Penn shut himself inside the Tanti Baci cottage, testing the double-entry doors he'd just hung at the entrance. The place was reasonably protected now—and a security company would complete the job later in the week. No more nights on the floor in the bridal boudoir, though he was thinking of putting up a brass plaque to honor what he and Alessandra had accomplished there two nights before.

No ghosts had appeared, but he sure as hell had seen stars.

Was there a more frustrating and more fabulous fuck than Alessandra Baci, the Nun of Napa? She pretended to hate the four-letter word he'd used for her, but he'd seen that gleam in her eyes. All the good girls liked to get dirty now and then, even though she continued to stifle her responses. But a lady who hadn't been laid since her teens was a special case.

A case he had a sudden hankering to attend to again, right this instant. While he'd spent another night in the cottage, last evening he'd been all alone. An affair to his mind didn't add up to two nights and one interlude in her office. Maybe he needed to explain that to her—all while he was kissing her until she was warm and wet and needy.

A little desperate himself, he yanked open the new door to go after her—and found himself face-to-face with Roger. Crap.

"Hey, Penn," his friend said, a big ol' grin stretching his thin face.

The big ol' grin made it clear that Roger was seeing a few stars himself, meaning Penn had to make a decision. He'd been able to avoid it for the past couple of days. With the cottage in disarray, the *Wedding Fever* producer and Lana had taken off to a bed-and-breakfast in Sonoma County, giving Penn a reprieve. But if they were back—so was his dilemma.

Did he tell Roger that the woman who spread that wide smile over his face was likely to rob him blind?

"Everything all right?" Roger asked, stepping into the cottage.

"Yeah."

"The place looks great." He ran his hand over the back of one of the handmade Craftsman-styled benches that Alessandra had ordered and that had been delivered the day before. Their honey finish was just a shade lighter than the gleaming hardwood floor recently refinished.

"Yeah," Penn said again, rubbing the back of his neck with his palm. "Did you, uh, have a good couple of days?"

"Lana loved a boutique she found in Healdsburg."

"I'm sure she did." Especially since it was most likely Penn's money she was spending at the place. He hadn't sicced the cops on Lana Lang because it had been so damn embarrassing just to think of how trusting he'd been that he couldn't imagine actually telling the police that he'd been duped. What if word of that had gotten around L.A.? He'd called himself a fool and accepted his losses as the price of a lesson well learned, never considering she'd move on to someone else—especially someone he knew.

Shit. Fooled again.

Blowing out a long breath, he shut the door to the cottage, giving him and Roger privacy. "Listen, I've got something important—"

The door popped open. In platform shoes and a bustier that looked more like club-wear than wine country-wear, Lana entered. "Honey," she said, her gaze lasering on Roger. "You got away from me."

She swished past Penn to reach the other man's side. Her hand found the crook of his arm and her mouth met the corner of Roger's. At the kiss's end, a faint smudge of her red lipstick remained, looking like she'd clipped the poor guy on the jaw.

The blow Penn had to deliver was going to be the one that really hurt. But hell, he couldn't keep quiet, even if he had to do this in front of Lana herself. Steeling his spine, he shut the door once more, then turned toward the couple. "Roger—"

Click. That damn door, open again. With a growl of frustration, he spun around. There stood Alessandra, framed in the doorway, and he felt like *he'd* taken an uppercut.

He didn't know what it was . . . the soft morning light surrounding her or maybe it was her looks in comparison to Lana's. The slender blonde was a beauty, but the brunette in front of him was apricots and plums and the juiciest of peaches. Dressed in an orangey-gold cotton dress that halter-tied around her neck, fitted close at her waist, then billowed past her knees, she looked like summer. Behind her, the vineyard showed a bountiful green, but nothing could look more lush or beautiful than Alessandra herself.

She pushed a handful of her coffee-dark hair over her shoulder. "I . . . I'm sorry." Her gaze darted from Penn to the couple. "Am I interrupting something?"

"Not at all," he hastened to assure her. No way would he admit his idiocy in front of Alessandra. He glanced at Roger and Lana. "You remember—"

"The Nun of Napa!" Lana crowed the phrase. "We had dinner at Oliver's last night after we returned to Edenville and heard all about you there."

"Including the wedding that wasn't," Roger said quietly. "We're sorry for your loss."

And Penn was damn sorry the other man had brought it up. She was moving on from that time and from Saint Tommy—or shit, maybe she wasn't, since as far as Penn could tell she wasn't ready to stop keeping her affair with him a secret.

She barely looked at him as she stepped into the main room. "Thank you." On strappy short-heeled sandals, she turned to regard the new doors. "These look good."

And so did her small toes, gleaming with a color that matched her dress. Their appeal—her toes!—pulled him to her side. "You're late this morning," he said, his voice rougher than he intended.

Her gaze flew toward him, color rising on her throat. "Well . . . um . . ."

With his fingertip, he drew a line along the slope of her smooth shoulder. She was so lovely she made him ache from his molars to his soles. Without thinking, he moved in, wanting a taste of that sweet mouth. His palm circled her upper arm. "Baby," he whispered.

Yet another shadow darkened the doorway. "Am I late?"

Sally Knowles, Saint Tommy's mother. Penn's hand dropped. Alessandra shifted out of his reach. "You're right on time, Sally," she said.

The older woman beamed at Penn. "We're going over the decorations for Clare's big day. It looks as if you're finished with the cottage."

"Just about," he replied, then turned to the other two in

the room. "Sally Knowles, this is Roger McCann and Lana Lang."

"The ones I told you about—from *Wedding Fever*," Alessandra added.

"*Wedding Fever!*" she exclaimed. "I'm such a fan of the show, particularly since my daughter Clare is getting married here in a few short days. The first wedding in the Tanti Baci cottage! Let me get your opinion . . ."

Apparently, assuming the couple were experts on marriage ceremonies, Sally waxed on about her plans. "Grapevine swags along the benches to frame the center aisle. We're having real grape clusters—chardonnay, not that it matters, because at this time in the growing season even the cab grapes are pale green—wired to the vines along with white roses. Those are Clare's colors—pale green and ivory."

White rose petals would carpet the walkway to the front of the cottage and the flower girls would scatter red petals on their way up the aisle. A few fairy lights "of course" would light the room, even though it was an afternoon wedding. Besides the unity candle the bride and groom would light, there would be another candle as well.

"It's to be in Tommy's honor," Sally said, her expression losing some of its excitement. "My son who died on his wedding day."

"We heard about that," Roger murmured, his forefinger rubbing over his chin. Penn had known him for long time, and there was something turning in the back of the man's mind.

Sally spun toward Alessandra. "And we'll have you light it, Allie."

She started. "What? I thought Clare—"

"Being stubborn." Sally waved a hand. "Following the bride's processional and after the minister welcomes the guests, you'll move to Tommy's candle. It will be as if he's right here with us."

Christ. The stricken look on Alessandra's face pierced Penn through the chest. Couldn't she have a moment when she wasn't Tommy's girl? He moved toward her, thinking to offer her comfort, and maybe show Sally that the Nun of Napa had another man on her mind now.

"Lana . . ." The speculation in Roger's voice halted his steps.

Oh no, Penn thought. He glanced back at his friend, who was clearly working on a plan. As one of the best of the production team at *Build Me Up* for the first three seasons, Roger had worn that exact same expression many times.

"Lana, see if you can get a hold of Dom and Kenny. That is—" Roger glanced at Sally and smiled.

Penn had forgotten his friend's charming yet crafty smile.

Sally blinked. "That is?"

"If you think your daughter and her fiancé wouldn't mind if we filmed the ceremony. We were planning a short segment on Tanti Baci, but if we stretch it we can give more attention to the winery and give our audience another tug to the heart by honoring Tommy's memory."

Sally's reaction was instant, overwhelming delight. Alessandra, on the other hand—from the frozen expression on her face—was torn between being happy about the extra attention for Tanti Baci and dismay at the focus it would put on her own disastrous day.

Swearing under his breath, Penn strode to her, catching sight of the tears in her eyes as she turned her back. With Sally involved in enthusiastic conversation with Roger and Lana, he took the chance to run his hand down the length of Alessandra's long hair. "Honey . . ." he whispered.

"I'm fine," she said, her voice tight, her back stiff. "This is great. Terrific publicity for Tanti Baci."

His heart ached for her. What a good little soldier. "Are you sure? Look, I can talk to Roger . . . I'll tell him . . ."

Oh, hell. He did have things to tell Roger—and now that was a much bigger problem.

If Alessandra was determined to go through with this filming, then he'd have to keep the truth about Lana to himself for a while longer. In reaction to the news, Roger might head back to L.A., and Penn wasn't going to risk ruining this opportunity for Alessandra.

He'd do anything for her.

The thought startled him. What? Anything?

Dude, you're surprised? a voice inside him said. *Face it, you'd do anything for the girl because—*

Alessandra suddenly swung to face him. Startled again, he stepped back, though he was damn glad of the interruption to that dangerous "because."

"You should talk to someone, Penn," she said, her voice low and insistent.

"What?"

Her hand grasped his. "And I don't mean Roger. Life's short, you know. Very, very short. If you care for her, if you love her, you should let her know."

He did love her, damn it.

God. His heart pounded, thumping against his chest wall. He was in love. He was in love with Alessandra.

"Let Lana know, Penn."

Let Lana know?

And then he understood, and oh, it was almost funny. Or completely screwed up. Because the woman he just realized he loved was convinced he cared for someone else. Alessandra was still squeezing his right hand so he used his left to cover his eyes. He couldn't let her see.

He couldn't tell her the truth.

The way things were now, Lana was an obstacle between Alessandra and himself. And he needed all the obstacles he could get. Anything that might squelch these feelings he had for Alessandra Baci. Because it was beyond inconvenient to be in love with the Nun of Napa, the woman who was forever connected—through love and community—to another man.

~

Clare stood on a platform in the middle of Susie Lee's Alterations as Susie herself bustled about, checking the final fit of the wedding gown. The tiny, crowded shop was wedged between a trendy bistro and an elegant wine shop. Typical Edenville, with the pleasurable existing side-by-side with the practical.

"You look fabulous," Allie said from a tiny chair set beside a tall stack of fashion magazines. "You love it, don't you?"

Clare inspected her reflection, not ready to commit to "loving" it. She ran her fingers over the new stays that had been sewn into the bodice before meeting the layers of petticoat and ivory fabric that created the full, ballet-length skirt. It had been her grandmother's dress, which they'd updated by removing the long fitted sleeves of chiffon as well as the matching material that had been sewn from the sweetheart neckline to the throat. Now it was a simple, strapless garment that clung to her breasts, ribs, and waist until belling into that frothy skirt at the hipline.

From the chair beside Allie's, her mother sighed.

Clare suppressed hers. "I'm sorry, again, Mom, that we couldn't use your dress. But that tear in the skirt—"

"No, no, no," Sally said. "I'm not thinking about that at all anymore. I'm just basking in how perfect this is turning out to be."

Both Clare and Allie stared at the older woman. She'd been dithering and anxious about the upcoming wedding for months. Nothing—from the invitations to the favors—had been found completely suitable.

"Mom . . ." Clare shook her head. "Did Dad prescribe you a tranquilizer or something?"

"No." Sally laughed. "Though I confess I sampled a

bottle of the Tanti Baci *blanc de blancs* after talking to those *Wedding Fever* people."

Clare stifled a groan. The idea of her ceremony being filmed for the television program made her belly flip like a pancake, but it thrilled her mother. Not only that, but Allie had confessed that the additional exposure would be fabulous for the winery and though Jordan had claimed he didn't care whether they had five witnesses or five million, she'd heard the lilt of excitement in his mother's cultured voice when Clare had floated the idea by her via telephone. So she hadn't voiced her objections.

Everyone was in a good mood about the upcoming day but Clare. At this moment the idea of walking down the aisle was daunting, with or without cameras watching. But she'd stepped aboard the marriage train months ago and there was no disembarking now.

Susie climbed onto a stepladder to arrange the veil on Clare's head. This was her mother's, a long fall of tulle that would be tucked under a simple top knot.

Gasping, Sally rose to her feet. "Oh, Clare."

The refrain of her life.

Oh, Clare, you're not still watching that old TV show.

Oh, Clare, why can't you be more like your brother.

Oh, Clare, you're not bringing that Italian boy home yet again.

"Oh, Clare," her mother said again now, tears starting to roll down her cheeks.

"Mom . . ." Lifting her skirt, she made to hop off the platform.

"No, no. Stay right there," Sally implored. Her palms covered her heart. "Let me soak in this sight."

Tears of joy? But they must be, because that was a smile on her mother's face, a wide smile that Clare hadn't seen in five years, not since her brother Tommy died.

It was impossible not to smile back. "It looks okay?"

"It looks wonderful. You look wonderful. I'm so happy."

"Get your cell phone out, Allie. Take a picture. Mom's happy." She was teasing, but really, the photo wasn't a bad idea. They'd walked through shadows for months upon months, years now, and for the first time Clare believed they might see the sun again.

Her mom even laughed. "I know it's been a long time coming, but today . . . today I think I am finally, finally moving on."

Clare's breath caught in her chest. "I'm so glad," she said, her voice breaking.

"You and Jordan marrying," Sally said, "that's going to be the signal for all of us to start living again."

Her own mood almost giddy now, Clare itched to get to her own phone to pass along the good news. Gil would . . . Guilt stopped that line of thought.

Jordan was the one she'd call. He'd been so busy at work that she'd spent little time with him during the last two months. She didn't think they'd ever been alone. But give her a few minutes of privacy and she'd phone her fiancé and impart the astounding news that her mother, who had been ready for the rubber room and the straitjacket—or who had gotten Clare ready for those two items anyway— was at last relaxed.

And because of that, so was the bride.

She looked at herself in the long mirror. Flushed, bright-eyed, focused on the future.

But five minutes later, down a short hall and behind a dressing room door, doubts flooded in again. With Allie gone back to the winery and her mother engrossed in conversation with Susie out front, Clare had those moments of privacy she'd sought. In two breaths she had her cell in hand and it was on instinct alone that her trembling finger punched a number.

"I need to see you. I need to see you right this minute." She pressed her fingers to her temple. "Don't say anything yet, just go to the alley door behind Susie Lee's tailoring shop."

Still dressed in the gown, she slipped out of the dressing room and unlatched the door leading to the alley, opening it scant inches. When she caught sight of him, she grabbed his arm and yanked his body through the opening, the door shutting behind him.

She towed him to the dressing room and locked them inside. "Clare," Gil said, shoving a hand through his hair. Shaking his head, he looked her over. "Isn't this bad luck or something . . . ?"

Bad luck or something was the day she started seeing her best friend in a new light. In the tiny room, his shoulders seemed to touch both walls and her full skirt brushed his knees. His body heat radiated toward her and she wanted to move into it, press herself against the hard block of his chest, feel the stubble of his dark whiskers against her face.

"Clare? Why did you call?"

Questions tumbled in her head and she grabbed for one. "What happened?" she asked him. "What happened the night of my bachelorette party?"

Gil froze. "What?"

Another thought bubbled to the surface of her troubled mind. "My mom's happy, Gil."

"Okay," he replied, his tone cautious. "That's good, right?"

"It's great." She bobbed her head. "What isn't so great is this hole I have in my memory bank, the nights that I'm not sleeping, the—" She broke off, staring at him. Her heart seized and she had to swallow, hard. "The way that you're looking at me right now."

He cleared his throat. "Because I don't quite know how to tell you this . . . I, uh, I brought someone with me, Clare."

"What? Here?"

"Here," he confirmed. "Someone I ran into on my way over. Someone I . . . convinced to come with me."

Her hands fisted. "Your new girlfriend?" It killed her to say it. She wanted him all for herself, always just hers. If it was only as her friend, so be it, but she could imagine so much more. Her brain had been imagining it, night after night, replaying the way he'd held her on Daphne's couch, how sweetly they'd fit, two puzzle pieces—

"I have to get him, Clare," Gil said, slipping out the door.

Him? And then that "him" was in the small dressing room facing her. Jordan. The man she'd promised to marry. Gil hovered in the doorway behind his back, like her bodyguard . . . or maybe more like an enforcer.

Jordan slipped his hands in the pockets of his slacks, his pose a study in cool sophistication. "So Clare . . ."

Her gaze flicked to Gil's blank face, then back to Jordan's. An easy smile turned up his mouth. "I need to confess, babe."

"You haven't done anything wrong."

His laugh was easy, too, but he glanced over his shoulder as if Gil was making him nervous. "That's true—it's what I think anyway. It was just an . . . aberration. A little bit of . . . guy fun before we married."

Guy fun? "You put money on a horse race? Took up Texas Hold'em and lost our honeymoon fund?" Jordan never gambled; a vow he'd made to straitlaced Grandmère when he was fourteen. She gave him five grand every year he kept his promise.

"Heh heh." He withdrew a hand from his pocket and wiped his mouth. Another nervous gesture.

"Jordan?"

"I've been seeing someone. A woman." He followed the words with a shrug. "Nothing important. No big deal. Has nothing to do with the two of us at all."

"You've been seeing someone. A woman."

"Yeah. No big deal. Like . . . like you see big Gil back there," he said, gesturing over his shoulder with his thumb. "Except . . . except we have sex."

Like you see big Gil back there . . . except we have sex.

Her gaze lifted to the man in the doorway, as recall filled that hole that had been hanging in her memory, one Technicolor drop at a time. In Gil's arms. On Gil's lap. Gil's mouth on hers.

". . . last fling."

Her eyes cut back to Jordan, who was still talking. "What did you say?"

"I'm saying I hope you won't hold that last fling against me. Really, it was nothing more, say, than . . . than a lap dance."

And there it was again, the vision of herself on Gil's lap, his arms around her, her voice pleading. *Last. Single. Girl. Fling. You.* He'd kissed her, caressed her, then stopped. In the end, he hadn't wanted her that way.

Jordan was speaking again. "You understand, right, Clare?"

She almost laughed. "Yes." *Better than you suspect.*

"So we're good? Going forward?"

"Moving on," she said slowly, repeating her mother's words as more of them echoed in her head. *You and Jordan marrying, that's going to be the signal for all of us to start living again.*

Going forward. Moving on. No more doubts. Gil didn't want more than her friendship, so the train wasn't even slowing down.

16

After closing the garage for the day, Gil had picked up his Man of Honor tux at the rental place. He'd been too grimy to try it on there, so he'd ducked in the shower as soon as he arrived home. The girl at the counter had taken one look at him and urged he put the pieces on before the big day. "With someone your size . . . there are no guarantees."

Yeah, he got that no guarantees thing, he thought as he wrapped his towel around his waist. A friendship could change, a woman could forgive when she shouldn't, a man could learn love didn't have a reciprocal clause. Walking into the bedroom, he tried not to glance at the bed. He shouldn't expect that, either, because every time he'd crossed the threshold the last few weeks he'd checked for Clare on his unmade bed. *Don't look*, he told himself yet again . . . and yet again failed.

She was there, a key ring spinning on her forefinger, her gaze on his body. "Pretty," she mused, in a repeat of that other day.

It was his imagination. That key he'd taken away from her weeks ago. Ignoring the apparition, he pulled open his dresser drawer and rummaged for a pair of boxer-briefs.

"Hey," the Clare-specter said.

Still ignoring her, he dropped the towel.

"*Hey.*"

The squeaky sound of the word sent him whirling around. Clare squeaked again—it *was* Clare!—and he scooped up the fallen terrycloth and held it to his genitals.

"What the hell are you doing here?" he demanded.

Her hand was pressed to her chest. "Well, if it was to experience a shock to my system, I think I just checked that off the list."

His gaze went to the key, because it was much safer than staring at pretty Clare in the very place he'd been imagining her for months. Her bronze sandals had short heels, there was a light tan on her bare legs, and above a short skirt, she wore a little T-shirt. He smelled her, too, that sexy floral scent that made him want to seek out every pulse point where she'd applied the stuff.

"Since when do you wear perfume around me? And where the hell did you get that key?"

"It's the one you gave Stevie. As for the perfume . . ." She frowned. "You don't like the way it makes me smell?"

"What happened to kindergarten paste and waxy crayons?" he muttered to himself, ducking into the bathroom. He yanked up his underwear, but realized he had nothing else to cover himself with but a very damp towel. To hell with it. This was *his* place.

He stalked back into the bedroom. "What do you want, Clare?" he asked, crossing his arms over his chest.

She shoved higher on the bed, an uncharacteristic spark in her eyes. "Don't try that with me."

"Try what?"

"Try going all big, half-naked he-man. It won't change the fact that I'm pissed at you."

His jaw dropped. "What did I ever do to you?"

"That's an interesting question all by itself."

She was talking nonsense and he struggled to control his Italian temper. "I did nothing! Nothing! I've always been your friend. Hell, I agreed to the Man of Honor thing, as ridiculous as I'll feel in a pink cummerbund."

"How long did you know about Jordan's extracurricular activities?"

Crap. Figured that out, had she? He'd wondered if and when she'd recall it was he who'd brought her fiancé to the big confession. Clearly he'd known what Jordan was up to.

Rubbing his hand over the back of his neck, Gil tried brazening it out. "What does it matter? You forgave him."

"I don't know if I forgive *you*."

"Damn it, Clare." His whole body was hot now. "None of this is my fault—"

"You should have told me the truth."

That only made him hotter. Because she was right. Maybe if he'd told her himself, maybe if he hadn't given Jordan the Jerk the chance to spew his bullshit—"less than a lap dance"—then Clare could have seen Gil's outrage on her behalf. How horrified he'd been to know what a worm she was marrying. How horrified he'd been that she was marrying . . . someone else.

He turned his back on her again and reached into his second drawer for a pair of jeans.

"What else have you lied to me about?" she asked.

Silent, he shook his head. Then he shoved his feet in the denim legs and yanked the pants to his hips.

"I've been thinking about all this—about everything— a lot."

Gil closed his eyes. If he knew Clare-the-Geek, she'd

probably consulted dictionaries, encyclopedias, and the *Star Trek* episode guidebook to get her through. It didn't matter how smoothly Jordan tried to cover over what he'd done, Gil was sure it had pierced Clare's ego.

"Two things stand out. You owe me—"

"I don't!" He turned to face her.

"—for keeping my fiancé's secret."

He pinched the bridge of his nose. "Fuck, Clare."

"Exactly," she said. "You owe me, and by doing that, you can settle the other issue that's bothering me."

"Doing that, what?"

"There's an imbalance of power, as I see it. Jordan had his last fling. I didn't get mine."

Turning away again, Gil remembered the night of the bachelorette party. The soft and willing warmth of his best buddy in his arms. He was a beast in comparison to her slight figure, but he'd been prepared to cherish her. Treasure every inch of her sleek skin, show her what she meant to him by being gentle with the rough pads of his fingertips and soothing with kisses the wet scrape of his tongue. But it would have given too much away. He couldn't imagine going through the rest of his life with that memory in his head, knowing it was the first and last time.

The only thing that would make it worse would be if she guessed how he felt about her.

A hand touched the small of his back. He jumped, spinning on his bare feet and crashing into the dresser with his ass. The lamp sitting on top of it fell over, crashing to the floor. Moving to pick it up, he yelped as he stubbed his toe on a book that had somehow fallen to the floor as well.

She was staring at him, eyebrows raised. "Hard to believe you were the county's leading quarterback."

"I wasn't always successful," he grumbled, avoiding her gaze by setting the lamp and book to rights.

"Junior year. Versus the Crestmont Cougars. You thought you'd lost our team the big game."

God, that had been a miserable time. His mother hospitalized with a serious infection, his father preoccupied with the illness and keeping the family in clean clothes. That night had been the last straw. On the bus ride back to school, he'd slumped in the bench seat at the back, ignoring everyone, his mood steeping in hurt and shame.

Clare had been waiting for him on the hood of his car. Bundled in her puffy stadium coat and a beanie, she'd looked like the kindergartner she'd once been. Big eyes, pink nose, and a bag full of Milky Ways.

She hadn't said a word to him about the game. Nothing about how it wasn't his fault or how the defensive line had let him down. She'd just stuffed him into his letterman's jacket and sat in the front seat of his muscled '69 T-bird, peeling wrappers off the candy bars like they were bananas. He'd crammed one after another into his mouth until he thought the sick feeling in his gut was from the chocolate and not from the loss.

They'd stayed out late and Clare had missed her curfew. She'd been grounded and he'd apologized for that . . .

He should apologize now. With a sigh, he glanced at his best friend, waiting patiently for him to compose himself, just as she'd done that night. "I'm sorry. I'm so damn sorry."

He saw her swallow. Then she stepped closer. "Make it up to me, then. Jordan got his, now you give me mine."

His eyes closed. Damn it. Damn them both. He refused to look at her.

So he felt her next step instead of seeing it. Felt her naked toes bump his. When had she taken off her shoes? Then her hands slipped around his ribs and yanked his body against hers. Her body naked except for bra and panties.

When had she taken off her clothes?

Without his permission, his hand cupped the back of her head and brought her face against his chest. "I don't know if I can do this, Clare."

Her hand slid to his crotch, into the notch of his open jeans and right over his hard shaft. "Feels like you're perfectly able to me."

He groaned, pushing his hips into her unfair caress. "This isn't right."

Her mouth pressed a kiss on top of the slamming pound of his heart. Her tongue gave him a delicate lick.

His control broke. He scooped her up in his arms, then bore her down on the bed. She gasped, her eyes wide and fixed on his face.

Oh, crap. Gentle, gentle, he told himself and loosened his hold on her. He lifted his weight so he wasn't pinning her. "Are you breathing?" he asked, anxious. He had to outweigh her by more than a hundred pounds.

"I don't think so," she whispered, her voice hoarse. But her arms twined around his head and brought her mouth to his. "Who needs air?"

Yeah. Who needs air? She didn't allow him any, either, as she took him into a series of hot, wet, deep kisses. There wasn't any air between their bodies, either, thanks to the slim legs wrapped around his thighs. The rasp of the lace of her bra was an aphrodisiac in itself, the thought of what was beneath her panties enough to get him burning, and desperate to shuck his jeans.

But she was like a clinging vine, a limpet, her skin and limbs sticking to him like they'd stuck together all their lives. He laughed, burying his face in the crook of her neck and breathing in her intoxicating scent. "This has gotta be done clothes-free, Clare."

"What?"

He loved the dazzle in her eyes and rolled so that she was on top. "C'mon, pretty woman, show me what you've got."

Her hands went to the clasp of her bra at her back. A blush rushed over her face. "I . . . we never played doctor. Weird, huh?"

He sat up so that he could handle the fasteners himself. "We were saving it for when we had something worth exploring." The bra dropped to the bed and his breath caught. "Oh, Clare."

She was small and delicate, and her whole body shuddered when he covered her little mounds with his big hands. Her nipples were pebbles, smaller than pebbles, against his palms. So much blood rushed out of his head, he had to fall back to the pillows.

Then Clare, so, so pretty, went to work, her breasts swaying as she kissed down his torso, paying attention to the ridges of white flesh on his ribs that were the aftermath of a shirtless skateboarding spill. When she reached his waistband, she drew free both his jeans and underwear, her mouth following the path of the retreating cotton. When she placed tiny kisses along the line of his knee-surgery scar, he almost came.

"Get up here," he growled. And then he yanked her to the head of the bed himself and went about proving he knew all her secret spots, too. There was the tiny mole on the underside of her chin, the tracery of blue veins in the inner crook of her elbow, the old softball injury on her kneecap, the—

Her fingers took hold of his hair. "What do you have there?" she whispered.

He glanced up at her. "The blast-off button."

She laughed. "What?"

"Trust me, I'm a mechanic." And she did trust him, she let him have everything, her legs pushed wide, her heels in the mattress, her arms welcoming as, after he'd made her cry out in climax, he slid inside her, one quarter inch at a time.

"You're hung like a horse," she said, her voice breathless.

"No, just proportional." But he slowed his progress into the hot tightness of her, knowing with each small increment gained that she was cemented more firmly in his heart.

"Gil?"

But he was afraid to look at her. He was getting too close, they were getting too close, and he couldn't risk her knowing that this would be the pinnacle of his sexual life. And wasn't that depressing? One night with the woman he loved.

"Ahh." He groaned as he stroked the final distance. They were groin-to-groin, breast-to-chest, and he couldn't regret it. Wouldn't.

They moved together easily. She clung tightly to him through every swing of his hips, but when he was only holding on by his pride, he managed to work a hand between them. To touch her again and take her high.

His own release exploded as she came.

"Blast off," she murmured as they lay next to each catching their breath. "Can you make it like that every time?"

"Oh—" But he swallowed the "yeah" he wanted to add. This wasn't an ongoing state of affairs. This was a payback affair. Her way to settle the score with—

"Jordan," she said, reading Gil's mind again.

"How do you do that?" he asked. He lifted on an elbow and pushed the hair off her forehead with a finger.

"You're hung like a horse," she said, "and your mind works in obvious ways."

"Hmph." He dropped back to the pillows.

"It's why I know that you're in love with me."

Oh, shit.

"You wouldn't have done this with me unless you were."

"I've slept with plenty of women I didn't feel the slightest thing for," he blustered, then shut up, realizing how low that made him sound.

She laughed.

"You know what I mean," he grumbled.

"But none of them were me."

The pooch was screwed. He didn't even know what the

hell that phrase meant—and if he hadn't just had sex with his best friend, he would have asked the brainiac for the answer.

"But don't you worry," she added. "I know this will all work out. I'll even forgive you for lying to me."

"I thought I was getting forgiveness for lying *with* you," he said drily.

"Hung like a horse and sometimes funny, too." Clare sat up, holding the sheet to her breasts. Her gaze met his. "But it's okay with us now because I lied to you, too."

He was wary. "How's that?"

"This wasn't about a power balance with Jordan. I gave him back his engagement ring this afternoon." She held up her bare left hand.

Huh. He hadn't noticed. His heartbeat started picking up. His mouth dried. "So . . . so what was this about then?"

She shrugged. "I wanted to see if you were any good in the sack before I committed myself to saying that I'm in love with you, too."

He stared at her. That beating heart was in his throat, his ears, shooting around his insides like a pinball. "Clare . . . Don't kid me."

She threw herself on him. "I love you I love you I love you." Her mouth peppered his face with kisses. "But you know *that* already. Listen, my BFF, and believe. I'm in love with you."

Oh, God. He cradled her in his arms, holding her against his trembling body. Made weak by 110 pounds of geeky girl. He'd be her bodyguard, and a damn close one. She was never getting away from him again.

"I'm so damn scared," he whispered against her hair.

But she heard him. Her head lifted and she gazed on him, puzzled. "Why? And why didn't you say anything since . . ."

"Since those three hellish nights on Daphne's couch," he admitted.

She smiled at him, tracing his mouth with her finger. "Why didn't you say anything since those three hellish nights at Daphne's?"

"First, tell me when you fell in love with me."

"I can't tell you *when* I fell in love with you—that might be on Daphne's couch or at a softball game or maybe the night you took me to the prom. I can say I realized it when I kept replaying in my mind your toast at my bachelorette party. 'Be happy,' you said. 'Be healthy. Be yourself.' And I realized the man who saw me for myself, who cared for me *for* myself, was you."

He wanted to write that she loved him in the sky. Take out a full-page ad in the newspaper. Call up everyone in the skinny Edenville phone book and leave that exact message on their answering machine. *Clare loves me.* Instead he kissed her, but she still wasn't giving up on her question.

"Why?" she asked again.

Why hadn't he let her know.

Sighing, he cupped her face in his hands. He'd been a coward. "Because I was afraid, Clare. Telling you would be risking everything we've had all these years. Did I dare that? If this didn't work out between us—who was going to comfort me through the fall?" It could still go wrong.

"That's not going to happen," she said, reading his mind again. Her arms tightened on him, as if the geek was the bodyguard after all. "And furthermore, if there is any trouble, we'll be falling together. My mom's going to be homicidal when I tell her I'm canceling the wedding."

17

"Build me up!" the crowd of boys and girls shouted, their voices echoing off the cinderblock walls of the Edenville Kids' Club, essentially a large rec room with linoleum floor, beanbag chairs, and a Ping-Pong table. Penn grinned at them and Alessandra took that as her cue to pass out the T-shirts advertising his show. Len Withers caught her eye and nodded with approval. An old family friend who ran the community rec center, he'd hit her up for an introduction to the TV star.

It was clear from the call he'd made to her that Len had an agenda, and his wish had been granted, because here stood Penn Bennett for a special evening with the kids and their parents. First he gave a short demonstration of simple home repairs that a grown-up could accomplish with a child's assistance. Following that he gave an even shorter speech aimed directly at the kids that was less about repairs and more about reliance on self.

If the smoothness of his delivery didn't confirm he'd done something similar before, the fact that he concluded the visit with yet another freebie did. Out of a cardboard box he'd lugged in from his truck, he pulled small plastic cases stamped with his show's logo. They held a selection of basic tools.

Alessandra wished she hadn't tagged along for the event. Every smooth move he made, every practiced smile that flitted across his face soured her mood. She couldn't wait to get home and get away from him.

The last attendee trooped out, a five-year-old charmer in platinum pigtails who had given him a hug and a kiss in exchange for the kit. Restless and still irritable, Alessandra sidled up to him as he swung the door shut behind the child. "It's always about the blondes with you, isn't it?"

He swung toward her, his eyebrows arched. "What bug bit the nun on the ass?"

Her glare should have melted his half-smile. "I'm no nun, as you very well know," she muttered.

"What bug bit the nymphomaniac on the ass?"

She wasn't that, either. Hadn't she stayed clear of Penn and sex for the last few days? She should have stayed clear of him tonight, too, but she'd hoped for a distraction from her fractious mood. She couldn't explain her edginess. Jules was committed to Tanti Baci now, the cottage was nearly ready for its debut, and Penn . . .

Frowning, Alessandra watched him fiddle with the rheostat light switch by the door. "What are you doing?"

He crossed to the box of tool kits and yanked one out. "Hey, Len," he said to the older man who was tidying the puzzles and books at the back of the room. "You mind if I fix this switch? I also noticed the sink back there is dripping . . ."

"I'll be grateful for whatever you can do," Len said, approaching the exit with car keys in hand. "But I'm expected at my daughter-in-law's for dessert. Can you two turn off the lights before you leave? The door locks automatically."

"Gotcha," Penn said, and went back to his repair as the other man left the premises.

Leaving her alone with the infuriating handyman for additional minutes. Dropping to one of the small tables, Alessandra contemplated his efficient movements, his confident stance, how handsome he was in worn jeans and distressed-leather moccasins. All Mr. Hollywood, she thought, her lip curling, her mood starting to smoke. She crossed her arms over her chest. "My, my, my. You're quite the hero, aren't you?" she said.

He glanced at her again, that surprise once more on his face. "What?"

"It's a comment. About how good you are at playing the leading man."

He narrowed his eyes at her. "Where's this coming from? I did this gig as a favor to you."

Other favors, too. Finishing the cottage. Ending her five-year celibacy. Each pricked at her. "And it's why I felt obligated to assist tonight. But the fact is, you sop up the attention." She knew she sounded surly, but she didn't care. "Don't you ever get tired of people fawning over you?"

"What the hell?" He turned and folded his arms over his chest. He looked a little hot under the collar, too. "Is it that you're afraid I'm going to push Saint Tommy off the Edenville pedestal?"

Her temper felt like a weight that hung from her eyebrows, pulling at her head and making it ache. "Don't talk about Tommy," she snapped.

"Or maybe it's you." The edge to his voice matched hers. "You don't want to lose your standing to someone else. The Nun of Napa has been revered here for five long years, thanks to her tragic loss and subsequent martyrdom."

"I—"

"Did you ever think it might be better for all concerned to take off that damn weepy wedding dress you metaphorically don every day and start living your life again?"

Her throat closed, but she refused to let him see he'd made her angry enough to cry. So she turned away, tamping down her ire as she crossed to the teacher-sized desk at the back of the room. There was a calendar there and some stacked notes. Obviously where Len did his paperwork. She pretended an interest in a garishly painted rock paperweight, holding down a check.

"I'm just making the point," she mumbled, aware of her pettiness, but powerless to stop it, "that you don't need to personally fix every leaky faucet and faulty light. You could just donate some money or something."

She heard his sigh from across the room. "Why are we fighting?"

"I don't know." Moody, miserable, she idly nudged the rock paperweight.

"Well, whatever, whyever, let's get over it, huh? I'm only here until Sunday, and I don't want to be constantly trading snipes these few short days left."

His words didn't sink in as she stared at the check anchored to the desk. Oh, wouldn't you know. It was made out to the kids' club. Five figures. A personal check signed by Penn.

You could just donate some money or something.

Great, now she felt both crabby *and* small. Wait . . . what had he just said? Short. A few short days left. Something cramped inside her at the spot between her breasts.

"You're . . . you're going?" She should be relieved, she thought. Even if she was stuck here with him now, soon he'd be gone for good.

"On Sunday. But don't worry, until then I'll be available for any emergency fixes at the cottage."

"My personal handyman."

He pressed the rheostat on, off, then spun the dial. It didn't stutter or blink, but performed without a flaw. Shoving the screwdriver in his back pocket, he turned to face her. A faint smile crossed his face. "Like I told you, I'm good with my hands."

She tilted her head, struck by a new thought. "How come?"

He headed for the sink at the back of the room. "How come I'm good with my hands? I'm guessing you don't want to hear about those Lights Out parties I went to in seventh grade."

Seventh grade? Yeesh. "No. I'm being serious."

"In college, I got a bachelor's in Commercial Construction," he said, fiddling with the faucet handle. "But my real education came from living in a sequence of crappy apartments. On TV they have supers in tool belts who live in the building. In real life, you better learn to fix the toilet and sink yourself. And if you're poor, the toaster, the TV the neighbor's throwing out, and the hole in the drywall the cockroaches are using as a hallway."

Alessandra repressed her shudder. She thought of Liam and Seth who had grown up with luxuries and comfort. Without cockroaches. "It would be natural to resent your half brothers," she mused aloud.

"What?" He turned to face her. "No. It's no more their fault than mine who contributed half our DNA and how Calvin Bennett handled that."

"You must have wanted a father."

He shrugged. "I made one up. Yeah, I felt the lack when the other kids in school had dads to talk about—even if their folks were divorced. So I created one of my own. He was a soldier, stationed in Hawaii, which made him too far away to visit."

"Hawaii?" she repeated with a little laugh.

Penn shrugged again. "Might as well have been Timbuktu as far as my mom's ability to pay for airline tickets was concerned. Plus it sounded exotic. Waikiki. Diamond Head. Pearl Harbor."

Poor kid. Though she knew Penn the successful television star wouldn't welcome her pity, she couldn't help but feel for Penn-the-boy, who had learned to fix things in his world as best he could. Another ache had her rubbing her chest and she bowed her head, exhausted by the emotional overload. Since the day he'd shown up in her life, she felt as if she'd been swinging between depression and delight, never quite finding her balance.

Would that sensation go away when he did?

Because he *was* going away. In a few short days.

Her head lifted. "You'll be back though, right? You don't blame Liam and Seth, so you'll be back for weekends, holidays . . ." Her words died off as she read the answer on his face. "You're leaving Edenville forever?"

"This is not my place, Alessandra. I've got a job, a life in L.A."

"But here you have family. The Bennett businesses, even Tanti Baci—"

"No."

Her head was hurting again, her chest aching, and she didn't understand why. "This place—"

"Is beautiful," he said softly. "But it's not mine."

She kept coming back to the same thing, despite what he said. "You have brothers. You can't go back and pretend you don't know about them, that they're not your flesh and blood."

"I told you I like them. And I'm sure a sentimental soul like yourself thinks it would be nice if we meshed into a family unit. Maybe for a moment I thought so, too. But the truth is, I don't do 'nice,' Alessandra. My mother was 'nice' and look where that got her. I was 'nice' to Lana—" He broke off. "Let's just say that in my personal dictionary, 'nice' is spelled c-h-u-m-p."

"Lana." There it was, she decided, the source of all her aggravation. The vapid blonde and Penn's passion for her—despite his ability to get passionate with Alessandra on occasion—made her want to break something.

He crossed to the cardboard box at the front of the room

and dumped the tool kit he'd used back inside. "Are you ready to go?"

They were in his truck and almost home before she trusted her voice. The man was lovesick, and she was mad instead of understanding about it. What kind of . . . *friend* did that make her?

"You don't want to ever come back here because of Lana," she said, bringing it out in the open as he braked in front of her farmhouse. "Seeing her here with Roger, it makes Tanti Baci the place where your heart was broken."

Silence reined in the dark cab. "Oh, God," he finally groaned. "What a sap you are. Is that the silly story you're telling yourself?"

She bristled. "It's not my fault you fell in love with the wrong woman."

There was another long silence, then he groaned again. "Jesus, Alessandra. You gotta use your head instead of your marshmallow heart, honey."

There it was again. Everyone always considering her a sentimental fool. If only they knew . . . She unlatched her seat belt, desperate to get away from him now. She shouldn't be around him anymore. "Never mind. I'm out of—"

"No, you're not." In a sudden movement, he hauled her across the bench seat. "Not until we get this straight."

"Get what straight?" she said, trying to slide toward her door.

He groaned again. His voice lowered. "I can't believe I'm telling you this."

Alessandra froze. Telling her what? *Telling her what?* All evening she'd been wishing herself away from him. Now, nothing could make her leave.

～

I can't believe I'm telling you this. The words echoed in Penn's head. He shouldn't tell her anything because that might lead to the one thing she could never know.

"Never mind," he said, removing his hand from her arm and nudging her toward the passenger door.

She sat unmoving on the seat beside him, her thigh two inches from his. "Never mind? You're kidding me. You can't say that."

"I just did."

He would have laughed at the way she flounced on the seat, except she ended up closer to his side. The full fabric of her skirt brushed over his leg and a long lock of her flower-scented hair clung to his shirt sleeve.

"It's one of the first rules of sibling-hood," Alessandra replied. "Maybe you don't know it, since you grew up as an only child. But the fact is, you can't start to tell something and then renege."

"I'm not your sibling," he pointed out, "so your little rule doesn't apply."

"The Bennetts grew up next door to us," she countered. "Our families have been partners for a hundred years. You're almost like my brother."

He choked on that.

She thumped him between the shoulder blades. "See? It's not healthy to hold things back."

God, he loved her. He was never going to get to have her, and he was going to miss like hell how she made him laugh. Her fist was still pounding on him and he had to twist and reach back to enclose it in one of his own. "I like my lungs right where they are."

Alessandra's hand in his felt so damn right. He touched his forehead to hers, driven by the need to touch her, to have of her what he could until he went away. Her stifled-sneeze response to good sex was still something to be overcome, after all.

"Honey," he said, and then kissed her nose, her mouth, each of her cheeks. "I just had a great idea. You've got nothing to do tonight, I've got nothing to do tonight . . ."

"So you've got no excuse not to finish what you started to tell me."

Stubborn woman. He tried kissing it away, doing his best to be coaxing and not demanding.

She was clutching his shoulders, but still not capitulating. "Penn—"

"Think about it, my lady. When's the next time an iterant tinker is going to arrive in the enchanted forest to fill all the holes"—she stiffened—"in your cookware? It could be a long time before another strong and silent type comes around to service you . . . I mean your castle."

Her eyes rolled. "You are ridiculous."

"But even after all your earlier sniping, you say that with fondness," he pointed out, a finger tapping the end of her nose. "And don't forget, there's still those velvet handcuffs."

His mouth touched hers again. Sweet, with just a swipe of tongue against her lower lip. "We could play some *very* adult games with them."

Her breath hitched. That word, *adult*, always got her. An image filled his head: a big bed, a television, Alessandra, and an adult film. He had to haul in a deep breath to keep from hauling her into his arms. "Alessandra?"

"Um . . ."

Say yes.

She was glancing up at him through her lashes, the little flirt. "Only if you tell me your secret."

His secret? God, no.

"About Lana . . ." she started.

He groaned, then a far off ringing phone startled them both. They looked around, Alessandra groping for her purse, Penn putting his hand over his pocket where his cell phone sat. Then she frowned.

"It's the house's landline." She was already sliding across the bench seat. "Nobody ever calls that anymore."

Of course he followed her inside. After all, it got him that much closer to her bed and those handcuffs. The wall phone in her old-fashioned kitchen had stopped ringing, but he didn't mind, except that she was frowning again. And then looking annoyed at the cell phone she dug out of her purse. "I turned it off during your talk," she said. "Maybe whoever called here left a message on my cell phone first."

"Let's forget whoever called you," he said. "Let's forget about everything but us." *Of course there is no 'us,'* he reminded himself, even as he took her in his arms.

She didn't seem to notice, because her attention was still focused on her cell. "Clare called a couple of times," she said, then glanced at the big-faced school clock hanging across the room. "It's not too late."

"It's much too late," Penn murmured, shuffling her toward the staircase.

This is when that chemistry thing was such a boon. He could read the objections and reservations on her face, but he could distract her from them by trailing his fingertip across her cheek. Sucking on her bottom lip. Caressing the small of her back as they ascended the stairs.

And the gods were smiling on him, because those furry handcuffs were tossed on the antique ash dresser she had angled in one corner of her room. He snagged them as he slow-danced her toward the bed, her mouth going soft under his.

Pressing her to the mattress, he dropped them between the pillows. She looked up at him through slumberous eyes. So dark, and their exotic tilt made her look mysterious. Except she wasn't. He knew her to her marrow.

Alessandra Baci. The darling of Edenville. Tommy's girl. The Nun of Napa, devoting herself to grief and one boy's memory. It was all true, and remembering it made him feel as if someone was taking a log splitter to his chest. Still, Penn couldn't take his gaze off her.

She stretched luxuriously, her arms overhead. The movement lifted the frilly little shirt she was wearing, exposing a wedge of her golden-skinned belly. He went down on his knees beside the bed, distracting himself from the pain by placing a string of kisses from rib to rib.

Wiggling, she laughed. "That tickles."

"It won't when you're naked."

She believed such outrageous things. Maybe it was part of her romantic soul. In any case, she let him undress her, until her clothes were flung aside and it was only Alessandra, bare, on the white sheets.

His heart seized.

Her phone rang, a distinctive tune. The *Star Trek* theme.

"Clare," Alessandra said, her head rolling toward her cell, lying on the bedside table beside her purse.

"I should—"

She yelped as he yanked her by the ankles, down to the edge of the mattress. He went back to his position on the floor and then used his fingers to open her for his mouth.

She yelped again, sweeter now, because it was followed by a moaning sigh. Yeah. Yeah, this was the only conversation anyone needed to have tonight. The only truth he was willing to tell. His lips to her heart.

He held her hips in his hands. God, if women knew how much a man loved to feel them tremble in excitement, to taste the arousal that was the result of the strokes of his tongue and fingers, they'd know how much power they held in their palms and in their mouths, and in their—

"Penn," she whispered, and her hips moved against the shackles of his hands. "*Penn.*"

Oh, baby. She came, subdued as always. As he slid up her boneless form, he shoved away his frustration and only murmured "Gesundheit," on the way to her mouth.

But she was satisfyingly pliant as she watched him undress through half-lidded eyes. Sated, but still interested.

He came down on one elbow, kissing her again. Her hands tunneled through his hair, slid down his shoulders, stroked along one arm, from bicep to wrist.

He settled on his back and she obligingly moved on top, kissing more. Her hands caressed his chest, his other arm, her fingers stroking the cup of his palm. That touch went straight to his cock. He groaned, but kept still, letting her kiss him until he had to run his hand along her back to her ass—but he couldn't. Stilling, he tipped up his chin. "Damn it," he said, staring at the cuffs that she'd attached to his wrists and to the headboard.

She smiled at him, all cat-with-cream. "My turn."

Then she drew her tongue down his chest. A wave of heat traveled over his skin to meet her wet stroke and he closed his eyes. She blew a cooling breath along the path, and more blistering heat rushed over him.

"Alessandra?" His eyes opened. Oh, God, oh, God.

She was positioned over his erection, gaze on his face, her tongue poised to taste. She licked him.

Killed him.

He groaned as she blew another delicate breath along the wet line she'd created. Then she did the whole thing again . . . and drew away. He tugged at the cuffs to no avail. "Mean," he managed out of his dry mouth.

But not for long, because soon she was back, the ends of her hair tickling his groin as her mouth explored with teasing strokes and tiny licks. Her hands fondled his balls and he felt them tighten, draw close to his body and her sweet, wet mouth.

When she sucked on him, his fisted hands flexed in re-flexive response. Velcro tore. His arms came free of the cuffs. She giggled.

He loved the sound.

God, he loved her so much.

"Get ready for retribution, sweet thing," he said.

She obligingly fell flat on her back and he donned a

condom with jerky movements. He crawled onto her body, cradling her beautiful face in his palms.

A wave of emotion came over him. He swallowed, his muscles tensing. This wasn't right. His body pulled away from hers. "I can't believe I'm telling you this," he said slowly.

"What?" She arched a brow. "Now? You're going to finally finish that conversation *now*?"

"Yeah." Because it seemed wrong, a kind of betrayal, to come inside her, while knowing she thought he cared for another woman. "I'm not in love with Lana, okay?" There. Shit. That wasn't so bad. That wasn't the bad part. The stupid, foolish Penn part. "I was never even close to being in love with her."

"Oh." Alessandra, the perverse creature, looked disappointed.

"That's a problem for you?"

"Well, it means I didn't need to dislike her after all. I was all ready to discourage Roger—"

"You should still discourage Roger." His jaw tightened. "She's a con, a cheat, a grifter, okay?" Disgusted with himself and the situation, he started to move off the bed, but she wrapped her arms around him, and that embrace was stronger than any handcuff.

"What are you saying?"

"I met her through the show. She was a participant's sister-in-law. We went out a couple of times, true, but it wasn't love that brought us together. She had a sob story, okay? A story that I swallowed whole. I let her move into my pool house, I introduced her to people in the business, and then one day . . ."

She raised up on her elbows. "One day?"

"I came home to find she'd disappeared—but first she'd cleaned out what she could, including a household bank account that had an easy-to-guess password."

He sighed. After that, why not the rest? He explained

he hadn't called the cops because he'd wanted to put the incident behind him. Never had he anticipated she'd show up in Napa, on Roger's arm.

"And you didn't tell him right away because—" He saw the knowledge dawn in her eyes. "Because you thought it might jeopardize the winery's *Wedding Fever* publicity."

Her eyes closed. Then she drew him down and kissed him again, luscious, sweet . . . and salty. The flavor of her tears.

"Alessandra . . ."

"Shh," she said. Then she was kissing him some more, languorous, long exchanges. Her tongue rubbed slowly against his, her body undulated, her bare flesh pressing close to leaving indelible marks etched onto his skin. He rolled to his back, sinking into the mattress as he sank into her taste.

Then she was up on her knees, taking him inside her. This was languorous, too, not the near-frantic slaking that his body had clamored for the times before. This was a long ride to shore, on the perfect wave with the sun beating down and the day more perfect than any one known before.

Alessandra was moving, moaning, and he caressed her pretty breasts and pinched her nipples as her volume increased. This was her show, and he let her set the pace, even as he felt that inevitable tug on his senses. He wasn't going to last.

But she broke first, her body shaking, her pelvis grinding, her passion sounding—loud!—in the room. "*Penn!*"

Triumph rose from his heart to his throat, he wanted to shout, too, to take a victory lap with his fist in the air, but then his own release crashed over him.

He came to himself minutes later, with his body beached on her sheets, his hands and legs wide, the Nun of Napa curled at his side. He rolled his head to kiss the top of her head. She returned a drowsy sound. "You nearly took the roof off, young lady," he said.

She made another little noise and burrowed her cheek on his chest. That beating organ inside of it tumbled. How had this happened? he asked himself.

How had Penn Bennett, who just months ago had been made fool of by another woman, been fool enough to fall in love with a beauty known far and wide as the Nun of Napa? She wasn't starchy or sinless, however. Instead it was worse. She was sweet and hot and such a to-the-marrow romantic that she would content herself to live on dreams of what couldn't be for the rest of her life.

Damn that legendary love story, the wedding wine, those bride-and-groom cake toppers. No wonder she was so sentimental. Starry-eyed to the soul.

Roll all that together with the ghost of Saint Tommy, and Penn didn't stand a chance.

Yet still . . .

"I can't believe I'm telling you this," he heard himself whisper. He had no idea if she was sentient, or if sleep had already taken her away.

"Alessandra." He kissed her head again, and then the thing he'd never meant to feel, let alone say, he freed from his heart. "Alessandra Baci, I love you."

18

By morning, Alessandra had forgiven Penn for that tossed off "I love you." He was from L.A., right? Hollywood. He couldn't know how his formulaic response to what they'd shared in her bed had bothered her. He was from the kingdom of air kisses and forty-two-hour marriages, wasn't he? When he said the word *love*, he probably meant the L-U-V kind and she counted herself lucky that he'd refrained from adding a "babe" at the end of the phrase.

But that was how he'd meant it, she decided as she stomped around the kitchen making coffee. She should have responded in kind. "Sure, sure, luv you, too, babe." She tried it out in an airy tone.

"Are you talking to me?"

With a jerky movement, she swung around to face him. He propped his shoulder against the doorjamb, wholly comfortable in damp hair, no shirt, jeans, and bare feet. A look that made her wholly *un*comfortable.

She plucked at the lapel of her fuzzy robe. "It's a little warm in here, isn't it?"

His smile grew slowly, as if he knew exactly what—who—was the source of all her heat. The rat. His naked feet took him closer to her, and her pulse sped up.

"Maybe we should get you out of all these"—fingering the fabric belt tied around her waist, he focused on the pink figures cavorting about the pale blue plush and his smile widened—"flamingoes?"

Embarrassment crawled over her skin. She'd never spent an entire night with a man in her bed. After jolting awake, she'd raced to the shower and then raced downstairs in her usual morning-wear while he was still sleeping. She didn't have any fancy negligees, just her scruffy slippers and her fuzzy flamingoes.

"I don't have anything sexy," she blurted out.

His palm brushed her hair off her forehead. "I hate to argue with such a beautiful girl on such a beautiful morning. However . . ." His other hand loosened the belt and the robe parted at the center. His fingertips tickled her belly and then slid up to cup her breast. "You're wrong," he said, tweaking her nipple.

She moaned, and in her own ears it sounded overloud. His half smile grew smug. "Music to my ears," he whispered against one of hers.

Her knees wobbled. "Penn." Was his name a plea or an admonishment? She leaned into him, still not sure. *"Penn . . ."*

The sound of rubber tires on the gravel outside the house had her leaping back. She yanked the sides of her robe together again. "Someone's here."

He strolled to the back door and pulled the gingham curtains covering the glass aside in order to glance through. "You're right."

She'd already retied her robe. Now she shooed him in the direction of the staircase. "Go on, go on," she urged.

Knuckles rapped on wood just as she was pouring from the pot of fresh coffee. Taking deep breaths, she crossed to the door and pulled it open. On the other side stood Tommy's mother.

"Sally." The tips of her ears felt hot and she resisted the urge to peek over her shoulder to make sure Penn wasn't loitering nearby. "You're an early riser this morning."

"And you are, too," the woman said, stepping into the room with a large box in her arms. "I feel like there's so much to do before Saturday."

"You'll get everything done," Alessandra assured her. "The wedding will be perfect."

From somewhere above, a loud thump sounded. Her stomach tumbled, but she gave the older woman her most serene smile, as if every day invisible elephants dropped hand weights overhead. "Would you like a cup of coffee?"

"Love it," Sally answered, sliding the box she held onto the kitchen table. "And I'd love the chance to talk to Penn, too."

Another stomach somersault. "How, um, why would you think, uh . . ." Did Sally know he was here? Alessandra thought frantically. Of course Sally couldn't know he was here. "Maybe later . . ."

"Now works for me," Penn said, strolling into the room.

Alessandra wanted to scream. What was he doing? She was wearing her thick-as-a-rug, utilitarian robe and Penn appeared as relaxed as any morning visitor—thank God he'd put on his shirt—but it wouldn't be a huge leap to imagine they'd spent the night together doing all sorts of un-nun-like activities. It was possible she'd never forgive him for not staying hidden upstairs.

Sally smiled at him. "I recognized your truck out front."

Damn. Damn! Caught red-faced, and it was all his fault.

He glanced at Alessandra, his eyebrows slightly raised and she knew he could read her mind. "Had to do some minor repairs here this morning," he said. "Now there's a new washer in the faucet."

On the way to the coffeemaker he passed by Alessandra, leaning close. "And you're almost out of toothpaste," he said in a near-soundless whisper. His fingers gave her behind a teasing caress.

She had to swallow her squeak. And her indignation, she supposed, because Sally didn't seem to suspect a thing as he poured a mug of coffee for her as well as for himself. The two chatted about the weather.

Still nervous that the older woman might guess the truth, Alessandra tried getting rid of one of the guilty parties in the room. "Penn, thanks so much for dropping by this morning, but didn't you say you had to be leaving ASAP?"

He cut her another look that she pretended not to see. She didn't understand it, anyway. Surely he wasn't displeased with her attempt at pretense. Hadn't they agreed from the beginning that this would be their secret?

After a moment, he gave a little shrug, then glanced down. "Sure. I'll just go collect my . . . tools."

Shoes! He meant shoes! He was still barefoot, and if Sally caught on to that . . . Alessandra rubbed her forehead as Penn headed out of the kitchen. "Did you just drop by, Sally, or . . ."

"Oh!" The older woman laughed. "I brought something for you. Can you believe I almost forgot?" She set her mug beside the cardboard box she'd arrived with and then placed her palms on either side of it.

Alessandra didn't have a clue. "Well?"

"It's been such a wonderful few days," Tommy's mother said. "I'm so thrilled with the plans for Clare's wedding, and I . . ." She ran her hands over the box, almost caressing the cardboard. "I have a few things that I think I'm ready to pass on to you. No. That I *know* that I'm ready to pass on to you."

Alessandra's skin went hot, then icy. Pinpricks burst along the nape of her neck. "What . . . what kind of things?"

"Keepsakes of Tommy's. Of course I have many that I've put away for the family, but I thought these might be of special meaning to you." She pushed the box toward Alessandra.

It seemed to writhe and rattle like a snake. Her hand white-knuckled the back of a kitchen chair to keep from falling . . . or running.

Sally was still smiling. "Aren't you going to open it?"

A warm hand wrapped one of Alessandra's hands fisted around the chair. Penn. She looked up at him, offering to give him a thousand pardons if he could get her out of this. He squeezed her fingers.

"I thought since you're here, Sally, I could take you down for another look at the cottage," he said. "Make sure it's all to your satisfaction. I have a few extra minutes."

"Oh." The inch-and-a-half of assorted gold bracelets on the older woman's slender wrist jingled as she gestured toward the boxed belongings. "But I wanted Alessandra to look through these—"

"I'm sure you'll agree it can wait. Clare's wedding, on the other hand . . ."

That prod carried the exact right voltage to get Sally moving. "Of course, of course," she answered, already heading for the door.

Penn and Alessandra trailed behind. "I'll stay here and get dressed," she whispered to him. "Thanks."

His smile was perfunctory and he strode ahead to catch up with Sally. Alessandra descended the steps in their wake.

The older woman tucked her hand in his arm. "Is there something in particular that needs my attention?" she asked Penn.

Before he could answer, another car came speeding toward the farmhouse. Clare's Camry. It came to a smooth stop, so quiet that it reminded Alessandra she needed to get her sedan into Gil's shop. Her brakes were squealing. And hey, maybe she could make an appointment right then and there, because it was her cousin who was getting out of the passenger seat of Clare's car. He looked great, brawny and bold and . . . happy.

Happy?

Her gaze snapped to Clare whose wide eyes were trained on her mother as she climbed from her seat. "Mom." She swallowed. "I was going to come by and see you later."

A questioning note entered her voice as she turned to Alessandra. "I called you last night. Your cell wasn't on this morning."

"Oh. Sorry." Guilt had her glancing at Penn. But he was focused on the couple by the car, and . . .

The couple by the car.

A premonition slithered down her spine. Her feet moved backward, her heels bumping against the first tread of the stairway. "I've got to get back inside . . ." She made a vague gesture with her arm.

Clare frowned. "But I came to speak with you."

"Your mom's here," Alessandra said, feeling her way up two steps. "Visit with your mom."

Penn moved quickly, catching her arm. "She's here for you," he reiterated.

But she didn't want to hear what Clare had to say! She tried shaking free of his hold, shooting him a glare. "Her mother—"

"Should probably learn this at the same time as you, anyway," Clare offered. She looked up as Gil came to stand beside her. The smile she sent him was sweet.

It made Alessandra's stomach hurt. She tried moving again, but Penn kept her tight to his side.

Clare's gaze cut again to her mother. "Mom, I'm not marrying Jordan."

Sally stepped back. Alessandra, too, stumbling against the next step. Penn caught her arm to steady her.

"But . . . but . . ." Sally said. "The wedding is just days away. You've never hinted . . ."

"I know." Clare gave a weak smile. "But it's like this *Star Trek* episode," she said. "It's titled 'This Side of Paradise,' and the *Enterprise* lands on an agricultural colony to evacuate the colonists endangered by fatal Berthold rays. No one wants to leave—"

"Clare." Alessandra's voice was firm. "*Star Trek* isn't a guidebook for life."

"Wait," Penn said. "I know this one. Spock got all hot and bothered with an old love interest, which made it pretty memorable. But the main idea was that everyone on the planet was affected by a plant that made them abnormally happy—happy enough to risk certain death by refusing to leave. It took them experiencing strong emotion to shake them back to reality and themselves."

Clare was nodding. "I was just going along with the marriage plans until something shook me up."

"What?" Sally slid a look toward Gil. "Did—"

"Jordan was cheating on me, Mom." Color flagged Clare's cheeks. "For the last few months he's found time to be intimate with someone else, though he was always too busy for us to be alone. I don't think that's right, even if he said it didn't have any more meaning to him than a lap dance."

"Cheating on you?" Sally blinked, obviously trying to absorb the news and its ramifications. "This can't be. I don't. . . . Oh, Clare."

Her daughter's voice hardened. " 'Oh, Clare' isn't the right response, Mom. *I* didn't disappoint you."

"No. Well . . ." Sally put her hand to her head. "But Jordan's parents, Grandmère—"

"I suspect Grandmère understands Jordan better than we did," Clare replied. "It explains why she gives him an annual stipend as an incentive not to gamble. She knows he wants to. She knows he's into risky behavior."

"But . . . but . . . he's a stockbroker!" Sally protested.

"Mom," Clare said on a sigh. "That's exactly what I'm trying to tell you."

Penn laughed, then covered up the sound with a cough. "Or maybe he's just a selfish jerk, Clare. I think you have dodged a bullet."

"Thank you," Clare said. "And there's more. More that everyone should know."

Alessandra tried retreating toward the kitchen again. Penn let her make it to the small back porch before his hold tightened again. "Stay put," he said.

Clare straightened her spine. "Like I said, I'm not marrying Jordan." Then she looked over at Gil and he smiled at her, that happy clear on his face. Alessandra felt another weird cramp in her chest.

"We're getting married—and right away," Gil said, taking hold of Clare's hand. "Clare and I are in love and we want to spend the rest of our lives together, not just as best friends, but as husband and wife."

Sally didn't crumple, but her expression signaled her dismay. "I . . . oh . . . You know what I think . . ."

"I think you're being foolish," Clare said, and her eyes were hard and her voice tight. "I think you should be listening to me and trying to understand how I feel."

"Oh, Clare." Sally's hands fluttered at her sides and her gaze flickered between her daughter and Gil.

"Congratulate us, Mom," Clare said, steely again. "This time, say 'Oh, Clare, I think you finally have it right.' "

Gil shook his head at her, and his voice softened. "Baby, don't throw out ultimatums and don't put words in her mouth. It doesn't matter—"

"Oh, Clare, I think you finally have it right," Sally broke in, breathless.

"Mom?" Clare blinked. Gil appeared poleaxed.

"I've lost one child." Tommy's mother sounded fierce. "I still don't understand that. But this I *do* know. I'm not about to lose another. Not like this. Not because of love." Then she turned to Gil and straightened her shoulders. "Congratulations. If there's one thing I believe about you, it's that you have my daughter's happiness at the forefront of your mind."

"Whoa. Class act," Penn murmured in Alessandra's ear. "And I think that's our cue to leave the stage."

But Clare held them up again. She looked to Allie, then back to her mom. "One last thing. Our wedding—mine and Gil's—won't be here at Tanti Baci on Saturday."

Sally gasped. "But—"

"That ceremony was orchestrated by you, Mom, and that's not the way I plan to start my new life. My wedding will be my own."

For a moment Alessandra considered cheering. Clare, standing up for herself! But then the words sank in—and she realized they were the ones she'd dreaded hearing since her friend drove up with Gil. *The wedding won't be here at Tanti Baci on Saturday.*

She broke Penn's grasp and flew down the steps. There had to be a wedding at Tanti Baci on Saturday! "It's all set," she cried out. "Everything in place."

It's how we're going to save the winery!

She felt the sting of tears in her eyes, and she looked from Clare to Gil as they rolled down her cheeks. "Don't you see? Don't you understand?"

A strong arm slid around her waist. Penn's arm. "Congratulations!" he said in a hearty voice, then lifted her off her feet. "We'd stay and chat, but Alessandra has to . . . has something to do."

He was carrying her toward the house, even as she was trying to formulate the right words to say to the couple. Or maybe that was the wrong way to go about this.

"Should I phone Jordan?" she called to Clare over Penn's

shoulder. "We have to have that wedding, and if he grovels enough would you consider—"

The kitchen door cut off her proposition. Penn dumped her on her feet on the floor, then stared her down, blocking her path to the outside and any resolution to this fresh problem.

"You don't understand," she told him. "I have to talk to Clare about Jordan."

"You've got the first part right," he said grimly. "I sure as hell don't understand why the Daydream Believer is giving a pass to some asshat who was cheating on his bride-to-be just days before their wedding."

"He said it was like a lap dance," she protested.

Penn crossed his arms over his chest. "Sex *isn't* a lap dance. And even then . . . when I go to bachelor parties I consider it my sworn duty as a friend to keep even the drunkest groom from doing so much as tucking a ten-spot into a G-string."

She waved his comment away. "We have a ceremony scheduled for Saturday"—*the ceremony that was going to save the winery!*—"and—"

"This isn't about a ceremony, Alessandra. This is about Clare and Gil and about their ever-after. That happy thing." He glared at her. "Don't look at me like I've grown a unicorn's horn in the middle of my forehead. Maybe I'm not the most obvious spokesman for the bridal brigade, but someone's got to talk sense when you're throwing love under the bus for your business."

Tanti Baci wasn't just a business. It was where she'd lost the best of her heart and buried the brightness of her future. "Penn—"

"No." He leaned against the door. "You won't be talking to Clare."

She opened her mouth to reason with him. To rage at him, if need be. Then she heard both Sally and Clare's cars start up. Alessandra ran to the kitchen window to see them drive away. "I might never forgive you for this," she told Penn.

But from the look on his face, she had the oddest feeling that she was close to the line that *he* might find unforgivable.

～

"She made me move the box, Stevie," Giuliana said, a note of censure in her voice.

"I didn't want to touch it." Alessandra appealed to the middle Baci sister. The memories it might invoke were too scary to contemplate. Weren't the letters enough? "You understand."

"Really? No." Stevie tucked her hair behind her ears and scanned the surroundings. The sidewalk tables outside Barely Bistro offered a good view of the town square and the tourists and locals going about their summer midday business. "This was a good idea. When was the last time we went to lunch together?"

Alessandra had called them both after Penn left that morning. She and her oldest sister had ridden to town together, but first she'd begged Jules to stuff the box Sally had brought into the hall closet.

Maybe she'd be ready to deal with Tommy's things by the time she needed her umbrella and raincoat. Probably not.

"Looking through those things could heal you, Allie. Don't you think you should give it a try?" Giuliana sent a pointed look across the small table. "Because you know avoiding unpleasant things never works."

"Says the voice of experience," Stevie added drily. "Considering Jules spent a decade on the run from Liam."

"Don't change the subject," Giuliana said. "Allie, I'm right, and you should listen to me."

After their mother died, Jules had taken on a maternal role with her two younger sisters, particularly Alessandra.

But she didn't remember her sister being so bossy and she definitely wasn't in the mood for a lecture now. "You know what? Your mothering skills stink."

Giuliana froze, her expression revealing sudden pain.

"What?" Annoyance forgotten, Alessandra half-rose from her chair. "What hurts?"

Her older sister shook herself. "Nothing. I don't know what you're talking about."

Their waitress came out with their food and once they were served and their iced teas topped off, Giuliana was again wearing a stubborn expression. "Back to what we were talking about . . ."

Alessandra shook her head. She'd decided to give herself an indefinite pass on the box, because there was a more pressing matter. And her sisters weren't going to like this, either. "There's a bigger problem."

Stevie glanced at her glass. "Are we going to wish we'd ordered wine?"

"Clare isn't marrying Jordan," Alessandra said flatly. "He's been cheating on her."

"No—" Stevie clapped her palm over her mouth, her eyes wide. Then her hand dropped to her lap. "But—"

"I think she and Gil are planning to elope."

Her sister's hand snapped back up, then she let her hand fall again. "That means there's nothing for the *Wedding Fever* people to film on Saturday."

"Got it in one." Alessandra attempted a weak smile. "Should I order that bottle?"

Giuliana snatched up the leather-covered wine list, and both Alessandra and Stevie stared at her. "I was kidding," Alessandra said.

"It wouldn't help anyway," Jules answered, dropping it back to the table. "We're in trouble."

"Without the *Wedding Fever* publicity, we don't stand a chance of keeping Tanti Baci," Stevie said.

Jules nodded. "And knowing those TV people like I

now do, I doubt they'll even film the shorter segment. I bet they pack up and roll on back to La-La Land. Cut their losses."

Alessandra's fingers curled around her sweating iced tea. She trusted her oldest sister's assessment because she'd been the one working closest with the television team, a small group that included camera person, sound guy, and a makeup artist. "We can't let that happen. What bright ideas do you two have to prevent it?"

The silence at the table wasn't promising.

"Allie . . ." Stevie finally ventured.

She didn't look at her sister. "We *have* to save it. We promised Papa."

There was a disturbance across the square, near the hardware store. A shout, a car suddenly stopped, people looked toward the commotion, including Alessandra and her sisters.

"Build me up!" floated across the street. Something flew up in the air—

"Is that a bra?" Jules wondered aloud.

A long wolf whistle pierced the air.

"I'd say that's a safe assumption." Alessandra turned her back on the action. Half-naked girls throwing themselves—and their clothing—at Penn were his lot in life. No wonder he treated everything so casually.

Alessandra, I love you.

She thrust aside the ache of the memory to focus on the issue at hand. "Well?" she asked her sisters again. "Who has a bright idea that will keep the *Wedding Fever* people interested?"

"We'd better come up with something quickly," Jules grumbled. "Word that the wedding's called off will get around fast."

"Presumably Sally's already canceling the food and flowers."

"Which means there'll be bouquets and baby quiches

ready to be snatched up at bargain prices," Stevie mused. "The orders and the work will already be half-done."

Jules sighed. "What we need is another wedding for Saturday."

Alessandra sat straighter in her chair. "Something splashy."

"The Latisse twins left for Maui last night," Stevie said with a regretful shake of her head. "The mermaids have flown—swum?—the coop."

All three sisters sipped from their tea. "If not splashy, something with a good story behind it at least," Alessandra ventured. "That's what Roger liked about Clare's wedding."

Her gaze turned on Giuliana.

She was already shaking her head. "Don't look at me. No story here other than I'm done with men and would not consider marrying one to save my life—or the winery."

Stevie brightened. "Hey, Liam and Seth know an actual prince!"

A little thrill ran through Alessandra. "Really?"

"Really. He's single. They went to college with him." She wilted. "But I don't think he's local and I doubt he's the marrying kind."

"Hmm." Alessandra took another sip. "Do you think if we found a way to contact him you could turn on your charm and get him to change his mind by Saturday?"

"And marry who?"

"You, silly," Alessandra said.

"You're kidding."

"Not so much. Men always go for you, you know that." Stevie had a posse of guys she hung out with.

"Because I like football and working on cars," Stevie said. "But a prince . . . no. I had my shot at bucking the social order and it ended ugly."

Curse Emerson Platt, Alessandra thought. Curse that snobby SOB.

Giuliana was shaking her head at the two of them. "I can't believe we're having this conversation. Some prince we don't even know!"

"Well, I already considered calling Jordan and getting him to grovel," Alessandra said. "But Penn—" She broke off, noting her sisters' astounded expressions. "What?"

"Miss Most Romantic, Miss Starry Eyes and Dreamy Soul contemplated encouraging our friend Clare to marry a cheater?" Jules said.

Stevie pointed a finger at her. "Not to mention cutting out our cousin Gil."

"I was just being practical," Alessandra muttered.

"Heartless, more like."

There was that, too, but now wasn't the time to shatter her sisters' perception of her. She looked away, her attention snagged by a pod of early teens passing by in short shorts and baby doll tops. They were all talking, their mouths slick with sticky gloss and their fingernails painted in the dreadful shades of banana yellow and moldy green. High-pitched conversation floated over the Baci sisters' table.

"My mom checked Rocky Reed into the Valley Ridge Resort. He's here until Sunday. She loves listening to the gossip on his radio show and she thinks he's so cute. But she thinks Stephen Colbert is cute, too . . ."

"Face it, Gwen. Your mom has weird taste in guys."

"Not always. She has it bad for Penn Bennett."

"*I* think Penn Bennett is cute," another voice said.

"Exactly."

Yet another girl chimed in. "And guess what? Penn paid for the Little League to get new bleachers. And my brother says the high school Key Club got him to volunteer for the dunking booth on Market Day like he did for the band. Michael said he was really nice about it, too, and . . ."

He was really nice about it.

Bam!

Alessandra set her iced tea on the tabletop with a sharp

clack. "I have an idea." Her brain humming, her nerves singing, she looked over at Giuliana. "Can you handle the *Wedding Fever* people?"

"What?"

The words bubbled out of her, heated by her excitement. "Convince them we have a replacement wedding—with a story behind it that's even better."

Giuliana's eyes narrowed. "You're scaring me. Do you know what you're doing?"

I'm scaring myself. "Just answer me, Jules. Can you try to get them to stay until Saturday?"

Calculation narrowed her sister's eyes. "I'll do one better. I'll guarantee they'll be here Saturday, *if* you promise to open that box before then."

Alessandra's blood chilled. She'd said she'd do anything to save Tanti Baci . . . but open the box? A shudder raced down her back.

Fine. All right. Okay. She'd open the box.

Ignoring the second shudder rolling down her spine, she held out her hand to her sister. "We have a deal." Because really, facing the contents of the cardboard carton was nothing compared to the other risk she was planning to take.

19

Alessandra carefully set the stage, certain that a man in the entertainment business would appreciate the effort. Beneath the spreading oak that shaded Anne and Alonzo's cottage, she arranged a crisp tablecloth over a small table and then unpacked the picnic basket she'd put together in the farmhouse kitchen. Place settings for two, a small vase of colorful country flowers, the covered bowls of green salad and the famous Baci summer pasta. A crusty loaf of sourdough. From a thermos she poured cold water into two glasses. In a thermal pouch at her feet was a bottle of chilled wine.

It had been twenty-four very busy hours since lunch with her sisters. Later, she'd be in town, representing Tanti Baci during Edenville's Market Day. This morning she'd made phone calls, cajoling various suppliers and making mysterious promises. After that, she'd prepared the meal she was going to serve, then dressed for the occasion in a gauzy sundress of deep turquoise and sandals with small heels. Her hair was in loose waves around her shoulders.

The whole effect was pretty, she'd decided as the make-up person had applied a third coat of mascara. Appealing. And most importantly, telegenic.

So she hoped.

There were comings and goings of tourists in and out of the tasting room and they cast curious glances across the gravel parking lot as she sat down to wait for her guest. Pic-nickers were directed to the tables under the arbor along-side the winery offices, so clearly this was a more special event. Aware that she had a part to play, she let her lips curve in a serene smile and didn't allow a single nervous glance toward the cottage to betray her.

A small dust cloud in the distance signaled that he was nearing. She rose to her feet as his truck stopped in the dappled light under another tree at the edge of the winery's parking lot. Her pulse rocketed, making her a little dizzy as he approached, a frown on his face.

"What's wrong?" Penn demanded, not seeming to no-tice the lovely setting she'd worked so hard to create. "I was told there's an emergency here?"

Oops. Maybe the message should have downplayed emergency and up-played better clothes. It was a jeans kind of day for Penn, with a button-down shirt thrown over, tails out and sleeves rolled up. Except he looked good in any-thing, she conceded, walking forward to give him a peck of a kiss on the cheek.

He always smelled so good.

His hands clamped on her elbows and he pushed her away. "What's going on?" His gaze shifted to the table be-hind her, then drifted toward the cottage.

Panic stampeded through her belly. Grabbing his hand, she towed him toward the lunch table. "Look here! Look at this nice food I have ready for us."

"What?" His brows drew together. "Why?"

"I . . . I wanted to thank you and to celebrate that we, uh, finished the cottage."

He took in the bowls of pasta and salad as she pulled his chair out for him. "I suppose I could eat," he said warily, settling into his seat.

She took her place across from him and reached for her napkin to blot her damp palms. Maybe she should talk first and they could lunch later. Her stomach wasn't up to a meal at this moment, that was for sure. He reached for a bowl.

She put her palm on the cling wrap covering. "Wait. I wanted to tell you . . . *ask* you something . . ." Oh, this was harder than she'd thought! At the bistro yesterday, and in her bed last night, it had seemed to make sense. But right now the words refused to roll off the tip of her tongue.

"Yeah?" Penn said. "I should let you know I've been trying to reach Roger all day. No luck so far, but as soon as I make contact I'm going to tell him about Lana. I don't know if the *Wedding Fever* crew is still in town—"

"They're still here." Oops.

Penn sat back in his chair. "Well, good. It's time I told him the truth."

Alessandra found herself nodding. "Excellent. Sure. I agree."

"I don't know how it will affect *Wedding Fever*'s plans for Tanti Baci—"

"Don't worry about that." She brushed away the concern as well as an inquisitive fly. "You've got to do what you've got to do."

He nodded, then looked at her expectantly.

Raising her eyebrows, she put her hand on her chest. "Me?" Oh, yes, she'd claimed she had something to tell him, too. But again, the words refused to form.

"Let me serve you some of the famous Baci pasta," she said, reaching for the bowl. "Both my mother and father claimed to have developed the recipe, but it's so simple. Tomatoes, garlic, basil leaves straight off the plant, a good parmesan. You rough chop the skinned tomatoes, smash the garlic, and heat them both together in a little olive oil before tossing with cooked spaghetti. No simmering . . . it's supposed to taste from-the-garden fresh. I think it's best served at room temperature."

She scattered the slivered basil and parmesan shavings over the pasta, then passed the plate back to him. He was looking at her, though, and not the food.

"Mangia," she said, shifting her attention to her own plate. "Eat."

The colors were pretty, the smell of the food divine, but her stomach still couldn't handle a bite. So she toyed with her fork and watched him chew and swallow.

"Oh," he groaned. "You should have said. You should have said this is really, really good."

"Yeah?" She smiled at him.

He smiled back and his hand reached across the table so his forefinger could brush her cheek. "There it is. Your dimple's been AWOL since I showed up."

It dug again into her cheek and a flush of warmth rolled over her skin. "You compliment my cooking, you get my best smile. Of the three of us, I'm the only Baci sister who likes to spend time in the kitchen. Papa taught me that recipe himself."

"Daddy's girl, huh?"

"Oh, yeah." She twirled her fork in the spaghetti. "My mom died when I was twelve, so I turned to my father. He took me into the kitchen and into the vines, anyplace where he could pass along his loves: for food, for the land, for the magical wine we produce." Oh, God, was she laying it on too thick, what with her cooking abilities and then the pitch for the family business?

Glancing up, she noticed he was working his way through his plate. Soon he'd be finished and she'd *have* to get down to it.

Nerves had her babbling again. "Did I tell you what happened here during Prohibition?"

He shook his head.

"Well, of course it was illegal to make and sell alcohol, so my family planted and grew plums, pears, and apples amongst the vines. Still, some whispered that you could come to the back door of the winery and take home a jug or two." This was part his history, too, though she didn't think he considered himself a Napa Bennett . . . not yet.

"Was it true?"

She could see her father telling the story, his barrel chest, his expansive gesture, the twinkle in his eyes. "One year, federal agents raided the winery and dumped thousands of gallons of wine into the creek. It was a popular spot, the night the water ran red."

"What? Did everyone come out with their ladles and soup pots?"

She shrugged. "That's the first half of the story, that the red wine was dispatched into the creek. However, even then the Bacis were experimenting with a sparkling white, and it's said that the daughter of the federal agent in charge of the raid was getting married in San Francisco the very next weekend. Rumor has it that the reception was a rip-roaring—and very bubbly—party."

"Weddings even then," Penn murmured.

"Even then." She blotted her palms on her napkin again. "Did you know that my great-grandfather married a woman after only three arranged dates? She was the sister of one of the restaurateurs to whom he delivered Baci wine."

"That doesn't sound very romantic."

"There's all kinds of reasons for two people to get married."

"Or not get married," Penn added.

She cursed herself, because of course his mind would lead him to his mother and the philandering Calvin Bennett. "Yes, well . . . It's really a very modern idea that people marry for love, you know. Dynastic reasons, reasons that involved land and power were much more common for most of history."

" 'It is a truth universally acknowledged, that a single man in possession of a good fortune must be in want of a wife.' "

She stared at him. "Did you just quote Austen?"

"In one of last season's episodes, there was a fourteen-year-old in the family whose home we remodeled," he said, shrugging. "Austen addict, that kid. The designer planned stenciling that line across the wall above her door, and then she sprained her ankle, so it was me up on that ladder."

She continued staring at him, and in the center of her chest, the coal-lump that was her heart cracked, leaking something foreign and warm. He'd quoted Austen!

"Episode seven," he said helpfully. "One of our most popular."

She couldn't look away from him. Blindly, she groped on the ground by her feet, finding the bottle of wine. "I . . . uh . . . I'll have to look for it." She managed to pull the 2006 Bella Amore *blanc de blancs* from its pouch and remove the cage over the cork, all while still keeping it out of sight. Then she was frozen again.

Penn noticed. He set down his fork. "Alessandra?"

"This is hard. Awkward." She laughed but the sound held the sharp edge of her nerves. "Maybe even exciting."

"Exciting?" He gave her a teasing smile. "Is this about some other little toy you picked up at a bachelorette party?"

"No!" Her face burned. "But that part . . . that part's good, right? Between us, that part's good."

He stilled. "I'll never forget holding you in my arms."

"We can make more memories," she offered, heat waving over her again. "I mean, it doesn't have to end like this. It doesn't have to end at all."

Penn's eyes narrowed. "What are you talking about?"

With a breath, she lifted the wine bottle to the table. "This, this is the wedding wine," she told him. She sneaked a glance back at the cottage. They still had privacy. The signal was when she let the cork fly. "We could serve it on Saturday."

"Serve it where?"

Now or never. Sink or swim. Die or fly. "At our wedding." She reached across the table to grab his hand. "What do you say, Penn? Will you marry me?"

The blank expression on his face rattled her. Had he lost his hearing? Had she not said it right? Was the sex not as good as she thought?

He continued staring at her, his hand frozen beneath hers.

"P-Penn?" She held her breath, willing him to agree. This was the only plan she'd come up with to save the winery. "Say yes."

His hand withdrew from hers. He leaned back in his chair, his arms folding over his chest. The laugh he released was short and distinctly unamused. "What sort of joke is this?"

~

Nearby, tires ran over gravel and Penn whipped his head toward the sound, relieved to see a vehicle was leaving the winery, not arriving. The last thing he wanted was to have witnesses to this ridiculous conversation.

"Alessandra, who put you up to this gag?"

"I . . ." She glanced over her shoulder, suddenly looking as jumpy as he felt.

"Let's get out of here," he said, half-rising.

"No, no!" Sounding alarmed, she gestured him back to his seat. "I just thought . . . We get along so well together."

"Yeah," he scoffed, starting to wonder if she'd been tasting wines all morning. "So well that we've had to keep our 'relationship,' such as it is, a secret."

"That could change," she said quickly.

He laughed again, then looked around him. "This *is*

a joke. Liam and Seth don't seem the types, particularly Liam, but are the Bennett brothers out to punk me?"

"*You're* a Bennett brother." She went all Vanna White on him and made a graceful gesture toward the rolling rows of vineyard surrounding them. "This is part of your legacy, too."

The view distracted him for a moment. So different than L.A., with its golden beaches and rockier, taller mountains. There, the valleys were filled with houses and malls. And though it had rural spaces, too, where flowers and strawberries and peppers grew, they weren't like these verdant acres. Maybe it was the way the vines stretched to embrace each other or perhaps it was the close boundaries of the mountains, but it all felt so personal here. Intimate. Where families committed to each other and to the land.

No wonder the bastard kid from a crappy apartment in downtown Burbank didn't fit in.

"You like it," Alessandra said. "You . . . you like me."

His focus switched to the sexy little nun who was going to be so damn hard to forget. Yeah, he liked her. He liked how hard she worked to keep things going here at Tanti Baci. He liked her loyalty to her family and even, God help him, her devotion to Saint Tommy. A woman like that wouldn't let you down.

But she couldn't be *his* woman, because there was that aforementioned love of her life.

"So we could get married," she said. Her hand ran up and down the neck of the wine bottle on the table between them. "It would be so easy."

"Easy?" He shook his head, still not quite believing they were having this conversation. "You think marriage—I don't care who the couple might be—is easy? I didn't have a father, but even I know marriage can't be called that."

"Not the marriage," she corrected. "The wedding. I've already done everything. We're all set for Saturday. You invite your brothers, I'll tell my sisters, we can both ask anyone else we want. The famous Penn Bennett and me, the Nun of Napa."

He blinked. "I thought you didn't think I was famous."

Her thumb caressed the neck of the wine bottle. "I've changed my mind about a lot of things."

"Yeah?"

"Yes." She leaned forward. "Look, just think of the *Wedding Fever* piece . . . think of the story Roger can tell with it when we're the bride and groom."

He stared at her. "You're serious?" He'd really been thinking this was some sort of odd good-bye gag on her part, but there was an intensity to her expression that wasn't the least bit funny. "Jesus. You're serious."

"Of course I'm serious." A smile turned up that luscious doll mouth of hers. "Maybe we could go to a nearby B and B for our honeymoon—Roger might be interested in filming that, too."

A honeymoon? His mind was reeling with all the implications of what she was saying, but that last word slowed his brain, nearly stopped it. Honeymoon. It spread out like a banquet in his head. White sheets, golden skin, the flavor of her juicy mouth and the juicier center he found between her legs. No more stifled sneezes for his Alessandra. He knew how to get her mindless with passion. He knew how to unleash the bad girl that shivered and cried and came in his arms.

Afterward, he'd slide down the sheets and soothe her aftershocks by sucking on her breasts, tender and soft, until her hands would cup his head against her and she'd whisper, "I love you, Penn Bennett. I love you."

Then his brain started working again.

Think of the story Roger can tell with it. The famous Penn Bennett and me, the Nun of Napa.

The fantasy shattered.

Maybe we could go to a nearby B and B for our

honeymoon—Roger might be interested in filming that, too.

It was all clear to Penn now.

"This is part of a PR plan?" he asked, anger crawling up his back. "You think I'd get myself hitched as part of your plot to save the winery?"

She winced. " 'Plot' sounds a bit harsh, don't you think? As for hitched . . . really, Penn, did you see yourself as single for the rest of your life?"

Well, fuck yeah, he did. The woman he wanted was out of his reach. He didn't think he'd find another, and frankly, falling in love had not much to recommend it.

Anger morphed to an ugly monkey, now digging into his shoulder. "Why did you think I'd go along with this?" he asked, his voice harsh. There was a ringing in his ears, claws digging into his flesh, shame burning outward from his chest, to leave a smoking hole over his heart. "What could possibly have convinced you that I'd agree to your plan?"

She swallowed. Her exotic eyes blinked, lashes falling up and down rapidly. "I . . ." She worried that wine bottle again, running her thumb to the cork and then back down again. "I . . ."

She'd heard him that night in her bed. He knew that now. They'd never mentioned it, and he'd hoped like hell she thought it was just one of those things that men said when they'd gotten their rocks off—and felt guilty for the thought, as a matter of fact. But now he didn't feel guilty, he just felt pissed.

Humiliated, like when Lana had cleaned him out.

Enraged, like when he'd discovered that he and his mother had existed in near poverty for years when his father, Calvin Bennett, had been livin' large four hundred miles away.

He shoved his hand through his hair. How had it come to this? There were women who'd come through his life.

Dozens, right? Models, supermodels, actresses, designers, the barista at his local coffee shop. And he had to pull a dumbass move of falling in love with the one woman who represented the life he hadn't lived and the love he'd never have.

"Why?" he demanded again. "I'm asking you why you thought I'd say yes?"

"Because . . ." Her thumb circled the cork of the wine bottle, a nervous gesture. "Because, uh . . . Because you're nice."

"*What?*"

His roar caused her thumb to twitch. The cork flew from the *blanc de blancs*, arcing into the overhanging branches of the oak.

Penn barely noticed. Nice? "*Nice?*" Though focused on her face, he was aware of people bursting out of the cottage. Camera people. Sound people. All gathering around them.

"Think about all the things you do, Penn," Alessandra said, her expression earnest. "You go out of your way for people. Even Lana. I know she stole from you, that you feel humiliated that you didn't read her right, and then she ripped you off . . ."

A gasp came from the people surrounding them. The *Wedding Fever* crew, he realized now. But Roger's startled expression and Lana's white face barely had time to register before Penn was hearing Alessandra again and she was repeating that word.

That damn word.

"Goes to show how nice you are."

"Don't say it again," he ground out. "When it comes to Lana, I was a mark, a dupe, a sucker." He shoved back his chair to stand, and it toppled onto the uneven ground. He glanced at it, his gaze finding Rocky Reed hovering behind him, obviously soaking in every word.

An acid mix of ire and shame erupted from his heart.

He whipped his focus back to Alessandra. "What the hell have you done?"

She came to her feet, too. A flush rushed over her cheeks, then faded. "Penn. I . . ."

"What have you done?" But he knew. *Wedding Fever*, Rocky Reed, she was using all of them, Penn included.

A sheen of tears brightened her eyes.

His gut clenched. "No. No, no, no. Those won't work this time."

"I can't help it." Tears starting tracking down her cheeks.

In some other dimension, he was aware of people listening, filming, capturing for posterity this inglorious, infuriating moment. "Your tears will not get you what you want."

"Penn—"

"You're a manipulator, Alessandra Baci. A con artist just like Lana."

"I don't know what you mean."

"Yeah. Maybe you don't." He grabbed the sparkling wine off the table and filled the two waiting flutes. "But we can toast to you, baby." Her hand curled around the glass he pressed into it.

His glass clacked against hers. "Once I told you I was in love with you, you decided to use that against me."

"No—"

"Yes." He quaffed half the bubbly in his own glass. "The starry-eyed, dreamy girl we all thought we knew proved she's really cold and calculating. You don't have a heart, do you, honey? You don't have the heart for a happy-ever-after."

Alessandra dropped her glass. It shattered against the tabletop.

He tossed the rest of the wine in his own onto the ground and let his glass follow. The damn stuff tasted bitter—or maybe that was just him.

"That's right, baby. It's all shattered now. You won't get your way."

She swayed on her feet and he repressed the urge to reach across and steady her. "When have I gotten what I wanted?" she whispered. "You tell me when. Tommy got sick, but I kept the faith. I believed and then we were getting married. But he died. How could I hold on to my belief in happy-ever-afters when all the ever-after I got for my believing was after a funeral?"

The heartbreak of that wasn't going to get to Penn, either.

With quick footsteps, he turned from her and made for his truck. A burning laugh bubbled up from the mass of lava in the middle of his chest. He understood his mother now. He'd thought her foolish for her love of his father—the real bastard in the situation. But now he realized that common sense and sentiment didn't operate on the same plane. That was the true foolishness—and danger—of falling in love.

Lucky that he was done with all that.

·

20

After the picnic-proposal debacle, Alessandra retreated to the farmhouse. Her kitchen still smelled of garlic and olive oil and though she would have found the familiar scent comforting in the past, now it sharply underscored all that she'd lost.

Everything.

When she'd stumbled off, the *Wedding Fever* crew were packing up their van. Rocky Reed was strolling to his Jag, working his iPhone at the same time. No one met her eyes, but she knew the truth.

The land would slip from their hands. The Tanti Baci label would be history.

And Penn would no longer think of her with any sort of fondness. "I'll never forget holding you in my arms," he'd said, but she'd ruined that.

Her body dropped bonelessly into a chair at the kitchen table. She stared ahead, unseeing.

It's all shattered now.

Her eyes squeezed shut on the thought, and her hand

rubbed hard at her breastbone. It ached there, had been aching since that night when Penn had whispered against her hair. *Alessandra Baci, I love you.*

She'd not believed a word of it, that was the truth, not until he'd refused to marry her twenty minutes ago. That's why her proposal had angered him, because he'd seen it as an insult to his feelings, when she'd meant it as a . . . as a . . .

Selfish plan to save the winery.

What had she been thinking?

With a sigh, she opened her eyes, her gaze finally taking in the cardboard box sitting on the kitchen table. Oh, God. The bargain she'd made with Giuliana. Her sister would handle the *Wedding Fever* contingent if Alessandra would examine the contents of Tommy's box.

Jules never forgot a thing.

Swallowing hard, Alessandra grasped the box and winced, as if the cardboard sides burned. She didn't want to touch the thing, but if she could get it back into the closet, maybe she could stuff all this new anguish in there alongside it.

The bottom was an inch off the table when the kitchen door flew open. Dropping the box, she gave a guilty start when her sisters rushed into the room.

"Are you all right?" Stevie asked, breathing fast. "Jules called and told me what happened. Damn it, Allie, you should have said something before you went through with this. We would have talked some sense into you. Proposing to Penn. For God's sake!"

"You didn't guess what she was up to yesterday?" Giuliana said. "It was obvious to me."

Stevie's eyes flashed as she turned to the eldest Baci sister. "What? Why didn't you say anything? Why didn't you stop her?"

She shrugged. "Because, maybe for once she was doing something *she* wanted, not something this town expected of her."

"Huh? Everyone loves Alessandra."

"Of course they do," Giuliana answered quietly. "Because we asked her to bear all our fears for Tommy when he was battling cancer, and all our grief when he lost."

"But . . ."

As her sisters continued to argue, Alessandra scooped up the box again and sidled toward the hall closet.

Giuliana's voice caught her. "Where are you going with that?"

Guilty again, Alessandra froze.

"For God's sake, Jules . . ." Stevie started. "Can't you leave her alone?"

"We had a bargain," she said, her tone not giving an inch. "Put the box on the table, Allie, and look inside."

"Good God." Stevie threw an angry look at Giuliana that reminded Alessandra of the spectacular quarrels her older siblings used to engage in. "Who died and made you the boss of her?"

"Mama," Giuliana answered. "I promised her I'd always take care of you, Allie, and I'm afraid I haven't done my job."

"I don't know what—"

"You were too young to get married."

Alessandra's gaze dropped from her sister's. She placed the box carefully on the table, as if she knew the contents were fragile. *She* felt fragile. "Don't blame yourself. Nothing could have stopped me."

"You've always had this . . . this magic, Allie. Tommy, the Knowles family, the whole town of Edenville figured you were the talisman to keep him safe."

That did it. Alessandra buried her face in her hands, the ache in her chest radiating outward from her tiny, hard heart. "I failed. I didn't keep Tommy alive. I haven't kept Tanti Baci alive, either."

Stevie rushed across the room to take her in her arms. "Neither one is your fault."

"Open the box," Giuliana insisted, though her voice was kind. "Give what's inside a chance to heal all that's hurting. It's like the letters, little sister. You know you have to."

The letters. What if there were more inside? She pressed her clenched fists to her breasts. *My Darling Allie* . . . "I can't do it," she whispered. "Penn was right. I'm heartless—nearly so, anyway. For five years I've been faking my faith in ever-after. Looking in the box won't change that."

Stevie tightened her hold. "We'll forget—"

"Allie, you have to do this," Giuliana insisted. "I honestly think you do. But the Mouseketeers have got your back." She pulled Alessandra out of Stevie's arms to tie one of the kitchen aprons around her neck like a cape.

"Hah!" Stevie's long arm snagged the colander from the counter where it had been set to dry. With a flourish, she put it on Alessandra's head. "Pretend it has ears."

A rough sound choked out of her throat. "Why am I laughing? This isn't funny." But Jules was right, it had to be done. Alessandra stared at the box another long moment, then she stepped toward it, catching the colander as it slipped on her hair.

Once it was settled again, her trembling hands released the intertwined top flaps. Scarlet wool caught her eye and her stomach jumped in nervous circles, even as she drew out the material.

"Tommy's letterman's jacket," Stevie said.

The leather sleeves were cool against her hands, the fabric scratchy. It was covered with patches and pins that spelled out Tommy's year of graduation, the sports he'd participated in, the accomplishments he'd been honored for. Alessandra folded it open and put her face against the satiny lining. It felt strangely warm, as if Tommy had just taken it off.

She could smell him.

Without thinking, she pushed her arms through the sleeves. The fit was much too big, of course, but it felt natural to her, because she'd worn it at Friday night football games, on cold mornings when she'd forgotten her jacket, any time her teenage self wanted to lay claim to the coolest boy on campus.

She smiled and laughed again, remembering. Remembering Tommy pulling her hair from beneath the collar and then linking his hand with hers as they strolled through the high school campus. She saw it from a distance, from above, perhaps how Tommy saw her now. *My Darling Allie . . .*

"What else is in the box?" Stevie asked.

With the colander, cape, and Tommy's jacket, she felt brave enough to explore. "Photographs," she said, reaching for them. With a sweep of her hand, she fanned them out on the scarred surface of the old wooden table.

Her sisters closed in as they all looked them over.

"Prom," she said, touching one with her finger. "Here's homecoming my freshman year. What was with those big chrysanthemum corsages? Remember we stuck an *E* made of pipe cleaners in their centers and sold them for two bucks?"

Giuliana shook her head. "Sometimes we stick with things—feelings, too—because . . . we don't know how to let them go."

There were no surprises in the rest of the photographs except that looking at them didn't hurt. Alessandra had her own similar set that she'd been afraid to gaze upon since she was twenty years old. Her hands didn't shake when she returned the box. Sliding off Tommy's jacket didn't feel like shedding her skin. She folded it back into its cardboard nest.

"You missed this one," Stevie said, handing her another photo.

Alessandra found herself smiling. "Sadie Hawkins

dance." The girl in the photo had long dark hair in braids and had blacked out one of her teeth. Fake black freckles peppered her nose. The handsome blond boy wore a gingham kerchief that matched the girl's short skirt. He sat on a straw bale and she sat on his lap.

"Look how cute they look," she said, holding the picture so Giuliana had a better view.

"They look very happy."

Alessandra smiled down at them again, and it was only then that it really sank in. Though that was she and Tommy, it didn't feel like herself at all. It was two young people, a girl and a boy, who had laughed and smiled and loved, once upon a time. The girl had lost that boy she'd loved, but that was in the past, too. With a final glance, she put the photo on top of the red jacket, like a memory held forever in the heart.

Inspiration suddenly struck. "Wait, wait," she said, and doffed the apron and colander, then raced upstairs to her bedroom. She was back in two minutes, carrying her white satin shoes, her tiara and veil, and the layers of white tulle that made up her wedding dress. They'd been in her closet for five years and it was time to put them away.

It took nothing to tuck the shoes and tiara beside the letterman's jacket. With the dress still over her arm, she folded the veil into a tiny package.

"Are you sure about this?" Giuliana asked.

She nodded. "Sure," she said, even as her pulse started to pick up.

Stevie found some tissue paper that she used to wrap the veil. It fit snugly into a corner.

Then Alessandra held up the dress.

Like that, pain hit, welling from the center of her breasts to fill her chest.

Crying out, she bowed into it, fisting the fabric against her. "Oh, God." *Oh, God.*

"Allie? What is it?"

She felt both Stevie's and Giuliana's hands on her, but their touch didn't alleviate the bursting, breaking, radiating hurt from where the kernel of her heart resided. It was expanding in her chest, its hard shell cracking so it could swell to a size that multiplied the aching pain.

Why? Her fingernails bit into her palms, even through the filmy fabric of the dress. Why now?

"Allie? Is it Tommy? Are you crying for Tommy? He wouldn't want this for you."

Shaking her head, Alessandra closed her eyes. There was a film playing in her head, and she couldn't turn it off. It kept looping, around and around and around, bringing wave after wave of anguish to wrack her body.

As it was resurrected, her renewed heart was breaking.

And the catalyst for her heart's regeneration and instantaneous fracture was the memory of her last time in this dress. Not that morning five-plus years ago when she'd learned of the death of her childhood sweetheart. But a month ago, when she went flying down the road to the cottage.

She saw this all from above, too, like a movie, the rolling rows of green vines, the thick branches of the oaks, the gray gravel that led to the dilapidated cottage where Liam's car was parked. A man was slouched against its side, his attention suddenly riveted by the woman running in his direction.

She'd noticed him, too, in one corner of her mind. Maybe she'd recognized him as her chance—or her fall.

They knew which one it was now.

Her gaze centered again on that high school photo nestled on the scarlet jacket. That girl had loved a boy she'd lost. The pain had finally faded.

But the woman, this woman who was Alessandra grown and who carried Alessandra's now beating but broken heart loved a man she'd pushed away by insulting the very feelings that tore at her right now. That mistake would never fade. The memory of it would stay with her forever.

~

Penn would have bailed if he hadn't promised the kids. But he'd agreed a week ago to man the dunk booth yet again on Market Day. It just went to show what reward the Good Samaritans of the world reaped, because he was fully aware that the teenagers of the Edenville High service club who were sponsoring the fundraiser would remind him way too much of Saint Tommy and the Nun of Napa, the wine country's very own Romeo and Juliet.

Christ, it made him want to stick a knife in his gut. From now on, he reminded himself, no more Mr. Nice Guy.

Reaching the end of Fir Street, he wondered if fate had sent him a reprieve. There was no tank/seat/target contraption in sight. "Hey," he said to a passerby. "Isn't the dunking booth usually here?"

The man paused. "I saw it set up in the square. Do you know—"

"Yeah, yeah. The town center." He reversed direction, trying to cheer himself with the thought that once he got this last obligation out of the way, he could head back to L.A.

L.A., where he'd be free of her dark-lashed eyes, her fall of coffee-colored hair, the lush curves and sweet scent of Alessandra Baci. His mood didn't lift.

Then he turned the next corner, and it sank lower. Damn. Hell. Fuck. He said every curse word he knew, then repeated them again, but the litany didn't act like the spell he'd hoped and make the woman he didn't want to love disappear. She was standing at the base of the booth, wearing that little turquoise dress she'd worn while proposing to him. The warm afternoon breeze pressed it close to her luscious body.

From this moment on and for the rest of his days, he was

going to be meaner than Scrooge. More flint-hearted than Mr. Potter in *It's a Wonderful Life.* A Grinch the likes of which Dr. Seuss had never imagined. Penn's good deeds had only led to great humiliation.

She spied him across the square. Their gazes met and his heart jolted in his chest, like a boat trying to loosen from its mooring. Humiliation—ha! The anguish of that was nothing compared to this gut-churning certainty. This knowledge that he'd never see her again.

He forced himself to walk in her direction. The square was crowded, forcing him to circumvent knots of people and step around strollers and kids on tiny bicycles that didn't reach his knees. He caught a whiff of grilling meat and passed a panoply of local goods, but nothing kept him from approaching his final destination.

Alessandra was short, he decided. Too short. After today, he was only going to date six-foot Playboy centerfolds.

Who was he kidding? He never wanted to date again.

When he was within hailing distance of her, she spun around and started clambering up the ladder to the seat suspended over the tank. Surprised, he halted in his tracks, wondering what the hell she was up to now.

A premonition skittered along his spine, and he spun around, looking for a *Wedding Fever* cameraman or maybe Rocky Reed's annoying mug, but if either was there, he was well-hidden by the growing crowd. And then it hit him . . . if there was another dunkee, he could go back to the Bennett house and dunk his troubles in a tank of beer instead.

His arm was caught just as he was about to turn. Stevie Baci smiled at him. "You're not going anywhere, are you?"

"I'm not needed here," he told her.

"That shows what you know," she muttered, towing him forward.

"Hey—"

"My little sister gets her chance," she said fiercely. "She

said she was willing to risk her own humiliation, and see if I don't make that happen."

The Baci girls, as he well knew, could be scary. So he, Penn decided, could be stoic. When Stevie released him a few feet from the tank, he planted his feet and crossed his arms over his chest. He could make it through this.

Instead of sitting on the seat, Alessandra stood on top of it in her little sandals. Her hemline fluttered just above her knees and Penn hoped like hell the two teenage guys standing nearby weren't looking up her skirt.

Then he remembered he didn't care about anything to do with her.

"Hey, everybody!" She waved her arms to get the attention of the crowd. More people turned toward her, some with barbecue beef sandwiches in hand, others clutching bags of local produce. "I want to introduce you to someone."

Oh, crap. He stepped back, only to be rammed in the kidneys by Stevie on one side and Giuliana on the other. He winced. Glancing around, he noticed Liam and Seth were nearby, too, obviously operating on the side of those devilish Bacis. They were part of a larger crowd. Edenville had a population of about six thousand and it seemed as if nearly all of them were attending Market Day.

Alessandra was gesturing again. "If you don't know him already, this is Penn Bennett."

Some people clapped. A little kid said, "Who?" and one of the high school kids from the service club started flinging T-shirts from the show into the growing audience. Cheers rose up.

Hell. But the showman had been beaten into him the last few years, so he found himself taking a step forward and raising a hand in acknowledgment. If he wasn't done with Alessandra, he'd have gotten her back for this.

She started talking again as the crowd quieted down. "He's the best, nicest man I know."

All he could do was shake his head. Nice? She knew how he hated that.

Her gaze touched his face. "I know you don't like me to point that out. But, friend, you're not as cynical or hard as you'd like to think. The band knows that, the Little League, the Kids' Club, the Key Club. The fact is, Penn, you can't run away from who you are—or what you've become. I know that now. And Edenville knows the good you've done here in the past month."

The high school kids applauded.

"See?" she said. "They could tell you. But I'll tell you more."

His feet shifted, but it was the Bennetts bracketing him this time. "Give her a chance," Liam murmured.

Seth nudged with his elbow. "Give yourself a chance, bro."

Alessandra swallowed. "You changed me, you presented possibilities I'd forgotten when you treated me like a woman." She smiled a little. "To tell the truth, I didn't want to be treated that way. That meant stepping out of my comfort zone, it meant feeling things I was afraid to experience."

Her gaze centered on his face and the honesty in it hit him like a wave. He stepped back. His brothers and her sisters were right there again, but he wasn't thinking of leaving. Not quite yet.

"Five years ago, I sort of . . . went to sleep, as Tommy's girl. But you woke me up, Penn. And I've grown up."

His pulse was pounding in his ears. He'd seen her as that enchanted princess in the grapevines, hadn't he? But he'd been wrong, too, underestimating what it would take to break that spell. What strength she had to find to get free.

"Sally." Alessandra's gaze skipped to the side, and there was Mrs. Knowles, standing frozen by the booth selling fresh corn and strawberries. "We'll never forget Tommy. None of us in Edenville. But I have to look toward the future now."

Stevie murmured in his ear. "For five years, she carried the town's grief. You get that, right?"

He got that. And it made his heart leak a little more pain, though he was glad if he helped her put down that heavy burden.

Alessandra looked at him again. Her face was flushed and the breeze played with her hair and the hem of her dress. "I did you wrong," she said. "I'm sorry. I'm sorry I kept secret something that was worth sharing. But I kept secrets from myself, too."

Penn's heart slammed against his breastbone. He couldn't breathe.

"Today, at Tanti Baci . . ." Her face went redder. "I hurt you by being dishonest with us both. I realize I set up that situation to give me an excuse not to say what I really wanted to say. Not to ask what I really wanted to ask . . ."

Maybe he was dying, because air wasn't making it to his lungs. But it wasn't so damn terrible a way to go.

"Penn Bennett . . ." She paused. "Would you, will you . . ."

The brat certainly knew how to build the tension.

Then her hopeful eyes smiled into his. "Build me up?"

You'd think he'd hesitate. Wasn't payback called for? But he wouldn't chance it, not when he understood exactly what she was saying. And while he might be nice, he wasn't stupid enough to postpone his own happiness.

"Build you up?" he repeated loud and clear as he moved toward her through the crowd, his arms outstretched to pull her off that platform. "Just for the rest of my life."

"Wait." Her grin blazed at him. "Wait. First you get to throw the balls."

Four were shoved into his hands.

The Nun of Napa had that wicked glint in her eyes he

found so irresistible. "Go ahead," she offered. "Dunk me. Get your revenge for what happened at the winery today. I deserve it."

Witch. He eyed her pretty clothes and matching shoes and shook his head. "After all that public praise, you know I couldn't possibly." And she'd already settled that score between them by risking her own public humiliation. Walking forward again, he pitifully tossed three balls, missing each time.

The fourth was snatched from his hands. "I'll do it," Stevie said. "I'm still mad that she cut the tails off every one of my My Little Ponies."

The ball hit the target, and with a shriek, Alessandra went down.

Surely she could swim. But Penn couldn't take the risk. In a blink, he ran up the ladder. He found her wrist, but she was an eel, he discovered.

Instead of pulling her out, he found himself in.

He didn't fight it really, because that's how he discovered this love thing was. You went in head first.

They came up, arms around each other, to the noise of cheers and applause and woots and whistles. All that static faded away as he looked into those big browns of hers, now framed by spiky lashes. *Everyone knows not to look in her eyes.*

But he wasn't worried, because for the very first time he saw Alessandra's heart in them.

"I'm in love with you," she said.

Emotion strangled his voice. Until he found it again, he hoped his kiss said all he couldn't.

~

They got married on Saturday. There were too many guests to sit inside the cottage, so they decided to say their vows outside it and set folding chairs on the lawn and the adjacent parking lot. Still, the event was standing room only. Penn, wearing linen slacks and a white Mexican wedding shirt, waited on Anne and Alonzo's front porch with the minister. Red rose petals delineated the aisle.

The bride scattered them with her bare feet as she walked to her groom. Her off-the-shoulder, ankle-length white eyelet dress had been found at a boutique in town. Her hair hung loose down her back, a circlet of baby's breath and red baby roses held it off her face.

As Alessandra approached the cottage, she glimpsed its interior. If Anne and Alonzo were there, she didn't see them. But other ghosts hovered nearby, she just knew it. Her parents. Tommy. She smiled for them and was sure they knew she was happy.

At the base of the steps, she handed her bouquet of more roses to her sisters. The plan was that she would mount the stairs by herself, but then Penn was there, taking her by the hand so they could climb together.

He smiled at her. "You are the most beautiful woman I've ever seen," he murmured.

"I used to hate how handsome and sexy you are." She'd thought her desire for him meant he'd infected her with a sickness, when instead this man had healed her.

"Yeah?" His brows rose over his laughing eyes. "What about now?"

"Now I think you'll show up marvelously well on TV." After all that, the *Wedding Fever* people were filming the event. While Lana had disappeared from Edenville, Roger and the rest had stayed put for the weekend. A few bottles of their Tanti Baci cabernet had helped the producer get over the breakup. Still, Alessandra had protested using her marriage to Penn for anything but their personal happiness.

Her groom-to-be had insisted.

Though their honeymoon would be private, allowing them to be blissfully, passionately alone, he'd said he wanted their wedding to kick off Tanti Baci's bid for success.

As together they approached the minister, he whispered again the words he'd used to convince her just two days before. "The famous Penn Bennett and Alessandra Baci, the Nun of Napa . . . face it, my love, that's a hell of a good story."

AUTHOR'S NOTE

To learn more about the Napa Valley, I point you to two books by James Conaway, *Napa* and *The Far Side of Eden*. Another excellent choice is *A Tale of Two Valleys: Wine, Wealth and the Battle for the Good Life in Napa and Sonoma* by Alan Deutschman. If you're in the mood for a movie, I think you'll enjoy *Bottle Shock*, which provides incredible cinematography, a great sound track, and an understanding of how Napa Valley became a celebrated area for wine.

But Napa isn't the only place where grapes are grown and fine wines are made. Many states have wine regions, and in California, you'll find wineries from north to south. Vintners are a friendly group and you can learn a lot by taking vineyard tours and participating in fun (and often free!) tastings on location. Of course, you don't have to go anywhere to enjoy an evening at home with a bottle of wine. Your local liquor store or gourmet grocer will have recommendations for every taste and price range.

And here's what I say (well, so do a lot of others, too): throw out the "rules"! Don't worry about whether or not it's okay to drink a white wine with your steak dinner. It's what *you* like and what tastes right to *you*. As to cost, we've participated in blind tastings and you'd be surprised how many times our group preferred the less expensive bottle over the pricier one. So . . . experiment and listen to recommendations, but ultimately follow your own palette.

Last, I want to acknowledge that due to Napa Valley's designation as an agricultural preserve, there are restrictions to the kinds of events that wineries may host (including weddings). As of this writing, changes to those restrictions are under discussion. For the purposes of the Three Kisses trilogy, the romantic "I-dos" go forward at beautiful Tanti Baci.

Keep reading for a preview of the next book

in the Three Kisses series from Christie Ridgway

Then He Kissed Me

Coming January 2011 from Berkley Sensation!

Leaning against the driver's door of a black stretch Cadillac, Stephania Baci crossed her arms over her pin-tucked white shirt and practiced pleading her case to a stern-faced judge wearing robes as dark as her own jacket and tailored trousers. "Put yourself in my shoes," she murmured, glancing down at her stiletto-heeled half-boots, ego-boosters bought for just this occasion. "Who wouldn't commit a crime when faced with chauffeuring an ex and his new fiancée on New Year's Eve?"

Forty feet away, the double doors to the Valley Ridge Resort opened. Even as her heart took an elevator-plunge, she shot up straight from her slouch. It wouldn't do for her posture to telegraph her low mood. The calm mask she'd donned tonight along with her limo driver's uniform was supposed to camouflage messy emotions—and hopefully smother any stray compulsion to carry out a high crime or misdemeanor.

A lone figure swept onto the portico, his long black overcoat swirling around his calves as he moved into a shadowy corner. Though her nerves were still jitterbugging, this wasn't the male half of the pair she was contracted to drive this evening. The tall man whose outline she could barely make out was wholly unfamiliar.

She ducked her head and studied him through the screen of her lashes, for some inexplicable reason intrigued. But the broad-shouldered silhouette didn't surrender any secrets. When a breeze kicked up, the only new information she established was the length of his hair: Long enough to be ruffled.

Nothing to pique her interest. No excuse for her still-chattering pulse, unless it was that faint note of expensive cologne that reached her on the next gust of air.

Stevie and rich men didn't mix with success.

The resort's doors opened once more, pulling her attention away from the stranger. Again, it was not the couple she was anticipating that strolled onto the covered porch. As this pair came closer, Stevie responded with an automatic smile.

"Rex and Janice!" Contemporaries of her late father's, she'd known the husband and wife all her life. "Happy New Year."

Rex beamed. "Back at you, Stevie. I take it the boss has to work the New Year's shift tonight?"

"Right." She didn't add that with the holidays nearly over and winter being the wine country's off season, there was little work for herself or her part-time, as-needed-only employees of Napa Princess Limousine. The two would guess as much. Their town of Edenville, in northern Napa Valley, was populated by just over six thousand friendly—read: nosy—souls.

"I heard about your sister," Janice said next, as if to prove Stevie's last thought. "Allie broke her foot?"

"This morning. She had surgery this afternoon." Stevie glanced over at the shadow in the corner, wondering if she imagined his attentiveness to their conversation. "Penn's keeping her in Malibu for the next few weeks. She'll be close to the surgeon and, unlike the Baci farmhouse at the winery, their beach place is a single story."

Rex and Janice made sympathetic noises. "That means you and Giuliana will have to pick up the slack, I suppose. Besides her PR duties, doesn't Allie handle all the details for the Tanti Baci weddings?"

"Mmm-hmm." The comment barely registered as Stevie couldn't shake the odd sense that Mystery Man continued to focus on them. The frowning glance she shot his phantomlike presence could neither confirm nor deny the feeling—yet it corroborated that odd awareness she had of him. She could swear she felt the intent of his return gaze, and the back of her neck prickled as a fight-or-flight spike of adrenaline kicked in.

The consequence of too much vampire fiction, she thought, suppressing the urge to cross herself as she waved Rex and Janice on their way. Not that she really believed in such dark creatures. No man could pierce one of Stevie Baci's veins and suck her blood.

The doors to the resort opened again, and the two now walking through made that statement fact. It was Emerson Platt and the woman who wore his ring on her finger. Given how he'd broken off his two-year relationship with Stevie—the why and the words that he'd used to do so— she should have been mortally wounded. Instead, she was still breathing, wasn't she? Her heart still beat.

She glanced toward the portico's corner again. It was pumping weirdly hard, as a matter of fact.

"Stevie." In a stylish tuxedo, the golden child of U.S. Senator Lois Platt moved down the portico steps, his fiancée's hand clasped in his. "You're already here."

"Can't keep the customer waiting," she replied, switching her focus to a spot just left of Emerson's elbow. As tempting as some misdeed tonight might be, she knew that maintaining an unruffled façade was in her own best interest.

Why give her ex the satisfaction of knowing he'd dented Stevie's psyche and battered her self-esteem? To that end, she'd created a mental picture of the bride-to-be, complete with wart on her nose, receding chin, and sausagelike cankles. Just in case her image didn't actually match the original, she'd decided against even passing her gaze over the other woman.

Spinning on her dominatrix boot heels, Stevie reached for the passenger door handle. It was cold under her fingers. Locked.

An anxious heat rose on her neck as she drew the remote from her pocket. "Just a moment," she murmured, fumbling with the buttons.

Bleeps. Clicks. Double bleeps. The lock stayed stubbornly seated.

The burn on her face intensified. She felt eyes on her: Emerson's, the warted bride's, and especially those of Mystery Man, which only made her fingers more clumsy. "In a second," she said, her voice tight, "I'll have you out of the cold."

She didn't need to see Emerson to hear the tender concern that entered his voice. "It *is* really cold," he said. "Roxanne, sweetheart, will you get too chilled on a winery crawl tonight?"

When he'd been with Stevie, icy temperatures would have had him exhorting her to man up and deal. But with Roxanne . . . what? Was he afraid his darling's endearing wart would freeze and fall off?

Emerson's shoes scraped on the pavement. "Did you say something, Stevie?"

Oh, God. Had she said that out loud? Her head swung around in order to deny the charge—and only at the last second did she remember her vow not to look upon the other woman. She turned away from the glimpse of silver-spangled skirt and breathed a sigh of relief as she heard the telltale snap of the limo's locks releasing.

With a professional flourish, she opened the door, making a last-minute inspection of the interior. Low lights, miles of leather cushions, two miniature crystal bud vases holding tiny white roses, a bottle chilling in a bucket. Harry Connick, Jr., crooned through the speakers.

Emerson and Roxanne would have their romantic New Year's Eve.

And Stevie, once seated behind the wheel with the privacy screen secure, would have her dignity intact and her cool façade unthreatened. After tonight, she'd make sure there was no reason that their path and hers ever crossed again.

"Go ahead," she urged the couple with a gesture. "Please get in."

A pair of glittery silver pumps paused beside her black boots. A light touch brushed the sleeve of her coat.

"I don't think we've been formally introduced," the other woman said.

Stevie stared at the diamond flashing on the slender hand touching her arm but didn't look up as Emerson cleared his throat. "That's right," he said. "Stevie—Stephania Baci, this is . . . uh, Roxanne."

"Princess Roxanne," Stevie corrected. Princess Roxanne Karina Marie Parini of Ardenia, a constitutional monarchy that rubbed shoulders—geographically speaking—with its cousin in style and language, Luxembourg. Stevie's ex hadn't dropped her for some generic other woman, but instead for European royalty—of a microstate, yes, but European royalty all the same.

She'd *better* have a wart.

"Roxy," the woman said now. "I'm half-American; I was mostly raised in America. Roxy is just fine." That diamond-toting set of fingers touched Stevie's sleeve again. "Especially as we'll be working so closely together."

Startled, Stevie forgot her promise and looked up into a pretty face surrounded by honey-gold hair. "Huh?"

"On the wedding."

"Huh?" Stevie said again. "What . . . what are you talking about?"

"Giuliana called us this afternoon," Emerson explained, in that hearty tone she remembered him using for breaking dates and conveying other bad news. "She wanted to be the first to tell us about Allie."

"She had surgery," Stevie said, still puzzled.

"Yes." More Mr. Hearty. "And Jules assured us that our wedding at the Tanti Baci winery—your family winery— at the end of the month will not be affected."

"Surely not," Stevie agreed. Six months ago, at Allie's instigation, they'd started offering the original founders' cottage as a venue for couples to exchange their vows. They'd been desperate for any revenue stream to keep the ailing family business afloat—still were, as a matter of fact—and the nuptials had taken off in a modest manner thanks to her younger sister's hard work and some well-timed TV promotion. "Your day will go as planned, I guarantee it."

"Exactly what Giuliana said." Emerson nodded. "Roxanne and I are sure you'll step in and do a fine job as our event coordinator."

"What?" Stevie's eyes widened. Event *coordinator*? Of course she knew that Allie had assumed more control over details of the ceremonies and receptions as time went on, but . . .

A new male voice entered the discussion. "We all look forward to working with you."

Stevie's gaze jerked to the man who'd come to stand behind the princess. It was her pseudo-vampire, her Mystery Man, the shadow from the corner of the portico. In the light he held no more secrets. Now she saw him as thirtysomething and dark-haired with handsome, chiseled features. Under his overcoat—cashmere?—he wore a tuxedo three times more elegant than Emerson's. He gazed on her with an attitude that struck her instantly as ten times more entitled.

There was no explaining it; no single precedent or simple reason for some man to, in an instant, make her feel as exposed as a raw nerve, but there it was. Everything about him rubbed her the wrong way, including his smile, set so clearly on charm.

Her hackles rose. "Who the hell are you?" she demanded.

A shallow dimple scored one lean cheek. "Definitely going to be a fun time," he murmured.

Underneath the starched cotton and black wool of her own clothes, a heat rash prickled her skin. "What's your name?" she asked again.

"Jack."

Still disliking the arrogant, amused gleam in his eyes, she raised a brow. "LaLanne? O'Lantern? In-the-Box?"

He had a husky laugh.

As it feathered down her spine, Stevie decided to ignore him and address the more salient issue. Turning back to Emerson, she attempted to force out the question. "Let's get this straight. Are you . . ." But she couldn't say it. She could barely *think* it. Hadn't she just promised herself that after tonight she'd have nothing whatsoever to do with her ex again?

Curling one hand into a fist, she tried once more for clarity. "Are you certain that Jules told you that I . . . that I . . ."

"Yes." It wasn't Emerson who answered. The handsome stranger was looking at her again with those knowing, smiling eyes. "Your sister promised that it's you who'll handle each and every fine point of the upcoming Parini-Platt nuptials."

~

With her clients inside their first stop of the evening, the Von Stroman winery, Stevie closed her eyes against the glare of the icicle lights dripping from its Alpine-inspired eaves. The back of her head bumped the cushioned rest and she tried visualizing herself removing the tension that clung to her spine like ivy climbing a trellis. She would never get coiled up like this again, she vowed.

New Year's Resolution #1: Stay away from men. Because if she'd avoided the species from the very beginning—

The passenger door popped open. Her nervous heart jolted, and she slapped a palm over it as she swiveled right. A body dropped into the seat beside hers.

"Surprise!" Her friend Mari Friday grinned at her, smile the same white as the uniform shirt she wore, a twin to Stevie's. "I'm parked right behind you."

A glance back confirmed a second limo had pulled up to her rear bumper. Mari moonlighted with Stevie's friendly competitor, Golden West Limousine, on occasion. "You scared me! I almost jumped out of my clothes."

"Hah. I'd like to witness Emerson's reaction to that."

Stevie slid a look toward the winery entrance. "You saw him?"

"Oh, yeah. And I demand a simple answer to a simple question. Why the hell do you have your unworthy ex and his princess bride in your backseat?"

Stevie hesitated.

It caused her friend to roll her eyes. "I get it. You don't want him to know he broke your heart."

"He didn't break my heart!" Stevie denied. Too loudly? "Look, Mari, if he wasn't embarrassed to book my services, how could I possibly refuse to provide them?"

"By saying, 'You're a smarmy two-timer and I wouldn't chauffeur your lying ass on a bet'?" the other woman suggested.

Except Emerson hadn't lied. He'd been honest—brutally—about why he'd broken it off with Stevie. The two-timing part wasn't true either. He'd dumped her eight months before and weeks had gone by before he'd been spotted in the area wrapped around another woman. It had taken even more time for word to filter back to her that Emerson's new honey had a "her highness" attached to her name.

The people of Edenville had wanted to protect her. They had a habit of that when it came to the Baci sisters, and it only made the situation more humiliating. By taking the job tonight she figured she'd shut down the pity party the whole town had kept going in her honor.

She was proving to them she didn't need it. That nobody, no how, could upset Stephania Baci's equilibrium. She was the brash Baci sister. The tomboy her mother had despaired about.

Stevie, where's your hair ribbon?
Is that grease on your dress?
Boys want a girl who acts like a lady.

"So who's the other guy?"

Once again, Mari gave Stevie a jolt. "Uh . . . other guy?"

"Tall, dark, and dashing?" her friend said. "Don't tell me you didn't notice."

She'd noticed. From the moment he'd stepped out of the resort. But tall, dark, and dashing didn't make up for rich, self-important, and rude. "He's haughty."

"I'll say," Mari agreed. "My sister gave me a Hottie-of-the-Month calendar for Christmas and I bet he's in there."

Stevie frowned. "Haughty, not hottie."

"That's what I said."

"I . . ." She shook her head. "Never mind."

"Just tell me his name," Mari urged. "I'll find out his phone number myself."

Another frown dug between Stevie's brows. Her friend

had a headful of blond spiral curls and a black book that rivaled any Hollywood bachelor's. But it was Stevie who had spied tall, dark, and dashing first, and didn't that give her . . .

No. Hottie, true. But the haughty got him permanently expunged from her own Bachelor Book, if she'd actually had one. And not to forget, there was that very recent resolution she'd just made. *Men are off-limits.*

"I think he's with the princess," Stevie said to her friend. When she'd told her clients they had to get moving or miss their tasting appointments, he'd climbed into the back with Emerson and his fiancée. "His name's Jack."

Mari gasped. "Jack! Of course! 'Jack' is Prince Jacques Christian Wilhelm Parini. I read about him in one of those magazines at the hairdresser's—you know, the pulpy ones with paparazzi pics of movie premieres and Euro trash boogeying down in flashy discotheques. He's some kind of notorious playboy and the Princess Bride's big brother."

That made sense. He struck Stevie as a royal pain in the ass because he *was* a royal pain in the ass. She loved being right.

Though she should have made the Jacques-Jack connection on her own. Blame it on her ex-anxiety. She knew of the man, not from a magazine, but because he was college friends with the Bennett brothers, childhood neighbors and not-so-silent partners in the Tanti Baci winery. Liam and Seth, she recalled, knew Jack through the University of California Davis Viticulture and Enology program and had mentioned during one of their regular poker nights that their old buddy was coming for a visit.

"It's a small world of wines," Stevie murmured.

"Yeah, and—" Mari's curls swung in an arc as her attention shifted to the side window. "Oops, gotta go. My peeps are coming out. Happy New Year!"

She was gone in a blast of chilled air, leaving Stevie

alone once again. Mari wasn't soothing company, but she missed her anyway, because now there was nothing else to think about besides that little threat she'd been putting off contemplating.

Your sister promised that it's you who'll handle each and every fine point of the upcoming Parini-Platt nuptials.

Closing her eyes, she groaned. Had Giuliana really made that guarantee? Could she actually expect Stevie to honor it?

The passenger door clicked open a second time. Stevie, eyes still shut, blessed her buddy and the distraction she'd prove to be. "Mari. Thank God, you're back. I—"

Her throat closed as heat prickles took another dash across her flesh and that weird hyperawareness she'd experienced at the resort tightened her belly. Opening her eyes, she saw a long male body fold onto the seat beside her. "Jack," she said.

He smiled at her, the wattage bright enough to bring up the temperature in the front seat. "You remember my name."

And his scent. It reached her again, subtle and smooth, a top-shelf cologne, one ounce likely costing more than her new boots—and probably her monthly rental check as well.

"What are you doing here? You belong there," she said, jerking her thumb toward the winery.

"I belong wherever I want to belong," he answered, smiling that easy smile he had as his body slid nearer to hers on the bench seat. "Just like I do whatever I want to do."

Stevie crowded close to the driver's door. It didn't stop his left thigh from grazing her right, his knee from bumping hers. One long finger reached out to adjust the heater that she'd left running.

Forcing her gaze off his lean hand, she narrowed her eyes at him. "And what you want to do is . . . ?"

Her suspicious tone didn't appear to offend. He relaxed against the leather seat, sliding an arm across its back, obviously comfortable in his own privileged skin. His charming smile deepened. "Nothing for you to worry about. I only thought we might take these few minutes to get better acquainted, *ma belle fille*."

Not for a winter's worth of bookings would she let him know that just for a second—a nanosecond—she found the soft foreign phrase as disarming as he most certainly intended. Even as her insides recovered from their quick melt, she made her expression blank and raised both brows in inquiry, all tomboy bumpkin.

His smile was rueful, his shrug European. "What can I say? I know five languages and how to compliment a beautiful woman in each and every one."

Wide-eyed, she pretended to appear impressed. "Wow." Then she dropped the innocent act. "I only know how to say screw you in Italian, Spanish, and Portuguese."

He blinked, then laughed.

"Oh, and in English it's fu—"

Leaning forward, he clamped his palm over her mouth. At the contact, they both froze and the smile on his face died. Her lips tingled, her skin burned, and another shot of adrenaline punched into her bloodstream. *Fight or flight.*

Uncertain which order to follow, her body twitched.

His hand dropped.

They stared at each other.

Refine that New Year's Resolution, Stevie thought, despising her breathlessness. *Stay away from* this *man.*

She cleared her throat. "You should go back to Emerson and your sister." *Please go back to Emerson and your sister.*

His gaze didn't move from her face. But he settled back in his seat and after a moment humor gleamed again in his eyes.

"What are you laughing at now?" she demanded.

He shrugged again. "Me, maybe."

Nothing felt the least bit funny to Stevie. She sent him another suspicious look, but his attention had shifted to a small item he was withdrawing from his jacket pocket.

A crystal bud vase.

A familiar crystal bud vase.

"That belongs in the back of the limo," she said, puzzled.

He glanced up. "I thought so. I found it outside. It must have fallen from the car."

Frowning, Stevie accepted it from his outstretched hand, careful to avoid another touch. Then she held it toward him. "If you wouldn't mind, you can return it to its place in the back."

His tall body didn't budge. He regarded her with another of those faint, almost-mocking smiles. "I wasn't kidding, you know."

"About what?"

"Until the end of the month I'm going to be your new best friend—"

"I don't think so."

He shrugged and that shallow dimple flashed again. "All right. The fly in your champagne. The thorn on your rose."

Champagne and roses. He was just that kind of guy, she supposed, barely suppressing a snort.

"Point is, I'm sticking close, *mon ange*."

Again with the French. Rolling her eyes, she ignored a second surge of traitorous warmth in her belly. "Why?"

"Why?" His smile disappeared; his expression turned coldly serious. "To ensure, of course, that you don't sabotage my sister's wedding."

Dirty Sexy Knitting

From *USA Today* bestselling author
CHRISTIE RIDGWAY

The conclusion to the trilogy that's
"the perfect combination of humor and heart"
(Susan Wiggs).

Malibu & Ewe's owner, Cassandra Riley, is about to turn thirty and wants to celebrate with her knitting club and her newfound half sisters, Nikki and Juliet, in a big birthday extravaganza. But with Juliet on her honeymoon and Nikki with her fiancé, it seems everyone's paired up—except for Cassandra. Until a series of near-death accidents causes Cassandra to run straight into the arms of the one man she's avoided most . . .

DISCARD

M625T1209